THE SKYBUM

SIMON FORBES

The Occasionally Diverting Adventures

Of Mostyn Zinctrumpet-Harris

Copyright © 2011 Simon Forbes

All rights reserved.

ISBN: 1463564465
ISBN-13: 978-1463564469

To the spirit of the free flier.

CONTENTS

There follows an account of a bizarre experiment that went horribly right.

A tale of perfidious chicanery, metaphysical speculation and cross-country paragliding.

It is the story of a highly confused young gentleman, facing down the shadowiest of sinister forces, armed only with savoir faire, a thoroughly blown mind and the race-tuned brain cells of his butler Reeves.

.

1 OUT OF THE BLUE

'When once you have tasted flight, you will walk the earth with your eyes turned skyward, for there you have been and there you will always long to return.'

Leonardo Da Vinci.

September the 24th 1999 arrived with all of the boisterous urgency of a puppy with a full bladder. It cared not one jot that I would happily have snoozed for a few more hours. It was heedless to the rather splendid dream that I'd been enjoying too - a dream which prominently featured the Swedish ladies' volleyball team - and worst of all, it was recklessly indifferent to the fearful hangover that loomed in prospect.

This is, of course, the sheerest folly. Surfacing too rapidly is a dicey business with little to recommend it, (ask any scuba diver) and this counts double when you are waking up after a big night out on the nasty. It is simply not a project to be hastened in any way.

Nevertheless, 24/09/99 clearly wasn't taking no for an answer, so, begrudgingly, I began to sift the stream of impressions making themselves known to me through various sensory avenues.

Actually, it was all pretty promising. For one thing, I detected in the air blowing in through the open French windows, the slight saltiness which, in Brighton, generally indicates an on-shore breeze. There was a distinct blueness to the sky too, which speaks of powerful convection and strong thermals. Most encouragingly of all perhaps, the cries of the seagulls wheeling aloft had that sonorous quality which told me that they weren't beating their wings but were gliding. Beneath all of this, as a sublime key-note, I divined the aroma of expertly grilled kippers. Even on this slender intelligence, two conclusions were surely inescapable:

Firstly, that the almighty had bestowed upon his creation, a late September morning that was absolutely bouncing with paragliding potential.

And secondly, that with the uncanny prescience with which all the finest butlers are endowed, Keanu Reeves had materialized in my bedroom, wielding a cooked breakfast.

Actually, it was this second development that really cheered me up. It really had been a more than usually bacchanalian night, trawling the low dives of Brighton, 'The city that sometimes sleeps,' and the cranium was absolutely bleating for the restorative effect of a good solid plate of the full English.

'Morning Reeves.' I yawned, sitting up.

'Jeez you're a lazy bastard.' rejoindered my gentleman's gentleman testily.

With almost infinitely less than the uncanny deftness of touch with which all of the finest butlers are endowed, Reeves plonked the vittles into the young masters lap. He then tapped the ash from his super-skunk speed-spliff into the Louis Quatorze silver ashtray by the bed and finally, casually, and as though as an afterthought, he indicated a folded note lying betwixt kipper and marmalade with the chilling words:

'Uh, yeah, this came in the mail.' Just like that, if you please!

It was a jarring moment, as I hardly need say! I regarded the item with a jaundiced eye, whilst pondering, not for the first time, Reeves' propensity for unveiling such developments at precisely the moment, and in exactly the manner, calculated to maximize the dramatic effect on the young master's beleaguered constitution.

My guard was down after all. I mean, one minute I am tooling down the highway of life, with no more weighty matter pressing upon my attention than that of deciding which silk cravat would set off my new purple paisley smoking jacket to the greatest advantage and the next moment I jam my foot into the pothole of fate and come the most horrendous purler, smack bang into the murky puddle of destiny.

This chain of events is by no means without precedent, as followers of my memoirs will aver[1] and always seems to be precipitated by the arrival of some

---

[1] See 'Zinctrumpet-Harris and the Danish Dachshund Debacle.

doubtful missive such as that which glared up at me now, in a manner more accusatory even than that of the kipper, which, it must be allowed, at least had reasonable grounds for feeling piqued.

I eyeballed the object further, decanting a measure of Lapsang Souchong to fortify the nerves. That it carried no obvious sign of having been dispatched by my Aunt Augusta was entirely to its credit. But then again there was absolutely no guarantee whatsoever, that the thing did not originate within Futwold Grange, a Hades that Dante would have hesitated to invent, and no really solid grounds to hope that its author was anyone other than that fearful hellcat, Aunt A.

September 24th 1999
Dearest Mostyn,
I trust that you are in good health dear boy.

Began the missive. - Hello? - Thought I, this striking me, on the whole, as a dashed promising first furlong by the seasons average. I mean, for my part, I would have preferred: 'Whato Mostyn old scream!' or: 'Tinkerty tonk Mosters old sock!' Nevertheless, it was a fairly matey opening gambit, given that communiqués from my aunt generally trip lightly over the social pleasantries, making a more or less immediate lunge for the jugular. Considerably bucked, I sloshed back a gulp of the old restorative and pressed on.

But even if you are at death's door, please do not imagine for a second that you will be excused from presenting yourself, here, tomorrow, at twelve o'clock sharp. There is a singular young woman staying with me at present, whom I wish you to meet.

Who knows? You may, even at this late stage, yet be rescued from a life of deplorable indolence.

Affectionately Yours,
Augusta Futwold.

I will own that with this lightening bolt, the legendary Zinctrumpet-Harris composure, for which my antecedents are legend, deserted me entirely. The jaw dropped. The eyes boggled. In fact so piscine was the combined effect, that in a less depleted state of vitality, my breakfast kipper would surely have hailed me heartily as a distantly related member of its kind.

'Hells bells!' I spluttered 'The balloon's gone up! Reeves, pack my steamer trunk and book a first class passage to Montevideo. I leave on the noon tide.'

'Ok.' replied the fellow oozing off.

'No hold hard Reeves, I didn't mean that literally.'

'No?'

'The remark was intended by way of hyper er hyper, what's the word Reeves?'

'Shit, I don't know. Hyper...' he paused uncertainly, '...dermic?'

'Good God Reeves! What in the name of Moroccan bottom-love are you blithering on about?' I cried aghast, 'Hypodermic Reeves? Jeepers! Hyperbole. That's the fellow. I was merely using hyperbole to emphasize the rumness of the 'rum do,' that appears to be threatening to queer the Zinctrumpet-Harris pitch.'

'Ah.'

'It's a conversational technique of which we British occasionally avail ourselves and with which I have, of late, been experimenting.'

'I often wondered how that was pronounced anyways.'

'Oh yes Reeves, most definitely hyperbole rather than hyperbole.'

'Or hyperbole, huh.'

'Snakes alive! Certainly not hyperbole Reeves.'

'Got it.'

'Edifying stuff what?'

'Yeah totally.' He yawned.

'Anyway the posish is this Reeves. Aunt Augusta demands my immediate transferral to the country pile.'

'Uh oh.'

''Uh,' as you rightly say Reeves, 'Oh.'' I affirmed, 'And when I tell you that she has apparently concocted another diabolic scheme to get me hitched, then I'm sure you will concur, that the 'do', as I have indicated, is indeed. 'Rum.''

'Hell yes.'

'Distinctly rum by crikey.'

'Distinctly,' he mused 'rum.'

'Any thoughts Reeves?'

'Well...'

'I dare say you will require further intelligence before formulating a stratagem, eh?'

'Well actually I...'

'Perhaps we ought to repair to Futters, in accordance with the dreaded A's wishes, before taking any steps.'

'Well,' he replied, after considering this, 'it wouldn't suck.'

'Play along for a while eh?'

'I guess.' He shrugged.

'Very well Reeves, in that case, throw a few things into a bag, just the barest essentials, I prefer to travel light.'

I picked and nibbled at my breakfast for a while longer but this recent disclosure that in spite of my unwavering opposition to the project, my Aunt remained resolutely determined to bring my care-free, one almost might say, caddish, reckless and self indulgent existence, beneath the umbrella of social respectability, rather took the joy out of the thing. I reflected, not for the first time, that waking up in the morning is a dicey business, with little to recommend it.

Abandoning the kipper, I fired up my first Turkish gasper of the day. Likewise the tiny aluminium portable computer that I had won in a game of mousetrap roulette on boat-race night, from a Belgian Lumberjack named Buddy Chevalier. I opened a truly salacious e-mail attachment from a young Austrian pen friend of mine and noting that she too was online, I engaged her in a brief exchange by means of a rather ingenious facility, not entirely unlike a light speed version of the post office telegram service, and known as the 'instant messenger'.

Shortly, Reeves re-appeared wielding a rather vulgar looking valise, constructed seemingly from artificial rhino hide and festooned with a collection of garish stripes and, mystifyingly, the word Reebok (why not kudu or Thompson's gazelle?)

I glanced inside to find a toothbrush, half a packet of cashew nuts, my novelty John Lee Hooker chillum pipe, which went 'boom boom boom boom,' when you inhaled, a hundred feet or so of orange nylon climbing rope and an extremely stale, hollowed-out section of baguette. Closer examination revealed that this last item had had inserted into it, a pair of slightly effete sunglasses based around the principle of the two way mirror.

I heaved a long sigh whilst formulating my next sentence.

Although he was without peer in butling circles, and whilst I had come to think of him as nothing less than my right hand, the art of extracting from Reeves the performance of which he was capable, without ruffling his sensibilities, had been, of late, rather more than usually taxing.

'Reeves old thing.'

'Yuh.'

'Whilst the alacrity with which you complied with my instruction, viz. To 'throw a few things into a bag'.

'Barest essentials' and so on, was nothing less than dazzling.'

'Uh huh.'

'Might I suggest one or two alterations to the inventory?'

'Go for it.'

'I ought to explain Reeves that I was, once again, employing the overstatement of understatement.'

'Oh right'.

'I didn't mean for you to literally toss a collection of randomly selected items into a small and unpleasant looking leatherette sports holdall.'

'Gotcha.'

'Perhaps I ought to have said, bung in all the usual chattels, the morning suit, the evening black tie, the grouse shooting tweeds and so on; only pass lightly over the string quartet and eschew entirely the half size billiard table.'

'Dammit! Sorry man.'

'Not at all Reeves the fault is entirely mine.'

'I'll be right back.'

'Oh and of course my new purple paisley smoking jacket.'

'Jeez no! You're not actually gonna wear that piece of shit?' Cried Reeves, fractionally inclining an eyebrow in such a way as to convey a sense of acute dismay.

'Certainly I intend to wear that, p. of s. Reeves. The item was described in 'The Cad' magazine {The Indispensable Monthly Companion to Dionysian Dandyism} as: 'The quintessence of sartorial vim.' Need I say more?'

Reeves oozed thither.

———————————

One of the more precipitous pitfalls with which the career path of Hollywood actors such as Reeves is beset, besides that of malicious paternity litigation and misadventurous rhinoplasty, is the risk of becoming typecast.

A sense begins to form in the mind of the viewing audience that the actor can only be truly believable in certain roles. Some artistes by sheer talent and versatility defy such categorizations, others though are forever confined by their past successes to endlessly inhabit the same persona.

Ho hum, I say, every rose has its thorn, every country its Basingstoke but Reeves seems to dwell upon this rather, perhaps due to his tendency to attract roles which call for the heroic, masculine and yet, shall we say, not especially cerebral type.

For this reason one doesn't like to draw attention to his more appalling gaffes viz. the wildebeest satchel and its contents, lest it rather rubs the old hooter in the fact that he is fairly widely, and in point of fact, completely inaccurately, regarded as being a couple of lengths off the pace in the intellectual maiden stakes.

In perhaps his most aptly cast role in the massively successful film 'The Matrix,' Reeves' character Neo seeks the advice of 'the Oracle' in order to settle, once and for all, the vexed question of whether or not he is in fact 'the One'. (The more percipient film-goer might intuit at this point that an eye for anagrams might have assisted him in penetrating this mystery {and by extension raise questions about a possible future role for Brian Eno in the fate of the universe} but there it is.) At any rate 'the Oracle' eyeballs the young computer hacker and man of destiny, and opens probably the choicest dialogue exchange in a film not overly burdened with proseity,

'You're cuter than I thought' She muses, 'I can see why she likes you.'

'Who?' Reeves rasps, and probably it ought to be mentioned here that, besides the Oracle, there is really only one other female character in the film.

'Not too bright though' retorts she.

It can't be easy for the poor devil.

2 THE LYCEUM

'I fly because it releases my mind from the tyranny of petty things.' Antoine de Saint-Exupery

Seated on a rock at the plateau's Northernmost tip, Les and Derek gazed out across the endless Australian desert.

Nothing was happening.

It had been happening relentlessly since lunchtime, swelling to a giddy crescendo of inactivity at about four o'clock, and, as the last evening of the millennium wore on, it showed no signs of letting up. Nothing unusual in that - the outback not being precisely noted as a riot of activity, by and large - it's just that, by local standards, the morning of December 31st 1999 had been pretty crowded with incident. The afternoon though, really had been very slow indeed.

For the longest time the pair continued to gaze at the incandescent, crimson sunset, smouldering on the Western horizon. They gazed too at the sepulchral, silver moon already rising in the East. And as they gazed, each was filled with an overwhelming and all consuming sense of not really giving two hoots one way or the other. They had seen it all before and, in truth, they weren't really especially interested. In fact they were at that time in their lives when nothing in the vast, arid landscape around them, engaged their enthusiasm as much as the occasional flying insect unlucky enough to stray within range of their sticky darting tongues.

By way of a comparison, a couple of human beings in their position, might have been rather enchanted by the splendour of the sky. In all probability they would have been pretty captivated by the moon too and perhaps a little haunted by the desert's eerie sense of emptiness. Where they would really have scored over the goannas though, is in noticing (and noticing almost immediately) that they were seated atop a simply gigantic column of rock, which, by some freak of geology, erupted vertically from the desert floor and thrusted dramatically hundreds of metres into the sky, before squaring off to form the sun baked plateau upon which Les and Derek had led their entire lives in blissful ignorance.

Of course, in the longer term, the people might have found the plateau a little wanting for diversion. Not so Les and Derek. For them the total absence of any discernable activity was precisely the feature of life in this part of the desert that most appealed. They were not, on the whole, positively disposed towards sudden developments in their lives. A few more flies to eat might have been a welcome improvement and perhaps the odd tiny lizard for a change but in general, everything was just as they would wish. Hence it was with a certain sense of foreboding that they were forced, reluctantly, to recognize, that the tiny speck in the indigo sky to the north, was incrementally growing in size.

As the evening wore on, the speck continued to grow - gradually resolving itself into two distinct shapes. The larger was the crescent shape of a wing, constructed entirely from fabric. Beneath the wing, suspended by hundreds of lines, hung a rather smaller object with arms and legs. The goannas had seen this before too, and hadn't been all that crazy about it on that occasion either. In fact they were decidedly inclined to the opinion that they could do without the distraction. Life on the plateau was quite hectic enough for them as it was.

Nevertheless the paraglider continued to draw nearer, descending gradually and then lazily circling in some rising air to gain a little height before resuming its long glide. In due course the pilot set up his final approach and shifted forwards in the harness easing his legs down beneath him in readiness for the landing. He was a young man, and on his extravagantly suntanned face he wore a sensational pencil moustache and an expression of rigid concentration. The moment his feet touched down softly on the plateau though, the intensity that gripped him, shattered like glass. He shuddered, almost convulsed, with a profound release of emotion - as though a gigantic charge of latent tension was being dissipated into the earth. Even as the glider's gossamer folds swirled lightly to the ground around him, he slowly crumpled to his knees and began to sob like a baby.

3 FUTWOLD GRANGE

'My boyfriend did that in Tenerife. They tow you behind a boat don't they?'

Brighton Hairdresser

As reported earlier, notwithstanding the occasional wobble, the Zinctrumpet-Harris composure is pretty formidable stuff. We are, on the whole, justly proud of the Iron resolve with which my great grandfather faced down four thousand spear-brandishing Zulus at Rorke's drift. And the impassive sangfroid maintained by great uncle Cecil as he charged with the first Light artillery at Balaclava is stamped upon the souls of all our breed.

In fact, one distant ancestor, Lord Frobisher 'Stiffy' Nutcutlet-Harris sported an upper lip so stiff that it withstood a direct hit from a Biafran sniper bullet, sustaining only minor moustache damage.

I mention this purely by way of indicating that it takes more than the prospect of certain death to wilt a Zinctrumpet-Harris's equanimity. Learning of the purgatory that awaited me at Futwold had been a nasty jolt certainly. In fact it was definitely a setback to rank alongside Dodgy Guru falling at the last in the Chepstow hurdle. On the basis of form however, it had not been entirely un-foreseeable. Aunt A had pulled similar stunts on at least half a dozen occasions in recent memory. In fact, as developments go, it was probably even more predictable than the denouement of 'Zinctrumpet-Harris And The Case Of The Butler Who Turned Out To Have Been Savaged By A Rottweiler.' (2002). The initial shock quickly passed therefore and once the ramifications of the proposal had been sieved through the little grey cells, it was a more sanguine Zinctrumpet-H that emerged. Grappling with a nameless dread certainly but outwardly composed, which is, of course, the really important thing.

Permit me to outline my thinking on the matter. And a pretty deft piece of reasoning it is too:

At the risk breaking modesty's well known injunction against ventilating ones own tri-valved brass wind instrument, I believe I can claim that in a number of highly regarded arenas of human endeavour, I have become, during my twenty nine years as a tenant upon this coil, if not exactly ept, then at least comfortably clear of being inept.

17

For example I can, whilst blindfolded and handcuffed, mix from its raw constituents, a sensational pineapple daiquiri, whilst simultaneously playing the left handed part of 'Hey Jude,' on a stylophone[2]. A feat, the mechanics of which, will not be explored for the moment, in the interests of dramatic suspense.

Furthermore my eerily plausible impersonation of the eminent rap artist Doggy Dogg Snoopy, was sufficiently authentic to bamboozle a certain distinguished public personage, in a momentarily diverting episode with an answering machine at a royal garden party[3]. And at the risk of over egging the pudding, let me divulge that I have gone head to head and puff for puff on a Moroccan hookah pipe extravagantly loaded with Afghani hashish against Otto 'the lungs' Shleswig Holstien Pils,' once acclaimed by 'Weed Magazine' {The Indispensable Monthly Companion to Pharmaceutical Recreation} as 'The hardest smoker in Bavaria.'[4]

A glittering portfolio of attributes then. Almost an embarrassment of riches you might think. And yet (and this realization was as sunshine breaking through the gloomy storm clouds) as the keen reader may already have intuited: depending upon where you stand on such things, the plenitude of qualities with which the lottery

---

2 See 'Zinctrumpet-Harris and the Schnauzer of Zanzibar.'

3 See 'Zinctrumpet-Harris and Da Dogg.'

4 See 'Zinctrumpet-Harris and the Munich Beer Cellar Pooch.'

of life has equipped young M. tend rather in the opposite direction to those viewed as ideal traits in a prospective husband. In much the same way that depending on where you stand, Andover is in rather the opposite direction to Mozambique.

Indeed when one stops to think about it, it would be no exaggeration to say that the view of Mostyn most commonly held among the female element, shares all of its main components with the view of rampaging rogue elephants prevalent amongst pigmies. At least in so far as it strongly motivates them to run, flat out, in the opposite direction.

As a consequence of this heartening realisation, I found myself pondering one of life's more pervasive platitudes. To wit, it is surely axiomatic, that the course a young man, seeking to insinuate himself into the affections of a young lady, ought most profitably to pursue, is to 'just be himself'. 'Just be yourself' is the very chorus of those whose counsel is sought by such fellows. And amongst those of my acquaintance who (for reasons as resistant to explanation as, say, why anyone would have their ears zinc plated) have entered into the state of holy matrimony, 'just being themselves,' has been the most frequently cited expedient.

It is one of the golden rules which, in company with 'Love thy neighbour as thyself,' and 'Watch out for seagulls!' form the holy trinity of life's imperatives.

Be yourself!

I found myself therefore on the nub of a bit of a paradox. Since the consensus of opinion indicated that 'being oneself,' represented the best policy in making a positive impression upon ones hearts desire, presumably it followed that being 'as though someone else,' was my best shot at avoiding the ghastly fate for which Aunt A had sketched me in.

On the other hand, bearing in mind the rebarbative effect most frequently produced in f.s of the s. by exposure to Mostyn's society, then being virtually anyone other than myself, logically had to be the approach most likely to succeed, and hence fail.

Which then was to be my philosophy? To rely upon my generally acknowledged propensity to send the non-chap element sprinting for the cliff edge? Or to deliberately invert the best available advice for acquiring a mate, and exploit the veracity of the golden rule, by breaking it?

I wondered which course of action Aunt Augusta's would favour. A degree of misrepresentation stopping not far short of total fiction, in all probability. She would no doubt propose playing down the gambling drinking and general idling side of the young Zinctrumpet-H. encouraging instead more of a conversational focus on the personal qualities of lovely little bunnies, the charm of rainbows and the appeal of pretty flowers and whatnot.

In this speculation though, later events were to reveal that I had erred, and erred badly. Oh yes.

In the end I evaded the quandary with the logical sleight of hand that whichever approach I adopted, I was almost guaranteed to fare pretty disastrously. Therefore I would simply present myself as a buffoonish fathead with all of the social graces of a flatulent Welshman. Duly I laid the subject to one side and concentrated on lacing-up the new handmade brogues that I had lately commissioned from Charles Thwaite of Jermyn Street London[5].

---

[5] *This is a red herring.*

4 SPLIF* ABUSE MORON

First light or thereabouts the next a.m. saw Reeves and I stumble from my Brighton pied-a-terre, pink of eye and sore of head. The echoes of a night of hallucinogenic debauchery were swirling still around our addled brains and maddeningly the song 'Boom Boom Boom Boom,' by the Venga Boys had now been lodged in my head for almost seventeen hours.

It had been a pretty intense night of psychedelic sensory discovery and general transcendental frolicking, which had climaxed in Reeves' shaven skull beginning, to me at least, to resemble one of those phrenology heads to which the Victorians were inclined - divided into sections according to the area of brain function thought to take place therein. At one stage, an area just above his left eyebrow, shaped rather like Luxembourg and

---

* Quite right.

labelled 'Belief,' in a confident, calligraphic hand, had acquired a purple paisley appearance. Reeves would not be drawn into an explanation of this though, in spite of my threat to feed his cannabis to the Chinchilla.

With difficulty we located the motor car in an adjacent street, next to the bank, without which, upon a bread crate and clad in malodorous rags, sat, as was his habit, a prolifically bearded fellow with a permanent expression of extreme astonishment upon his grizzled face. He wore his hair in the style popular amongst participants in Van der Graaf generator experiments.

'Any change?' shrieked this fragrant vagrant, as he always did. I appraised him for a long moment.

'Nope. Still barking mad as far as I can see.' I replied. No idea why he always asked me this. Not really my field.

Responding, no doubt, to a deeply ingrained conditioned reflex, I found myself inspecting the atmospheric conditions and noted wistfully that once again a munificent creator appeared to have arranged things expressly to excite the anticipation of that most splendid of fellows: The skybum! This truly was a first class sky for flying a paraglider. The almighty had opted for a variant on the flawless china blue theme, generously festooned with those fluffy, flat bottomed clouds resembling the blob of frothed milk on an inexpensive cappuccino. I felt a little tug at my soul, beckoning me whence I could not go.

Despite the tenderness of the hour, barely nine o'clock, the street swarmed with the unnamed masses. Hollow-eyed proles, bandy-legged stevedores and rat-faced urchins, loomed large. The flotsam of Brighton, 'the city that never sleeps but occasionally slips into unconsciousness'. Some of these hobbledehoys even had the bad grace to snigger at Reeves as he scraped the seagull droppings from the Triumph's windscreen with my Ben and Jerry's loyalty card whilst I warmed up the engine. I pulled down the earflaps of my leather flying helmet and stared fixedly ahead.

Notwithstanding the occasional, arresting flashback as trace levels of psychoactive drugs ebbed and flowed throughout my nervous system, the actual journey down the B2114 to Balcome that fateful autumn day, was not especially crowded with incident. In fact, as I look up from my writing now, some three years on, and gaze out from my perch on the upper terrace of the Darjeeling Paragliding club, noting with approval the inchoate early morning cumulus clouds already forming across the valley before me, I find that I can conjure to mind no real recollection whatsoever of that trip to Aunt A's besides that of being constantly and severely criticised for the excessive use of speed, by a hysterically indignant Reeves. An accusation, the unfairness of which (as I was obliged repeatedly to rehearse) dwelt in the fact that he, rather than I, was at the wheel.

We were, it is fair to say, a little wired as a result of the early morning toot that we had hoovered up to chase away the mescaline.

Now Futwold grange is a rum old pile. Or at least the house itself is fairly bobbish but there is something about the way in which it is stranded in that hinterland between the North and South Downs that is the Sussex Weald, which offends one's sense of Feng shui.

The place contrives to resemble some great biblical ark stuffed to the plimsoll line with a menagerie of gods creatures - or indeed washing machines for what difference it makes - a leviathan let's say, albeit designed by someone with a worrying ignorance of the principles of streamlining and hydrodynamics. A benighted hulk then in fact, whose progress in navigating some ancient river basin was arrested when the water unexpectedly and inconveniently evaporated.

This impression derives partly, one suspects, from its seemingly arbitrary orientation - a whisker to the West of West South West - which suggests that it has run aground at a slightly undignified angle and sunk into the mud up to its poop deck but that its captain is seeking to maintain the pretence of having merely stopped for a few minutes to let the elks stretch their legs.

Ditto the apparent pointlessness of Futwold's exact location is one calculated to depress even the most enterprisingly calumnious estate agent. It stands fairly close to a small unhealthy looking copse and about a mile or so from a, not wildly significant, little pond, in a manner rather suggestive of the widely known 'empty car park effect.' This little understood phenomenon dictates that the first motorist to arrive in an empty car park must overcome a significant inner struggle against simply pulling up and getting out of the car, due to the gnawing sense of having merely 'stopped' the vehicle rather than having truly achieved 'parking' with its satisfying sense of geometrical adjacency.

Though I must have made the pilgrimage down to Futters hundreds of times but the place still manages to creep up on me like a butler in pursuit of a pay rise. Thus it was with the peculiar jolt of the anticipated surprise which somehow still manages to jar, that as Reeves veered my howlingly shabby Triumph Herald round the last bend in the lane, we were confronted by the imposing gateway of my childhood perch. Its granite gateposts were connected by a proscenium arch, atop which, picked out in a filigree of wrought iron, were a few characters. Where Dante might, perhaps, have placed the legend: 'All hope abandon, ye who enter here' the arch, instead, announced the house beyond as Futwold Grange.

Timorously creeping up the gravel drive I recognised the solid figure in white, standing atop the steps like the figurehead on the petrified slave galleon of Futwold, as Aunt Augusta herself. In the manner of a Turkish gamekeeper setting the dogs upon a poacher and looking perfectly sinister in doing so, Aunt A. sternly bade her two uniformed flunkeys heave our cases from the Triumph's boot and favoured me with a look suggestive of having discovered, too late, that there was a slug in her lettuce.

'Whato Aunt A' chirped I, squeaking up the steps in my new brogues[7].

'Never mind all that young man', quoth the nephew mangler, histrionically consulting her watch and rolling her eyes, 'follow me.' I biffed along after her, reflecting as we toddled through the dusty corridors of the enormous house, that If ever aunt A should find herself in need of gainful employment (and the contingency is a remote one) then she might wish to punt her personality in cities such as Naples, which, cowering within the immediate neighbourhood of active volcanoes, may have need of something which could freeze lava.

After banging on at some length about how fortunate I ought to consider myself in having someone of Aunt A's estimable clout to line me up with opportunities of which others can only dream, and so on (strings pulled, favours called in, don't mess it up etc,) she deposited young Mostyn with, I thought, rather scant regard for the protocol appropriate to introductions of this sort, within a the small wooden panelled anti chamber immediately adjacent to her office.

'Now listen carefully.' barked the elderly relative as though addressing a simpleton, 'the reason that I have

---

[7] *Or is it?*

brought you here today, is that I very much wish to present you to Miss Ernestine Epswurf.'

'Righto.'

'Ernestine was a little doubtful about this Mostyn, owing to your relatively advanced age but I assured her that you are extremely immature.' She plucked from my mouth the Chuppa Chups lollipop I had been sucking and deposited it in a wastepaper basket. 'and she has kindly agreed to this meeting as a special favour to me.'

'Capital Aunt A'

'And for once' she said 'If at all possible, do you think you could just be yourself?'

'Rather Aunt A.' chirped I. She heaved a sigh of acute resignation and beetled off.

I threw myself into the comfy leather sofa that had thoughtfully been provided, lit up a gasper, parked the merchandise of Charles Thwaite of Jermyn Street London on the coffee table[8], and began to mull over Aunt A's curious behaviour. I was a trifle peeved that, as on each of her half-dozen or so previous attempts to affiance me to a member of the sex, Aunt A. had chosen to park me *without* the chamber of this mysterious Ernestine. Surely a Pimms and croquet type of affair is more, the form, for such occasions. 'Ernestine, allow me to present my nephew Mostyn. Ernestine schools polo ponies Mostyn...' Furthermore I was nothing short of

---

[8] *Yep.*

bamboozled as to why Aunt A should counsel me to be of all things, myself! Very suggestive.

Whilst absently scrutinizing a mote of dust twinkling in a shaft of sunlight, I tried to formulate the most crassly gauche approach that an inept suitor might make to the object of his affections. A lumpen indifference to the charms of lovely little bunnies, struck me as a promising stance. Also a general lack of enthusiasm for poetry, rainbows and pretty flowers and a withering scorn for all things fluffy. Perhaps one or two mildly revolting personal habits too. A propensity to belch extravagantly after paying a complement, for instance - and maybe a Welsh accent. First impressions count after all and it was hence vitally important to make an extremely bad one.

My meditations were interrupted presently by the sound of an electric buzzer of the type that one seldom hears nowadays. Extinguishing my cigarette in the make-shift ashtray that I had fashioned from the no smoking sign on the coffee table, I glanced in its general direction and noticed for the first time that above the other door leading from the room were two lights, one red, one green. The green light was illuminated, bidding me hither. Curiouser and yet more curious. I stepped inside.

'Lock ze door please.' The female voice was low and calm with, to my surprise, a strong German accent. Its owner occupied the large leather swivel chair behind the expensive looking reddish, L shaped desk in the opposite corner of Aunt A's office.

As interiors go, the room was rather institutional in its theme, featuring a couple of filing cabinets, a couch of some species or other, a free standing cupboard and, it's only concession to decoration, a rather austere bust, perched upon a plinth, just beside the door. The chair and its occupant faced away from me and towards the computer. Above it spiralled a coil of blue smoke. Keyboard tapping could be heard.

I turned the key in the lock and approached the desk like a guilty schoolboy. As I drew near, my brogues made an unexpectedly flatulent noise on the wooden floor. More keystrokes. A pause. She revolved slowly around in the chair.

Holy Christ on a jet ski!

This was quite simply the most sensational looking woman upon whom my eyes had ever been clapped. She was attired in the familiar long white coat that enjoys such popularity amongst the ladies of Aunt Augusta's acquaintance. It was accessorized with a rectangular plastic brooch emblazoned with the legend Ernestine Epswurf Mpsy. But it was the way that she wore it, like a second skin, that so accentuated her deliciously feminine curves. She eased her Havana cigar into the cleft of the crystal ashtray and offered me her hand across the desk. To do this required her to lean slightly forward, providing me with a view from which it was inescapably obvious that besides this thrillingly ironic garment, she wore only a look as cool as a polar bear's outside loo.

'Mostyn,' I ventured, struggling to keep the Leslie Phillips effect from creeping into my voice 'Mostyn Zinctrumpet-Harris.' This woman was about as far from the prim, mousey, bespectacled types that Aunt A generally wheeled out, as Weymouth is from Alpha Centuri. 'If the skin on her hand is this soft', I found myself thinking, 'just imagine...'

'A pleasure Mostyn,' she replied, and in her mouth the word had a certain ring, I thought. Reaching down into an unsettlingly hideous leatherette holdall on the floor by the desk festooned with a collection of stripes and, mystifyingly, the word Reebok, (why not antelope or gnu?) she produced an over-sized egg timer which she placed on the desk. I sat down gingerly, like a Conservative M.P.

'We haven't long,' she said contemplating the item.

'We haven't?'

'Believe me you are, how do you say? on the back foot.' she said. 'The best thing you can do is try to keep up.'

'Righto.'

She gave me a long and level look, checking she had my full attention, inverted the timer and then she spoke.

'Mostyn,' she began 'how do you account for the dominance of the human species on this planet?'

Good gracious! I thought, pulling a face, Where's this going I wonder? As indicated, I had been planning on playing the buffoonish fathead card pretty strongly throughout the up-coming interview. Besides heaping derision upon poetry, rainbows and the disarming twitchy-nosiness of lovely little bunnies etc, the kind of conversational agenda that I had anticipated didn't extend very far beyond the weather, the test series and the advisability or otherwise of betting one's shirt on Dodgy Guru to win the Cheltenham Gold cup. Anthropology, by way of contrast, was rather towards the other end of the list of possibles. In fact, just above necrophilia and coprophagy[9].

'We are neither particularly fast nor strong nor robust,' she continued, 'how did we get so far up the tree?'

'Oh Lordy.' I sighed 'Well let me see. Isn't it opposable thumbs or something?'

'Partly, what else?'

I cast my eyes about the room as though for inspiration, noticing as I did so a length of orange nylon climbing rope hanging outside the window.

'Um. Intelligence?' I ventured. She appeared to consider this for a moment.

'Certainly we are more intelligent than most other animals but our range overlaps with that of higher apes. A five year old child has the equivalent intelligence of an

---

[9] *See Zinctrumpet-Harris and the Shanghai Shitsu Shenanigans.*

adult chimp, and yet our supremacy is totally disproportionate.'

I thought back to my days as a psychology undergraduate at the Polytechnic of Worthing, suddenly wishing I had paid closer attention to the ramblings of Professor Ludwig Cillit-Bang. 'Culture? Language?' I asked vaguely.

She surveyed me for a long moment with her mesmeric eyes. Twin lacunae, so dark the iris and pupil were indivisible.

'You're brighter than I thought.' she murmured at length. 'No wonder he likes you.'

'Who?' I enquired.

'Not too cute though.' She mused wrinkling her nose.

'Well really!' I blustered.

'The human race' she began, rolling the cigar between her fingers in a distracting manner, 'proliferates because, through language and in particular, through writing, its leading members can pass on the discoveries that they make. As a result, even the most unexceptional member of the species can directly benefit from their breakthroughs. It took the mind of Edward Jenner to make the logical leap that lead to the smallpox vaccine for example but as a direct consequence we are all immune from the disease.'

Again I found myself gazing with a sensation not unlike envy at the cigar as she caressed it with her fingers.

'This process of disseminating ideas,' she continued 'effectively equips us all with capabilities vastly in excess of our own and places at our disposal almost infinitely more knowledge than we could possibly acquire for ourselves in a lifetime. Thus we appear much more capable and intelligent than we are, because we are, as Newton professed himself to be, 'upon the shoulders of giants.''

'Righto.' I said cautiously. Although precisely what all this had to do with the market conditions relating to seafood, was still far from becoming apparent.

'The reality,' she said 'is that ninety nine point nine nine percent of humans are entirely intellectually negligible. Just husks really, like agar filled petri dishes for incubating d.n.a. Their only contribution to the species is as a reservoir of genetic heterogeneity.'

'Jeepers!' I gasped, 'you are Austrian aren't you?' She ignored this and continued.

'The key to mans supremacy relative to animals then, is that his achievements do not reflect the average capabilities of its members, rather the bar is pushed higher and higher by a very tiny but eminent minority.'

'This would be the point zero zero one percent of us that aren't husks, one supposes.'

The tiniest flash of anger flared momentarily within those heart-stopping eyes and she fixed me with a look that seemed to say, 'I happen to have gone to a lot of trouble to be here telling you something the significance of which could hardly be exaggerated, so just handle it o.k.!' No little amount to convey in a look, I would be the first to concede but, as indicated earlier, these were some pretty high calibre peepers.

'When the first stone-age man banged a couple of rocks together to make fire, three hundred thousand years ago,' she resumed. 'the other members of his tribe watched him and copied his idea. Since that moment mankind's social and technological development has been accelerating at a rate that is itself accelerating. Knowledge breeds knowledge.'

There is an old aphorism, Reeves would tell you who said it, that it is better to remain silent and be thought a fool, than to speak up and remove all doubt. I said nothing. And I said it like I meant it.

'The human brain is almost identical to that of our prehistoric ancestors, because biological evolution is a slow process,' she went on 'but unlike genes, ideas don't need generations to pervade the meme pool. They aren't inherited, they can be transmitted horizontally within a generation, through example, communication, culture, and now of course, they can travel at light speed through the internet.

Everywhere at once, ideas are like viruses, infecting the minds of their hosts, changing and adapting to circumvent the resistance deployed against them,'

Again I said nothing but this time I said it with more emphasis. There was a little more keyboard tapping.

'As far as governments are concerned Mostyn,' she continued 'really big ideas tend to be perceived as either an opportunity, or a threat. So if you come up with an idea to cure obesity, or a way to make petrol out of sand, you'll probably be hailed as the new messiah.'

'I dare say.'

'But ironically, if you unleash a breakthrough on the ideological level, then you are much more likely to be treated like the old one.'

'Nailed to a cross eh?'

'Exactly,'

'Cripes.' I pondered this.

'An idea can kill you Mostyn, as surely as a virus can. Because, like a virus, an idea doesn't care about the interests of its host, or even about its own survival. It merely exists. And if the environment happens to be favourable for it, it will continue to exist. And multiply. And its potential for multiplication is infinite.' She took a puff of her cigar. 'Take fascism,' she continued, 'in the thirties it existed at a low level, as tuberculosis does today, until suddenly conditions were right for it to flourish and then, aided by one particularly contagious carrier, it flared up in an epidemic, with results that were disastrous for all concerned.'

'So, erm, just to check I'm keeping up. Did you just compare Jesus to Hitler?'

'Yes.' she said without irony. 'Both men professed ideas which directly caused their deaths and the deaths of countless millions.'

'Well there is that I suppose.' I conceded. Pausing briefly she leant forward to ease the cap of ash from her Havana, giving me as she did so, a mildly indecent thrill.

'And because of the upheaval visited on society by the ideas of an eminent few in the past two centuries, the authorities naturally wish to keep an eye on anyone who may have anything comparably seditious in their head. Because every dangerous idea has its Typhoid Mary.'

'Ernestine, I suppose you do realize how dreadfully paranoid all of this sounds.'

'Ask yourself honestly Mostyn. What do you think the state would have done about Karl Marx if they had known for a fact the outcomes that would arise from his ideas about society? The upheaval that would be perpetrated in his name?'

'Erm. Popped him off you reckon?'

'Certainly.'

By this stage I had begun to develop a disquieting feeling in respect of this conversation. A feeling that will be familiar to anyone who has unsuccessfully run to catch a bus. It was the feeling that the whole thing was rather getting away from me.

'It's not that this isn't all jolly fascinating Ernestine but....'

'A lot of people are *jolly fascinated* by what makes these people different!' She interrupted with some force. 'And there are those who believe it cannot be coincidence that so many of them are from the German speaking world. Mozart, Kant, Haydn, Beethoven, Wittgenstein, Schubert, Goethe, Schopenhauer, Hegel, Marx, Brahms, Nietzsche, Wagner, Freud, Einstein...'

'But Ernestine old thing,' I soothed, interrupting her interruption, since the list showed no signs of abating until it reached Michael Schumacher. Actually the entire diatribe seemed to have a niggling familiarity to it and I was beginning to form a strong impression that she was telling me a story of which she was not the author. It goes without saying that I was also a trifle pipped by her heavy sarcasm. 'Not wishing to interrupt you in full flow,' I continued, 'I can't help wondering why you have gone to these, presumably considerable, lengths, to rehearse this theory of yours to...well, me.'

'Have you never felt that there was something different about you Mostyn? That you were here for a special reason that had yet to be revealed to you.'

I pondered this angle. 'Well, not really no. I mean that's just existential angst isn't it. Everybody has that.'

'Interesting.'

'Of course they do, that's why the plots of so many books and films hinge upon a character who, having previously assumed himself to be witheringly normal and having been considered by the gen. public at large to be a bit of a tick, suddenly discovers he can spin webs or dodge bullets or what have you.'

'But such fiction is popular with precisely the type of person who would love to be superman but is really Clark Kent.' She parried, 'You by contrast are more likely to read 'Fly Fishing by J. R. Hartley,' you have a self image to which nobody but yourself would aspire.'

'So why did you ask me if I thought I was special in some way?'

'What I asked you,' she said quietly 'was if you didn't.'

'And I don't.'

'Which means that, at least in that respect, you are.'

Her logic was inescapable, and it wasn't until some considerable time later, that it occurred to me how unlikely it was that a native Austrian would have heard of J.R. Hartley.

'Very well then,' I interjected feeling the need to chivvy things along towards their logical conclusion, 'am I to take it then Ernestine, that you are suggesting that I, Mostyn Zinc-trumpet Harris, am in fact one of these ubermenshen? These happy few with their world changing ideas?'

She favoured me with a look suggestive of having discovered a maggot in her apple, accompanied by a rather unflattering nasal sound, before throwing back her head and laughing like a drain. She revealed as she did so a set of teeth which rather put one in mind of Martina Navratilova, set in a jaw which suddenly seemed altogether more prognathous and masculine than at first I had realized.

'Something wrong? I enquired weakly as a wave of cigar halitosis reached me across the desk. She continued to convulse, issuing now a really strikingly plausible impression of a male whooper swan, trying across some distance to convey to a female whooper swan, his conviction that what this world really needed was a few more little whooper swans.

I am bound to say, that at this point love died. Actually it died a death that was both nauseating and unnecessarily gratuitous. In fact love hurled itself from the penthouse balcony of hope, accelerated rapidly past the twenty-five storeys of bitter experience, to be unrecognizably mangled on the keep-left sign of disillusionment.

'Mien Gott' gasped the stricken Teuton embarking on a display of sickeningly productive coughing, 'what you? Ha ha ha ha ha!' more coughing ensued, I could all too easily visualize the grey sputum being redistributed around her interior. 'you? Ha ha ha ha ha ha!'

I heaved a sigh folding my arms and noticed the sand was almost through the timer. One excruciating eternity later she had somewhat recovered.

'No Mostyn,' she said, giggling a little into my proffered pocket handkerchief and loudly blowing her nose 'you are not the one.' She took a deep breath at the end of which she was entirely composed, 'but perhaps in order to accept what I am telling you,' she continued 'It will be necessary for you to acknowledge who you really are.'

'Yes, well it's been a real pleasure Ernesti... I beg your pardon?!' This last remark caused me a spasm of acute anxiety. The conversation, it seemed, had reached a crossroads. In my experience, when someone invites you to acknowledge who you really are, they generally have one of two things on their mind. On the one hand they could be about to witter on at length about self knowledge and connecting with the inner child; A tedious but not unprecedented scenario round at Aunt A's place. Alternatively, and rather more worryingly, they could be on the point of denuding a chap of his assumed identity. A scenario of which, those of us who live behind a pseudonym, live in mortal dread. A molecule or two of lysergic acid, still adrift in my bloodstream from the previous night, may have become lodged in a synapse at this point, as, for a moment, Ernestine suddenly appeared to shimmer at the far end of a long and kaleidoscopic tunnel. This passed.

'The face that you present to the world Mostyn,' she resumed, 'is a mask. A crude cipher created by your subconscious and thrown around you like a cloak. It is a composite, assembled, it seems, from the works of P.G. Wodehouse, Captain W. E. Johns, Anthony Buckeridge, Enid Blyton, Agatha Christie, Evelyn Waugh. In fact you seem to have incorporated just about any fairly tweedy fictional influence from your childhood.' Gratefully, I breathed an inner sigh of relief. Clearly, this was to be merely more of the feeble psychobabble that seems to enjoy such favour amongst associates of Aunt A. For now, it seemed, my real identity was safe. I braced myself to play my part in this weary drama. To feign indignation at such slander. "Displaying resistance." "Evading my issues."

'Hellhounds of Hades!' I spluttered accordingly.

'Ah, plus Vivian Stanshall apparently.'

She took a lazy puff, indulging in a tiny smirk at what she presumably considered a deft jab. Tapping a few keys whilst I marshalled my thoughts.

'You see, the trouble with spending your childhood in a place like Futwold Grange' I began in due course, 'is that you have less chance of developing normally than an ant growing up in a flamenco school.'

'How so?'

'Well, I never knew my parents Ernestine, and grew up knowing nothing of them; so who was I to be? I had no sense of social or cultural identity and so, I suppose, I must have rather osmosed the upper class mindset of Aunt A.'

'And this is why you come across like some kind of nineteen thirties fop is it?'

'Well the thing is,' I replied, 'television was frowned upon by Aunt A. It was allowed on a strictly rationed basis but the way to gain approval was to eschew it entirely in favour of a dusty volume from Futwold.G.'s compendious library 'I gestured vaguely in the direction of the west wing by way of illustration, 'and by and large this suited me famously, as soap operas set in urban Manchester didn't speak loudly to a boy growing up in a house where the difference between who and whom was taken more seriously than that between City and United.' I was on familiar ground here, having trotted out this bilge numerous times in the past. 'Naturally therefore I found more to relate to in stories about the boarding school japes of Jennings and Darby and the adventures of The Famous Five.'

'Hmm.' she opined with a noncommittal air.

'Later I probably over-identified with the mythical England of Bertie Wooster, where mild mannered, latently homosexual vicars took part in sack races at village fetes. An England of cucumber sandwiches and Sopwith Camels and Wimbledon and open-top two-seaters haring along country lanes. I found I could relate to the stiffness of Wodehouse's characters. Their sense of emotional containment.'

'That they were grown-up versions of little boys.'

'That kind of thing.'

'So whilst other children aspired to be action heroes, secret agents and so on, you styled yourself on the emotionally constipated English nitwit?'

'Er, well pretty much, yes.'

'No doubt this affectation attracted a degree of ridicule.'

'Jeepers, I should say so.' I emitted a giggle the girlishness of which surpassed my expectations of it. 'By the time I arrived at university I had well and truly acquired the musty redolence of a cloistered upbringing. And it jarred rather with the zealous toff-bashing overnight socialists, I can tell you.'

'I can imagine.' She concurred. A little too emphatically for my liking but I let it go and pressed on.

'For instance, I'll never forget the remarks made by my college flatmate Jizzer on the occasion of our first acquaintance, having discovered that I had never heard of the eminent rap artist 'Snoopy Dog Dogg.'

'Pray tell.'

'Well, folding his arms across his chest this middle class white boy asked me: 'Where you coming from bro?' An enquiry which, as I recall, he swiftly followed up with the observation 'I ain't feeling you dude!' The irony of the situation was apparently lost on him but of course what I absolutely couldn't say, no matter how much I wanted to, was: 'How culturally authentic is your own vernacular Mr. J.? pillaged wholesale as it is, from urban Afro-American patois? Is that really 'where you are coming from bro'? Am I really any more or less the stuffy, tweedy home-counties twit of the nineteen thirties than you are genuinely the ghetto gangsta pimp that you appear to be imitating?'

'It's a tragic story Mostyn.' Ernestine sympathized.

'Well, one soldiers on don't you know.'

'Although perhaps a little bitter, just at the end there.'

'Well, one occasionally feels a little 'got at' Ernestine.' I rallied, 'I mean living at Futters makes it a bit of a challenge to cultivate a positive sense of regional identity, owing to the fact that harbouring anything approaching pride in coming from the rural South of England is to present oneself as the most frightful oligarch. Ditto to regard being white, male, able-bodied, heterosexual, atheistic, carnivorous and right-handed as anything other than a burden of guilt is, apparently, simply not done.'

'As I say, a tragic tale.' She repeated.

'That's about the strength of it.'

'If a little bitter.' She added.

'Think so?.'

'Plus of course it is also a complete lie.'

'Excuse me?'

'You see, I happen to know that all this 'bally tally ho' behaviour actually started much later on Mostyn.'

'Ah.'

'It began rather suddenly. Overnight in fact, following the climax of a sequence of profoundly psychologically devastating events which happened to you in 1994, when you were twenty one.' I started to sweat once more.

'It was something of a rough patch as I remember.' I said hollowly.

'Prior to which you were a relatively normal, well adjusted young man named Nigel Jenkins.

Bugger! She knew who I wasn't and she knew who I was. Did she know why?

'Ah well, then you have me.' I conceded.

'A socially inconspicuous sort of guy actually.'

'Just about.'

'No cut glass accent.'

'Not as such.'

'No upper crust pretensions.'

'Nope.'

'So, as I say, all this 'whato, tinkerty tonk' stuff really amounts to is a type of camouflage.' She ventured 'And it is absolutely typical of the kind of improvisations with which the subconscious mind protects itself.' She continued, 'In your case it generated a persona which, in passing, seems mildly colourful and has the effect of making you seem slightly aloof, slightly, what is it you English say?'

'Eccentric?' I offered.

'Fucked up,' she continued, 'but basically unthreatening, which is exactly what it's intended for.'

'No harm in it really.'

'Perhaps not but nevertheless, the authorities have been monitoring you since this behaviour started during your university years.'

'That is true.' I admitted ruefully. Inwardly though, I was squirming. Did she know or did she not?

'But did you also know,' she continued, 'that they have assigned a trusted figure in your life, who is also an employee of the state, to liaise with the series of mental health professionals whose mission it is to keep you under continuous psychological evaluation.'

A long silence followed this. And then a medium sized one, hot on its heels. She was watching me very closely indeed.

There were two more short pauses in quick succession, another long one, and then the schilling dropped.

'Aunt A?'

'Augusta Futwold.'

'You've got to be jo...'

'...But I'm not jo...!' She barked. 'I'm not jo... in the least!' The ashtray jumped as her fist smote the mahogany. 'We Austrians never jo... about such things!'

-Why do really beautiful girls- I asked myself not for the first time, -always so totally and utterly, mess with one's head?-

I still remember the occasion upon which this sage truth first suggested itself to me. It was the Friday night of my first week at Worthing Polytechnic. I was standing in the noisy, smoky student union bar, savouring a surreptitious cannabis cigarette, leaning against a wall festooned with flyers for anti poll tax demos, hunt sabs and naked amputee contemporary dance companies. She approached from across the crowded room her eyes locked on mine. A scintillatingly stylish specimen of the species with long shiny ebony hair. She wore leather trousers and one of those topless straps. Where I would have been jostled, the crowd parted to admit her. Where I would have slipped on the spilt cider she slinked as seductively as Jessica Rabbit on her way home from yoga.

My heart thumped like two midgets playing squash in a London taxi. I needed to blink but I didn't want to take my eyes off her in case she vanished.

Suddenly she was with me, fixing me with a look as cool as an Eskimo's ice box. Leaning into me, one hand against the wall above my shoulder, almost an embrace really. I breathed her in as she moved her mouth towards my ear, felt her breath on my neck the universe stood still.

'Is that what I think it is?' she purred, 'How can she see it from that angle? I thought. Then, realising she meant the forgotten spliff, smouldering in my hand, I passed it to her, trying like the dickens to think of something intelligent to say.

She kissed me on the tip of my nose and then with a coy backward glance, the wild and wonderful, completely beautiful, girl from out of nowhere, went back to where she belonged.

Elsewhere.

Suddenly the world had re-materialised around me, the bar the noise. The people that I had come with, my erstwhile housemates Stig, Jizzer and Spunky, had watched the entire thing and were finding it all wildly amusing.

They knew, it seemed, what I was only learning now, publicly and excruciatingly. They took as self evident what I spent two hours savagely torturing myself over as I masochistically stomped eight miles home in the rain having turned on my heel and marched out of the bar. They knew that a girl with that much sex appeal would see at a glance that she could take anything she wanted from me. And disappear in a puff of smoke.

Happy days.

I shrugged off my reverie and dealt the Austrian a hard stare. With a Herculean effort of will I managed to keep my voice steady with the result that the entire rest of me, quavered wildly.

'Well, since we are on the subject of people's true identities.' I managed at length.

'Who am I?'

'Well you're clearly no chum of my Aunt.'

'No.' she replied, 'I'm a chum of yours.' I blinked in incomprehension. 'You know me as Trinity' she said flatly.

I reeled.

'Hells bells!' I gasped, 'Trinity? Not Trinity from Vienna?'

'Yes' she confirmed. I reeled again, much bigger this time.

'Trinity with the... the thing about furry handcuffs?'

'The same'

More reeling, with perhaps a hint of boggling.

'Trinity from the internet? With the. The shaven...'

Yawning she slowly uncrossed her endless legs in such a way as to make it inescapably obvious that it was indeed she. I reeled with a practiced technique of which a champion deep sea fisherman would have been envious.

'Of course it's not my real name' she added, stubbing out her cigar in the ashtray.

'Well no. I suppose not' I became acutely conscious of a twitch in my eye.

'Any more than yours is really Badboy1975.'

'Ahem, well quite, er but why did you pretend to be. Epswurf?' I managed eventually.

'I never said I was Ernestine Epswurf.' She said mildly. I thought back through the interview. The facts appeared to be on her side.

'Ernestine Epswurf is the psychoanalyst currently assigned to your case,' she continued 'the authorities are most keen to keep an eye on people like you.'

'Like me how? They surely don't imagine I'm a terrorist?'

'Oh no, your potential is perceived not so much as a threat but as an opportunity.'

'How so?'

'Because you are the way.'

'The way where?'

'The way to the one'

'And the one is?'

'The one,' she said, 'is Bertrand Whisted.'

The silence that followed this thunderbolt hung in the air for a few moments like the aroma of a passing ticket inspector. This Trinity, it seemed, knew all. Clearly the bag was to be hitherto un-infested by cat. Where had it gone? Amongst the pigeons perhaps? Certainly it had the cream. Would it be killed by curiosity?

The dizzy silence endured a moment or two longer and was then suddenly shattered by an avalanche of urgent hammering on the office door behind me. Above the din the voice of Aunt Augusta distorted by panic and desperation, screamed to Doctor Epswurf.

In one smooth balletic movement Trinity rose from her chair, sprinted across the room with the measured strides of a gymnast steaming towards the vaulting horse, planted her hands on the sill and describing an arc of poetic beauty, launched herself, feet first, out of the window.

Finding myself at a loss to keep up with unfolding events I had barely arisen from my chair when the door burst open, violently smashing the bust of Carl Jung, and permitting the ingress of the two white coated henchpersons who had earlier attached themselves to my luggage, closely pursued by the howling virago that was Aunt A.

Of the moments that followed there are now only two surviving snapshots in the Zinctrumpet-Harris memory album. One shows the hypodermic needle being plunged into my arm. The other, slightly blurred, taken immediately after the cupboard door was forced open, shows the prim, mousey, bespectacled, personage of Doctor Ernestine Epswurf, as she slumped forward, onto the floor.

5 PRIM CRAZY MENTIONS TRUTHS

'Mr Wodehouse's idyllic world can never stale. He will continue to release future generations from captivity that may be more irksome than our own. He has made a world for us to live in and delight in.'

Evelyn Waugh (Of the Jeeves and Wooster stories).

In a twee little bookshop, in a market town, in the Sussex Weald, there reigns a dreamy sort of peace. The place is all tobacco and coffee, dust and mustiness. The white-haired, be-cardiganed proprietor potters about contentedly. His tabby cat dozes in a pool of sunlight.

Abruptly, a bell jangles and a young man bursts in, clad in tweeds and sporting a sensational pencil moustache. He wears a hunted look and his brow is beaded with sweat. It seems he is in the grip of an urgent lust for knowledge. The man sets about scouring the *shelves in an orgy of bibliophilia. Evidently his passions are much aroused - but what is it that so animates his bosom? Perhaps the tantalizing promise of coming across a leather-bound Trollope? No, he makes a frenzied lunge for the academic section. He rifles through the volumes, little knowing that fate has placed in his path something decidedly sinister. Something lurking furtively amongst the respectable volumes of serious learning. Something as poisonous as anything a heroin addict might leave on the steps of a junior school. Disaster strikes. He happens upon the object; a text on the subject of 'communication theory'. What to do? Ignore the thing? Clearly. Hasten from the establishment without a backwards glance? Certainly. Drop-kick the item to a safe distance and then burn down the bookshop? Possibly. But no. It's already too late for all of that. This young innocent has inadvertently scooped up the wretched thing. He is already holding it in his hand? The book falls open randomly at a page somewhere between 'hegemony' and 'gender studies'. He glances at it. Reads the words! Arrrrgh!*

I woke with a jolt, wrestling with the bedclothes, adrenaline coursing my veins. The ghastly nightmare was already melting, shrinking away before my gaze. Horribly disorientated I blinked furiously, striving to clear my head.

Eventually, albeit with no particular sense of commitment to the exercise, the world began to resolve itself into focus around me. The first fuzzy outline to emerge through the gathering twilight, turned out, rather disappointingly, to be a regency ceiling rose. The next was a large black and white object stationed beside the bed, which said:

'Fuck man! You look like shit.' as it tenderly dabbed at my fevered cranium with a cool flannel.

I took a deep breath, noting as I did so that the crisp cotton sheets surrounding me were infused with that clean, freshly-laundered aroma, which, I have concluded after protracted investigations into the matter, can only really be achieved by frequently washing them. Wherever I was, clearly I wasn't at home.

With a sense of frustration similar to that which one experiences when driving down a narrow road behind a fleet of senior citizens in Swedish motor cars, I waited for my fragmented recollections of recent events to ponderously shuffle themselves into some kind of meaningful sequence. At the conclusion of this exercise though, I immediately felt a good deal worse as two, highly disconcerting thoughts loomed large in my mind. The second most immediately alarming of these was the sobering realization that, following my encounter with the Austrian siren Trinity, I must surely rank as the prime suspect in the grisly murder of one Ernestine E.

Chilling though this idea was, it was rather eclipsed by another, even more arresting one. Actually, the thing was more like an impulse than an idea really. In fact, to be absolutely precise, that which occupied centre stage amongst my thoughts as the veil of Morpheus was whisked away by hand unseen, later that September day, was more in the way of being a compulsion. For the first time in five years, I had awoken with an uncharacteristically strong and focussed sense of purpose. I had a very clear objective in mind. A quest, in fact, the exact nature of which need not detain us at this juncture, except to say that it was a pretty epic one, and would involve a paraglider, a fair amount of personal mettle and quite a bit of mosquito repellent.

Clearly the very first thing to do, in the pursuit of this end, was to establish whether the chamber in which I had been installed, was my old bedroom in Futwold's East wing, or one of the discreet but secure isolation wards in the medical centre. I began squinting about the environs for further data. Presently, my curiosity was satisfied on this score, as I became gradually, blinkingly aware of the familiar, slightly nasty and highly whimsical watercolour of a French monastery which, throughout my childhood, had hung opposite the bed. The practical upshot of this was that absconding from my incarceration by the time honoured expedient of defenestration should present few problems. Such was the relief occasioned by this realisation that I immediately lapsed back into unconsciousness and then drifted in and out of it for what at the time seemed like forever but which subsequently turned out to be merely ages.

At length I washed up on sanity beach.

'Whato Reeves old prune.' I croaked to my faithful valet who had continued throughout to apply the soothing ministrations, 'The young master finds himself amidst a do, the rumness of which could only be further increased by adding coke and a small umbrella.' He nodded understandingly.

'Fuck yeah.' he observed.

Grateful for this sage counsel I began to ponder the dreadful bookshop nightmare. This was a recurring dream which had been troubling me for some years. It was generally set in a bookshop or library or similar citadel of learning, within which I would stumble upon a fount of arcane knowledge. It seemed to me to speak of a loss of innocence. An awakening.

Perhaps, in order to put the thing in its proper context, I ought first to sketch in a little of the mental landscape that characterised the Zinctrumpet-Harris mind-set during that last Autumn of the second millennium.

You see, following the sequence of fairly psychologically devastating events to which Trinity had referred – events which had played themselves out over the period of a year beginning in the spring of 1994; the techniques and mechanics of influence and persuasion had come to exert something of a morbid fascination for young Mostyn. In consequence, throughout this time I had left no stone un-turned in acquiring the weaponry with which to defend myself against them. For this reason I was ineluctably drawn, as a moth to the flame, to the dicey screed of communication studies. Now, if you have never strayed into this particular swamp of pseudo-academic folderol, let me go on record as recommending that you do not.

Not for all the china in tea shops.

But, if you do. If, perchance borne upon the wings of some giddy autodidactic fancy, you do recklessly pry open this Pandora's box, then you are likely to encounter, (listed somewhere between hegemony and gender studies), something called, (rather coincidentally) 'The Hypodermic Needle Theory'.

This notion, also known variously as 'The Magic Bullet theory,' 'The common sense theory,' and 'The waste of time theory,' offers a simple model to account for the way in which a message:

Buy one of these and women will like you - enters the consciousness of its recipient and controls his behaviour:

I'd like to buy one of those please.

The H.N theory is by a mile the least sophisticated of the models which have purported to anatomise this process. In fact, the mechanism at its heart more or less distils down to:

Monkey see - Monkey do.

Perhaps because of this simplicity, the theory has proved wildly popular. Particularly with the kind of people who bang on about violence on television causing violent crime in society.

An example often trotted out in support of this bilge, is that of John Hinckley Jr. the man who shot and wounded Ronald Reagan in 1981. The man was a certifiable maniac. A barely sentient, fanatical nut-job, and in all honesty Hinkley wasn't much better. Subsequent to his attempt to kill the president it was discovered that he had been obsessed with the film 'Taxi Driver' by Martin Scorsese, in which a psychologically disturbed Vietnam veteran and all-round loon, played memorably by Robert De'Niro, becomes similarly fixated upon some species of presidential candidate or senator or similar figure. Anyway, subscribers to the H. N. Theory, or the 'Stands to reason' theory, as they like to think of it, eagerly seize upon such cases as evidence of the inability of the consciousness of, (important bit coming up) *other people*, to successfully negotiate meaning in the face of a message powerfully suggested, one might almost say injected, into them.

(The film made him do it.)

This is of course the merest guff, the entirest piffle and the utterest of utter flim-flam. This hopeless dud of a theory is universally regarded as a busted flush by the right thinking element. No mechanism of causation has been established in it, there is no solid statistical or empirical support whatsoever. And yet, and here's the thing, it scores over rival theories in a couple of important respects:

One, it is easy to understand, and:

Two, it relieves the individual of the burden of responsibility by rather sportingly passing the buck to an outside agency. That amorphous entity; the media.

So, what of it? You may ask.

Is this strictly germane? You may enquire.

Is it entirely wise, you may wonder, to plunge into a potted history of theories of media effects and risk disrupting the flow of a narrative that is nothing short of a dramatic roller coaster? And the point is well taken. Indeed the only reason I bring up the whole hypodermic needle business at all, is simply because, at around this point in my life, guff or otherwise, this absolute floater of a theory always seemed to crop up rather prominently in a dream, whenever I became the target of a powerful and beguiling influence. It was like a tripwire for ideological stealth attacks. Apparently, even as I slept, my jaded subconscious had been busily booting up my cognitive immune system. This, it must be said, was something that it had to do pretty regularly during the years from 1995 to 1999 - A period that my butler came to refer to as my 'Socratic phase'.

According to Reeves, the ancient Greek philosopher Socrates Laertius, a fellow about whom he is liable to bang on at great length, was prone to biffing around the streets of Athens, clad in malodorous rags, engaging startled strangers in sensational philosophical exchanges aimed at undermining the assumptions upon which their world view was founded. Perhaps unsurprisingly this habit seems not to have endeared the chap greatly to the Athenians who, on some flimsy pretext, sentenced him to death by drinking hemlock (a form of execution that they reserved for the more extreme examples of clever-dickery). As I say, during this especially paranoiac episode my days too were spent in engineering just such scenes, although naturally I did not play the role of Socrates (oh dear me no!) rather I was cast as the startled stranger in the street. I was in the business of inviting the ideological sallies of professional persuaders, with the aim of acquiring some perspective and building up some kind of immunity.

For a while it became my habit to cruise the Scientologists in Tottenham Court Road in London, whilst attired in the shabby, drab garb of alienated youth. They would invariably size me up as a desperate soul in need of a belief system and buttonhole me with an approach, the internal logic of which was hard to resist.

'Do you ever feel that there is something holding you back?' they would ask.

'The sensation is not entirely foreign to me.' I would reply,

'Do you sometimes worry that you think too much but that something is preventing you from fulfilling your potential?'

'Such has occasionally been my anxiety.'

'Well there is a reason for this, they would say, a reason why you and as many as eighty per cent of people feel as you do, and (reassuring smile), a way to reverse it. Have you heard of the Church of Scientology?'

'I am vaguely sensible of the quasi-religious organization to which you refer.' I would feign.

'Well, if you've got a few minutes I would like to tell you a bit about the discoveries of L. Ron Hubbard.'

The millionaire L. R. H. it turns out, has discovered through rigorous and (he assures us) entirely scientifically respectable research, that the sense of impotence and alienation which bedevils the lives of a large and pecuniarily viable proportion of the population, results mainly from overheard snippets of suggestion or 'engrams' which become a form of subconscious programming beginning, he claims, even before birth.

Amongst the examples Mr. R.H. gives of these fragments, easily the most disturbing and ipso facto, the most potent are (are you ready?) the outbursts of frustration that a pregnant woman utters during a failed attempt at aborting her baby.

Yes I know but that is what he says.

'I can't do it!' the wretched wouldn't-be mother wails. A phrase which, because of the programmable nature of the brain, is destined to become your mantra for life.

During this period I became a habitué, not only of the scientologists headquarters in Tottenham Court Road but also their branches in Cambridge (the city that never slopes) and York, (so good they named it once). On each occasion I contrived to be targeted by a different agent, each time venturing a little further along the process of induction. Flirting with the sense of gravitational attraction that they exerted upon me. This produced a feeling of brinkmanship that I had not experienced since flying a paraglider perilously close to a towering cumulo-nimbus. (The irresistible up-draught of these immense storm clouds can rapidly pluck the insipient skybum from the comparative safety of cloud base and propel him vertically upwards through its turbulent interior before spitting him out at thirty thousand feet as a chap-shaped block of ice).

Of course the thing that drew me to the L. Ron H. brigade again and again and which, during that period, brought me to 'the Christadelphians,' 'the Socialist workers,' a network selling organisation with a name similar to 'Scamway' and indeed to anyone who approached me in the street trying to sell me a religion, an ideology or 'the Scamerican dream', was that these encounters were virtually interchangeable. As such they offered a delicious luxury seldom afforded in life. They provided an opportunity to fathom out where I had gone wrong in an argument and to re-run it from the top. In this way the anatomy of the proposal would be laid bare and its advocate, deprived of the advantage of surprise, was rendered vulnerable to counter attack. Like a close-up magician forced to repeat his trick slowly and deliberately until it is obvious how it is done. By this expedient I was able to gradually develop a sort of polemical cardio vascular fitness with which to at least keep pace with the argument. I became harder to wrong-foot. Less easily distracted by irrelevancies. I began to anticipate the tactics.

For instance, how often does an attractive member of the non-chap element approach a fellow in the street and strike up a conversation? It's not common. Indeed it's really rather rare. In fact if this happens, she is pretty certainly either a barking loon, a lady of negotiable affections or an undercover vice officer. Either way there is likely to be something on her mind besides merely shooting the breeze. And yet, In spite of this, a prehistoric mating instinct deep within a chap's soul will always oblige him to allow for the possibility that the rather becoming f. of the s. who strolls smilingly up and complements him on his suntan (been somewhere nice?) might simply wish pass the time of day in idle conversation. Or, at least, it causes him to suppress the overwhelming probability that she merely wishes to sign him up to a possibly cheaper utility company or pinch his cannabis cigarette.[10]

The disciples of L. Ron do use this gambit too but the real flattery is even more seductive. With a bit of the spin taken off it would read roughly: 'You are obviously an intelligent fellow who ought to be capable of great things. Perhaps your lack of purpose, focus, direction, confidence and social success arises, not from the patent

---

[10] *I'll never get over that.*

fact that you are an ineffectual mediocrity but due to factors beyond your control.' The point is to confirm what you had always privately suspected; that you are actually a very special but rather unfairly overlooked individual.

Another strategy widely used by professional persuaders is to smuggle the premise of the pitch into the target's consciousness upon a raft of reasonable sounding conjecture, the agent seeks to benefit from the 'seems to know what he's talking about,' effect. This also works well for politicians, prophets etc. and can be illustrated as follows:

'Did you know that we only use ten per cent of our mental potential?' asks the scientologist brandishing a flyer. This seemingly meaningless but strangely plausible statement appears in quotation marks beneath a picture of Albert Einstein (not actually the originator of this statement but certainly a right old clever clogs).

'You know don't you, that things we are told when very young are sometimes stored in our subconscious mind without our conscious awareness?' Again, this sounds reasonable. In fact didn't that famous brainbox Sigmund Freud say something rather similar? And then of course there's post-hypnotic suggestion and de ja vu which seem to be along the same lines. Yes this chap seems to know what he's talking about and no mistake.

If he continues finding points of agreement and exploiting the credibility of respected figures in superficially similar fields, the artful persuader ought to be able to slip the Achilles heel of his thesis past the credulous chap undetected. The wily chap though, will be able to spot this transition from objective to subjective due to its reliance on words like 'should' as in, for instance, John Prescotts 1998 claim 'There is no denying the scientific fact that cannabis is a dangerous drug which should be banned.' I gradually developed a peculiar horror of statements of this type. Opinions masquerading as facts. Such dogma is an example of what philosophers call 'the naturalistic fallacy' and constitutes a clear breach of the 'no ought from is,' rule, which seeks to expose the sloppy thinking at work in such statements.

To amplify the no o. from I. rule: that cannabis is deleterious to health may be a scientific fact but to assert that it follows from this alone that cannabis ought to be banned, is completely incorrect. It depends entirely on whether you accept the agenda that everything which can be scientifically shown to be harmful, ought to be banned. It simply does not automatically logically follow. Bona fide scientific facts never contain words like should or ought. These are the currency of opinions and value judgements. What Mr. Prescott perhaps should have said is that anything which is dangerous - *and which in his opinion doesn't serve a useful purpose,* - ought to be banned. In neglecting to include this caveat, his footling thesis would rather defeat its object, since it would logically extend to cover such fundamentals of civilised life as paragliding and cashew nuts, not to mention popular but dangerous leisure pursuits such as sex and childbirth. Hence in his efforts to protect us from ourselves, the ilk of Mr. Prescott would ultimately have no-one left to whom to condescend.

Of course it is no good overcoming or sneaking past a person's natural scepticism, shifting their paradigm and generally winning them over, only to have them immediately shuffle off and run the entire iffy proposal past a trusted pal who will doubtless see it as their role to talk some sense into them and get them to drop the whole shaky enterprise.

What the really switched on agent seeks to do therefore, having successfully installed their big idea in the subjects mind, is cut him off from such influences as might subsequently dislodge it by implicating them in the problem, to which the idea is the solution.

Conspiracy theories also work in this way, in that, the lack of evidence supporting the idea that, for example Princess Diana was assassinated by the British Secret service, as is widely believed everywhere outside Britain, is in fact completely consistent with the nature of a conspiracy and thus in a particularly obtuse twist of illogic the lack of evidence in support of the theory is in itself evidence in support of it and is therefore the last thing that we should allow to persuade us that it is false.

(But they would say that, wouldn't they.)

This gambit is seen in action in the Dianetics spiel too in the splendidly tasteless device of the abortion attempt scenario, in which the subject is heartened to discover what Phillip Larkin discovered before them and which the Hyperdermic Needlists knew all along, which is that nothing is your own fault because 'they fuck you up, your mum and dad.'

As a direct consequence of this crafty manoeuvre the scientologist not only panders to the target's most feeble inadequacies, he also cuts him off from probably the most significant support figure in his life, leaving a vacuum which the Church of Scientology, (as oxymoronically bogus a name as 'the National Socialists') will be only too happy to fill.

Anyway.

In view of all of this accumulated scepticism it was pretty hard for me not to see my encounter with Trinity within the framework of a pitch. It was all there; the use of sex appeal in the preamble, the 'sounds reasonable' softening-up process, and the implication in a conspiracy of Aunt A. the one person to whom I would, in all probability, turn for guidance in a crisis.

Exploring this theme further, it occurred to me that, through the alchemy of the microcomputer, Trinity could have established, with little difficulty, that the celebrated, Augusta Futwold wasn't my actual aunt in the biological sense, as I had always suggested in our chat-room sessions on the website, sexchatforum.com. Many children grow up calling somebody 'auntie' who is actually no such thing. In my case it was the principal of the orphanage for learning and behaviourally challenged children in which I spent my childhood following my parents' tragic deaths in a freak pancake tossing accident, a few days after my birth.

Ditto Trinity was, if rather lacking in delicacy, probably on fairly safe ground in speculating that my personality was little more than a pastiche of tweedy fictional characters. In fact everything she had said was there to be divined by a moderately observant person. I dare say that a half-way competent cold-reader such as a psychic or palmist could have intuited as much and more, merely from close observation of my telling physical reactions. The dilation of my pupils, demonstrative body language and so on. And from craftily constructed sentences which can become questions or statements according to the response given.

'Your mother isn't still alive is she?'

'No.'

'No I didn't think so?'

'Your mother isn't still alive is she?'

'Yes'

'Ah yes, I thought she probably was.'

On the other hand, one aspect of Trinity's yarn was absolutely right on the money: Bertrand Whisted. Certainly to make his acquaintance was to be immediately enchanted by his magnetism. To know the man was to recognise him as endowed with prodigious calibre. But to place him as a peer amongst the most significant figures in Western thought, could surely mean only one thing; Trinity was his acolyte and his emissary. Perhaps even his lover.

6 SANITY BEACH

How about making a run for it? - I asked myself a little later, while squinting from within my, still somewhat swimmily sedated, soporific state in the direction of the rectangular patch of evening gloom across the bedroom which was surely the window.

No point asking me. - I answered. We're the same person.

There is that. - I conceded and pondered asking Reeves instead.

Reeves, as it happens, is no stranger to seismic upheavals in his weltenschauung. In the astonishingly successful film, 'The Matrix,' (surely a Gnostic myth) Reeves' character Neo is approached by a group of stylish, leather clad, cyber guerrillas, or some such, who reveal to him that the fabric of his life is no more than a fiendishly plausible illusion, generated in a computer.

Reeves who, it comes as a surprise to many to learn, is actually a pretty deep thinker, bangs on endlessly about the philosophical implications of this.

'Course, Plato got there first, man.' He told me, one particularly uneventful Brighton afternoon.

'Plato you say?'

'Yeah Plato man. Socrates' favourite pupil and founder of the Academy, the most famous school of philosophy in ancient Athens. The father of Western philosophy dude!'

'Ah that Plato, Reeves.'

'Instead of a Matrix he came up with the allegory of 'the cave''. He continued.

'Then lay it before me without delay old cheese.'

'O.k.' said Reeves, formulating his thoughts. 'Imagine a cave with a pathway running through it. Along the pathway a steady stream of folk trudge back and forth. Goin' about their lives and doing their thing, right?'

'With you so far Reeves.'

'So, on one side of the path is a big fire, and on the other side is you.'

'Me?'

'You have been there all your life, chained up since birth, facing away from the path and towards the back wall on which the shadows of the people are cast by the firelight.'

'Bless my soul.'

'So of course you got no choice except to assume the flickering silhouettes are the extent of the real world.' He continued. 'Only by leaving the cave, or the Matrix or other self imposed slavery, can you learn the truth.'

And in this way Reeves had turned me on to metaphysics; the branch of philosophy that obsesses over questions like: How do we know what's real?

'So, how do we know what's real Reeves?' I enquired on another Brighton afternoon, similarly un-infested with incident.

'Well,' he began, barely pausing for breath 'Descartes, rocked the world with his famous cogito, (I think therefore I am) asserting that at least he can be sure of his own existence, because to be thinking, he must exist.'

'Well I'm blessed!' I enthused. 'Yes, I like that. That's really very clever.'

'He was a brilliant Guy.'

'If a little French.' I pointed out.

'Right. But the examples of the Matrix and the cave, show that any assumption about the real world based on the interior of your mind is highly suspect. You dig?'

'I'm right behind you old sock.'

'In the cogito, the argument depends upon it logically following from the premise that 'I think,' that I must exist in order to be thinking. Thoughts need a mind, a mind needs a brain, a brain needs a body Right?'

'One would think so certainly.'

But what kind of existence does this actually prove?'

'Well there is that of course.' I mused.

'Many sceptics have suggested that it doesn't prove an existence beyond that of being 'a thinking thing,' and as such really needs to be modified to 'I think, therefore I am a thinker' which, sadly, is only a rizla's breadth from: 'I think therefore I think,' which as near as makes no difference, is a tautology, cancelling neatly to 'I think'.

'Well I'll be.'

'And it is widely, although not universally accepted, that the only things that you can think into existence, are thoughts.'

'It's a fair point Reeves,' I agreed 'otherwise Batman would walk amongst us.

'And unicorns and the Easter bunny.'

'And the honest estate agent.'

'Any number of mythical creatures,' he agreed. 'Actually,' he added, warming to his theme 'more sceptical thinkers still, have argued that to be conscious of thoughts isn't necessarily the same as actually generating them. How, after all, can I be sure that these are actually my thoughts that I am having?

'Like de ja vu you mean?'

'Right. In de ja vu an experience is being wrongly addressed by the brain as a memory. If that's possible maybe a memory can be wrongly addressed as an original thought. Perhaps the thoughts are being played out of the brain like a c.d.rom and the impression that they are being conjured into being is an illusion. This means that the statement 'I perceive thoughts,' may be as far as you can go. Boil the whole thing down this far and it's probably logically unassailable but then again, in philosophical circles, the statement 'I perceive thoughts' is most likely to attract the criticism 'no shit Sherlock?'

Happy days.

There was no doubt about it, Reeves' mighty mental machinations were a beacon of hope in a world of gloom. If he couldn't find the solution to the frightful impasse in which I presently found myself, then my name wasn't an anagram of 'rich star, unzip my torments.'

'Reeves old legume' I chirped sitting up and swinging my legs out of bed.

'Wassup?' Enquired he, from behind his copy of Jean Paul Sartre's 'Being and Nothingness.'

'One is uncomfortably sensible of the sword of Diogenes hanging above one by a single hair.'

'That's Damocles man.'

'Quite so Reeves. In any event I shall be requiring your expert erudition. Pray knock me up a restorative martini and prepare yourself for a tale of perfidious chicanery.'

I laid the facts before him, omitting nothing. The entire interview with Trinity, her abrupt departure and Ernestine Epswurf's chilling fate. Throughout my narrative, my eyes toured those iconic, chiselled features, watching for any reaction, any clue. His face though, was a mask.

'Well Reeves?'

'It's possible you may have misinterpreted Aunt A's note? He ventured at length. What did Lady Futwold say to you before you went into Ms Epswurfs office'

I thought hard. 'Be yourself' I think it was.'

'Hmmm.' Said Reeves

'Hmmm Reeves?' Said I

'Well, they do say, only a fool lies to his doctor.'

'Expand Reeves.'

'No way dude, not after last time.'[11]

'I mean amplify your point viz the doctor and the foolishness of lying thereto.' Reeves minutely adjusted his features in such a way as to suggest profound relief.

'Well, whether Trinity is on the level or not; Lady F. sure has been keeping an eye on you since you graduated huh?'

'That's putting it mildly old sock' I agreed 'She's wheeled me out in front of more nerve specialists than I care to remember.' I paused for a moment picturing the procession of brainiologists, of whom, it had been my singular lack of pleasure, to make the acquaintance during the past five years.

Professor Antonia Wadge came immediately to mind, a psychotherapist so elastic in her approach that it occasionally seemed to be little more than a semantic exercise in redefining into non-existence the distinction between robust mental health and general loopiness, so as to leave the patient on whichever side of the divide he felt most comfortable.

The aim seemed to be to reconcile the wretch to his plight rather than to risk making it worse.

'After all what is normal Mostyn?' She had asked me in her opening panegyric which appeared to be pitched at lowering my expectations of the treatment,

---

[11] See 'Zinctrumpet-Harris and the Dagenham Dogging Disaster.'

'who is to say that anyone else's state of mind is abnormal?'

'Agreed,' I said. I hadn't actually used the term 'normal' myself although she nevertheless appeared to have heard it, 'similarly I wouldn't dream of describing somebody with Down's syndrome for example, as abnormal.' I added helpfully.

'Absolutely.'

'Although if you asked me what was the normal number of chromosomes for a human I would have to say forty six.'

'Not for a human with Down's syndrome.' she retorted.

'Does it follow then, that believing one's self to be Napoleon is perfectly normal behaviour for a mad person and hence is in fact no more or less mad than anyone else's beliefs?'

'It means that what's normal for one person is not normal for another. What can seem incredible to one person can seem totally real to another.'

'But that's the case for heterodoxy, not for a subjective reality isn't it?' I objected 'I mean, thinking that orange goes with pink or that it's rude to stare, is a subjective belief based on what one considers normal but believing oneself to be Napoleon is delusional. That's not to say that if it's true for you then it's true. It's not a subjective belief it's a wrong belief.'

'Everything is subjective Mostyn.' She said slowly in that infuriating way that contrives to suggest that if you don't agree, then you mustn't have properly understood.

I dare say that in my stead, Reeves would have unsheathed his razor sharp, Socratic rhetoric and rejoindered thus:

'But Ma'am, to say 'Everything is subjective' is in itself an attempt at an objective statement. And yet for it to be true then it follows that *it* must be subjective too, and hence only as true as it is held to be. And if it's false from any angle at all, then that means that not everything is subjective. For it to be true it has to be, at least in principle, capable of being untrue. It's logically impossible for everything to be subjective.'

'Tell me Mostyn,' Ms. Wadge had persisted, steepling her fingers, 'do you consider yourself to be delusional?'

'Well I do have Keanu Reeves for a butler.' I pipped.

Happy days.

'Reeves!' I ejaculated when my reverie had passed, 'Do you Suppose then, that I was summoned here for a consultation with some species of psychologist?'

'Well I guess if M's Epswurf was a consultant, maybe she wouldn't use the title doctor or professor or whatever.'

'An excellent point.' Reeves.

'And if her specialty was younger patients as implied by her personal friendship with Lady Futwold, the co-proprietress of a home for developmentally challenged orphans, then that explains lady F's remark that she wouldn't normally be interested in someone your age.'

'There is that too.'

'Plus', he added with the air of a magician producing a non-sawn-in-half assistant from a box, 'the last six women she's hauled you up here to meet, all of whom you wrongly assumed in your Bertie Woosterish way to be marriage prospects, have, in every case, turned out to be psychiatric doctors.'

You see what I mean about Reeves? What a brain!

'Bravo old cheese! I exclaimed leaping out of bed 'Well that's me off the hook and no mistake. No drippy popsy to marry after all, just a simple misunderstanding.'

'I guess.'

'Hurrah for you Reeves, I knew your race tuned grey matter would get me out of the soup.'

'No sweat man.'

'So, do you suppose it's too late for a spot of dinner Reeves?'

'Well, there is still the little matter of getting intercepted by this Trinity person and her tipping you off about this government conspiracy huh?'

'Oh yes, that business,' I mused 'I was forgetting. What's your council Reeves?'

'Escape.' He replied, without hesitation.

'Escape you say?'

'Hell yes.'

'In which case Reeves I rather regret my earlier haste in striking from the inventory that unpleasant vinyl sports holdall.'

Reeves coughed and removed a speck of dust from his sleeve in a very creditable affectation of a servile butler. 'Actually I gotta confession.'

'You interest me strangely Reeves.'

'I kinda packed it by mistake.'

'You don't say.'

'Mixed it up with that purple paisley number.'

'My smoking jacket?' I gasped.

'Sorry man.'

I swallowed hard. It was a bitter blow of course but not entirely without its sunny side.

'Don't give it another thought Reeves.' I breezed.

'O.k.'

'Strike it from your mind.'

'Cool.'

'The purple paisley smoking jacket does not signify.'

'Right.'

'This is not a moment for purple paisley smoking jackets.'

'I guess not.'

'This is an occasion for derring do.'

'Yup.'

And it is at this point that I embark upon the longer, stranger and almost infinitely second part of my tale. Mostyn the disreputable night-crawler you know. With Mostyn the shape shifting sybarite you are acquainted. And of Mostyn the unaccomplished sophist and utterer of flimsy unfocussed psychobabble, you are surely heartily sick.

But what of Mostyn the adventurer? What sayeth Mostyn the fearless man of action? And wherein dwells Mostyn the heroic crusader after truth? For in every man these are inalienable component parts, shrivelled undernourished and vestigial in all but a few cases but there nevertheless, awaiting the call.[12] And for this

---

12 *Possibly.*

estimable inner Mostyn, to lash a length of orange nylon climbing rope to a hat-stand and brace it against the window was but a trifle. To shin noiselessly down to the drive below, was the work of an instant. And to push the car across the drive and through the gates, noiselessly save for the crunching of gravel, was the merest bagatelle.

As we reached the lane I turned to take one last parting look at Futwold Grange. Its granite gateposts were connected by a proscenium arch, atop which, picked out in a filigree of wrought iron, were a few characters. Where Dante would, I dare say, have placed the legend 'All hope abandon ye who enter here' the arch instead simply displayed the name of the establishment. Or so I had always thought. I was mildly astonished therefore to notice for the first time in my life, an additional word that I had completely overlooked in the scores of times that I had casually glanced at it, whilst creaking past in the old Triumph. A small but positively crucial word in fact, which gave the sign an entirely different aspect. A word that I had missed entirely owing to the gaps being perhaps a trifle too small, between Futwold and and, and and and Grange.

Part 2

7 MANILLA N.S.W.

'Hmm. Tour tyrannizes script.'

Beating the dust from my clothes with my battered Panama, I waved to the ancient pick-up as it creaked off across the bridge which spanned the Namoi river. Hitch-hiking the last leg of my trip from Sydney had proved a purgatorial episode, and as grateful as I was to my avuncular benefactor and his charming if hallitotic dog 'Digger', it was nevertheless a relief to be finally at journey's end.

A cursory inspection of its non-bustling main street, disclosed that the pace of life in Manilla, New South Wales, was pretty far from blistering. In fact continental plates have been known to hoof about at a more reckless lick.

Squinting across the wide thoroughfare and beyond a strip of the only really green grass I had so far seen in this brown and pleasant land, upon which sprinklers made rainbows of the afternoon sunshine, I spied for the first time my Elysium, the Manilla Imperial Hotel.

It was an absolutely forgettable sight. A once undistinguished edifice which now seemed to reflect upon a long decline into utter decrepitude with an overwhelming air of not really giving a damn one way or the other. The vintage of this mouldy monument to mediocrity was proudly announced on a crest above the door as 1899. By Australian standards this was the caves at Lascaux.

In the shade of the hotel's lower terrace a brace of churls gazed at me as I hefted my enormous glider bag onto my back, and approached the drunken steps. 'Bit dusty in the back of that ute, eh?' Uttered the less ancient and rather more mad-eyed of the rustics infesting the veranda.

'On the contrary sir,' I replied genially, 'There is no more agreeable sensation than the wind in one's hair.'

'Jeez it's another one a them flamin' pom paragliders.' groaned the more wizened, and from an oncological point of view, interestingly ravaged specimen, sporting a crop of melanomas and a huge sweat stain with traces of hat.

'At your service gentlemen.' I tipped my headgear theatrically and moved on into the foyer. As my eyes adjusted to the gloom I dumped my backpack next to the door marked ublic Bar, doffed the Panama, took a deep breath and entered.

The place was an absolute hive of inactivity. Its interior, which was painted the colour of nicotine, featured more insects than actual patrons. The flies dodged the blades of the ceiling fans which slowly circulated the tobacco fug. The clientele were a sorry looking gang of veteran drinkers, attired in the uniform khaki shorts, their long socks stopping just short of the knee, leaving exposed a section of leg reminiscent of a chorizo sausage.

'Hello darling, I'm Colleen, what can I get you?' beamed the landlady, her face an extravagant celebration of scrotal wrinkles. She eyed the cut of my lightweight safari suit as she approached the bar.

'Madam, I am Sir Peregrine Axlerod,' I smiled, inventing a pseudonym designed to attract no attention, 'I am another one of 'them flamin' pom paraglider pilots' and I am desirous of board and lodging in your fine hostelry.'

'Ah reckon you met Les and Derek on your way in eh?'

'I believe they've had the pleasure.'

Briefly overcome by a fit of coughing my hostess turned to inspect the book which had been hitherto employed in supporting the corner of the pie warmer. I admired the way in which the blue print of her dress harmonized with the varicose veins that festooned her calves.

'D'ya think you'll get a Sheila love?'

I boggled.

'Double room or dormitory she explained epexegetically.'

I deposited a gratuity the largesse of which rendered my hostess speechless with gratitude and having trousered the room key, I duly became the newest resident at the Manilla Imperial Hotel.

'Now Pregrin have you met Otto?' Enquired Colleen, although pronouncing the word Oddo and indicating the enormous saturnine gent positioned at the bar, nursing a schooner of V.B. which looked comically miniature in his gigantic paws.

That Otto was not the most chipper of chaps was readily apparent. His overstuffed face was a study in melancholia and I felt for him keenly. After all, for any citizen of one of the great beer cultures of the world, being reduced to hoovering up the unsettlingly orange, vaguely lager-flavoured, soapy beverage which Australia goes by the name of Victoria Bitter, can surely only be a traumatic adjustment.

Otto had the unmistakable dress sense of the Teuton, luxuriant blonde hair of the type that always seems faintly indecent on a gentleman and he sported truly extravagant top lip shrubbery that can surely only have been designed to terrify the younger generation.

'You fly today.' he growled.

'Thanks bro', yo' pretty fine yo'self 'n' t'ing' I rejoindered in my eerily plausible Snoopy Dog Doggy impersonation[13]. Not a glimmer. It's true what they say about the Bosh you know.

In due course I heaved my colossal Glider bag up the stairs towards the bedrooms that lurk above every Aussie pub, having passed a few long minutes indulging, with Otto, in a conversation which, at a fraction of the cost, featured all of the entertainment value of root-canal surgery.

Nevertheless the skybum is, virtually by definition, an opportunist. As such he is inclined to court such types as these on the strength of the fact that having apparently just arrived in town, a clear two hours before the once daily bus from Tamworth and not appearing at first glance to have the temperament of the natural hitch hiker, Otto was most probably in possession of a certain, infinitely useful, commodity. Something which paraglider pilots, like heavy drinkers, never wish to own for themselves but definitely like other people to have; a car.

The quarters on the whole were a pleasant surprise. Clean and light with two windows facing North

---

13 See, I told you I could do that.

and a door that led to a huge covered balcony with a table and chairs upon which pilots could idle away the non flyable days and from which one could clearly see, fifteen kilometres distant, the distinctive silhouette of Mount Borah.

Of the six single beds available I selected the one furthest from the door and dumped my glider bag thereon, I then sat and regarded it for a long moment with that special sense of nostalgia reserved for things that are not yet in the past.

This strange outsized rucksack and its contents had been hoisted in and out of tuk-tuks, donkey carts and rickshaws from Cape Town to Canungra. It was dusted with the earth of every flyable mountain in between. And it now contained everything tangible that I owned in the world.

Following my escape from Futwold at three a.m. that morning in September '99, I had made a lightning sortie to the Brighton flat to extract such items as I would need for an open ended spell as a skybum and distributed a few of my remaining possessions amongst my bewildered neighbours.

Mrs. Colick in the basement had declared herself thrilled to give a home to Stumpy my no-legged chinchilla, and Lee the actor in flat one was the sleepily grateful beneficiary of a walnut sized piece of Moroccan and my entire collection of ganja paraphernalia. I switched everything off and left, popping the key through the letterbox on my way out.

Nine o'clock had seen me impatiently waiting without the car auction rooms in Shoreham where I entered my battered Triumph Herald for sale with no reserve price and left my bank details. I caught a hackney carriage to the railway station, took the train to the airport, bought a six flight, round the world ticket from the student travel exchange, nominated five destinations starting with Rio De Janeiro and hopped on the first plane out.

I am not, by nature, terribly comfortable with technology, and yet I am constantly impressed by how much of ones life nowadays can be organized via the internet. All of human knowledge is there, linked by a fibre optic nervous system, the collective consciousness of the species. By the time my boarding gate was called I had, by this expedient, paid off all of my utility bills, redirected my post, acquired a one year emergency medical insurance policy and subscribed to something that called itself a 'paragliding news group', the better to have ones ear to the ground.

I also picked up an emollient e.mail from Augusta Futwold, co-founder with Penelope Grange of 'Futwold and Grange' an institution for the care of developmentally challenged orphans. Whilst striking a generally conciliatory tone she urged me to contact her immediately since apparently Special Branch were most anxious to establish the identity of the mystery fiend who had stealthily crept through the window of her consulting room and chloroformed the unfortunate consultant psychiatrist, Ernestine Epswurf.

Three months, five airports and two hundred cross country hours later. It was a fitter, healthier, browner Mostyn who sat gazing at this hermit shell of a glider bag, reflecting upon how effortlessly he had collapsed his universe down to a singularity.

The Skybum, in common with his elemental soul brethren the surf-bum and the ski-bum, leads an itinerant existence. Typically his peregrinations will see him on five continents in a year in pursuit of favourable flying conditions around the globe and since he needs to be self sufficient and mobile he finds it expedient to confine himself to those chattels that he can actually physically carry. Ergo tweaking, paring down and rationalizing his kit tends to become a trifle obsessional and, as I flipped open the lid of the bag, I was embarking upon a routine that had evolved into something in the nature of a ritual.

Wedged into the top of the bag was my horrid and deceptively heavy Reebok pouchette (caribou? muntjac?), containing my radios, variometer, gps, camera, portable computer, batteries, the silver cocktail shaker I won in a game of cigar cutter roulette against Leonardo Ping (a Chinese gondolier that I met in Zanzibar) a pair of slightly effete sunglasses based around the principle of the two way mirror, a Rosie Cheeks novel and a heat reflective survival blanket.

These I strew upon an adjacent bed. Next my clothes, sandals, towel and flying suit.

Like a geologist excavating progressively deeper strata of rock I duly exposed my harness, now tatty and u.v. bleached, with its possibly still operable reserve parachute fitted. Lastly, packed into its protective inner bag the Glider itself, an elderly Edel Rainbow, an early and highly dangerous model that I had acquired on a part exchange basis in Cape Town from a dreadlock-festooned radical skydude with plaster casts on both legs, for the bargain price of five hundred South African Rand plus a low mileage John Lee Hooker novelty chillum pipe. It was wrapped around my excitingly technical carbon fibre crash helmet with it's built in radio headset which was itself stuffed with socks.

The rather draconian nature of airline baggage-weight limits, presents something of a challenge to the invariably impecunious skybum, since his flying kit alone is likely to weigh in at a shade over twenty kilos even before factoring in his clothes, shampoo, sandals, real poo, cashew nuts e.t.c. He is obliged therefore to exercise a certain degree of cunning and engage in a certain amount of theatre in order to avoid being penalized.

For example, when checking in at Zanzibar international airport three days previously, I had presented myself in the forty degree heat, attired in my flying boots and a coat, the pockets of which were stuffed with batteries, chargers, books and so on.

Meanwhile, the twenty kilo Reebok sports bag that I faux casually dangled before the implacable and heartbreakingly beautiful check-in clerk, was, unbeknownst to her, causing the muscles of my arm to tremble like the dickens.

Having exploded my possessions all around the room, I then reconfigured them in flying mode. I fitted the vario, gps and radio to the flight-deck which sits across my knees in flight. The back protection system and the flight-deck to the harness, and the harness to the glider. I then shoved the whole lot, plus helmet, flying suit, gloves and a few survival necessities, back into the bag, which now appeared precisely as it had before.

I was now technically re-jigged from travel mode to flying mode and ritual being what it is I had simultaneously made the psychological adjustment too.

All that remained was to install my mosquito net above the bed with four drawing pins and place a plastic drinks cup, pinched from the train, containing an inch of insect repellent under each of its legs. I showered and shaved, carefully re-delineating my sensational pencil moustache, changed into a fresh lightweight linen suit and kicked back on the veranda with a V.B. and a particularly racy Rosie Cheeks novel, until the sun went down and the fliers, like the flies, were drawn back to the lights of the town.

In the distance above the mountain a little swarm of gliders enjoyed an evening ridge soar. They floated on the updraft caused by the breeze as it swept up Borah's westerly slope and were buoyed up further by the restitution effect wherein the earth begins to release its warmth as sunset approaches. This was probably the second flight of the day for most of these chaps, having launched this morning when the thermals were building and tried their luck in the cross country lottery, by mid afternoon they would have been strewn across the countryside like confetti and by evening they would have hitched back to Manilla to share stories or indulge in a little twilight flight.

'Is the blighter up there, do you suppose?' I enquired of my right hand man as he decanted another beer into my glass.

'Whisted?' Reeves growled 'ridge soaring?' He incrementally inclined an eyebrow in such a manner as to suggest a lack of confidence in this theory.

I bridled at such scepticism. 'Stranger things have happened Reeves,' I protested 'remember when Dodgy Guru won the Gold Cup at 33/1?[14]' Reeves shook his head.

'No way!' He rasped, millimetrically re-arranging his features so as to crank up by another notch, the air of moody intensity for which he is noted. 'Not his style.' He added.

---

14 See 'Reeves at Worcester.'

He was of course quite correct. To Bertrand Whisted, as to any right-thinking aviator, swooping about at a hill site stood in the same relation to real flying as a picnic does to an expedition. It was the equivalent of an improvised guitar jam session next to the symphony of cross country flying. Like pulling wheelies on a trials bike compared with riding coast to coast on a Harley Davidson.

But it was to Manilla though, that I had been ineluctably drawn. I'd heard whispers about Whisted from Porterville to Valle De Bravo, missed him by a week in Zanzibar, it was late in the season and the best sky in the world right now was here, between Australia's Great Dividing Range and the vast desert of the red centre.

He was here alright, or my name wasn't an anagram of 'Crazy him torments turnips'.

8 SHREWD AND BITTER

The name of Bertrand Whisted first floated into my purview back in 1994. I was in my second year of a Psychology degree at the polytechnic of Worthing. 'The city that never wakes.' At the time I was a fledgling paraglider pilot, positively bursting with the zeal of the newly converted and I was, in those days, for reasons which it would be otiose to rehearse at this juncture, living under my original name of Nigel Jenkins.

Lamentably, after a promising first furlong, my academic career had conspicuously failed to hit mid season form, as often happens, I am told, in the second year of a bachelor degree. Whereas my fresher year had been entirely satisfactory, consisting of a head-spinning and highly stimulating gallop through the first principles of the subject, by the fourth term the going had become decidedly heavy. In particular my course tutor, Dr Ludwig Cillit Bang, whose unhappy assignment it was to

97

bathe me in the fountain of knowledge, was evidently no longer content with the one way flow of scholarship and began making overtures about receiving a return on his investment.

This was a worrying development as I hardly need say. I had always assumed that the professors were to be the wellspring of knowl' whilst the young master Jenkins was cast in the role of blank canvas or uncarved block or empty vessel. That type of thing. Why fix it if it ain't broke? Was my view. Why change it whilst it's all going so swimmingly? 'I go to college to be entertained' about summed up my attitude, 'if I had wanted to be educated, I would have gone to the theatre.'

Ultimately I suppose, I had been guilty of inadequate research.

That and being a dilettante.

And a lazy bum.

The unreasonableness of Dr. CB's demands, came to a head during the summer break before what was to be my third and final year at the P. of W. I was flying a good deal, biffing about in my ancient Triumph Herald, living at Futwold of course, in my old room in the East wing and generally trying to keep out of Lady F's way.

But what I was utterly failing to do, in spite of trying like the blazes, was to think of a decent idea for my final year project. I had until the end of the holidays to submit a preliminary proposal for a piece of research based around an original hypothesis.

One July morning as I loafed about in Aunt A's office while she did her rounds, idly flicking through the paragliding association's stridently forthright magazine 'Skythings' *{The Indispensable monthly Companion to Life's Up Tiddly Up Upness}* I turned to an article which completely changed my life. In fact to say that it changed my life would be to indulge in understatement on a par with saying that Mexico City would be a bit of a chore to paint in a weekend:

The Icarus Complex

By Professor Bertrand Whisted M.Psy.

On a recent visit to Austria to attend a psychology convention, I happened quite by chance, whilst walking one afternoon in the mountains near Westerndorf, to come upon a paragliding flying site and was intrigued to observe what struck me as the largest manifestation of dissociative neurosis I have ever encountered outside of an institution.

Of the many flyers with whom I conversed during the course of that afternoon (it was, I believe, rather insufficiently windy for really good gliding) not one was able to give me a reason for his involvement in the sport that seemed to me to be remotely proportionate to the time, expense and danger that it involves.

The evasiveness of their responses, of which a typical example was '(laughs) do you know I'm always asking myself that exact question,' put me in mind of one of the more powerful of the techniques available to the therapist. That of post-hypnotic suggestion.

With P.H.S. it is possible to appeal directly to the patient's subconscious whilst bypassing the often obfuscating mediation of the conscious mind. An example, with which you will be familiar, is that of the stage hypnotist, who will instruct the subject under hypnosis that upon leaving the trance state he should on no account reveal his name, if asked but also that he should have no recollection of this instruction. The inventive rationalisations that people can generate in such situations to cover their little understood but powerfully felt aversion to answering the question, are extraordinary and fascinating and serve to illustrate the fact that our stated reasons for doing something may in fact have little to do with our deeper motivations.

When a persons subconscious mind or unconscious as the Jungian psychologist prefers to call it, is significantly in conflict with the ego or conscious mind, then that person begins to experience the symptoms of dissociation. Typically the unconscious will strive to restore the balance through its capacity to generate symbolism, which expresses itself primarily in dreams as well as through mistakes in speech, unexpected memory loss, inexplicable compulsions, physical symptoms (in the case of neurosis) and also during free association. Indeed, in any behaviour in which the unconscious plays a role.

In the ancient world, the language of symbolism would have been more readily accessible and indeed was entrenched in all of the classical mythologies in which the collective racial wisdom of countless generations is repeatedly enacted. Thus through the conduit of a holy man or medicine man, visions dreams, hallucinations and so on could be interpreted and explained to provide a resolution to the individuals dissociation.

In the age of reason however, in which the conscious is king and any instinctive feelings are largely regarded as sinister and retrograde, a person who feels the urge to contemplate an enterprise such as paragliding, is apt to find a rationalisation to support it, rather than to recognise it for the symbolic and compensatory behaviour that it is.

One of the most persistent themes in mythologies of all cultures is the rite of passage myth, in which the hero achieves independence from his mother and thus gains the capacity to fully relate to women, through a trial of strength and courage often leading to his death through over-confidence. Theseus slew the minotour in the Cretan labyrinth (a maze is always the symbol for matriarchy in

Greek mythology) and went on to rescue Ariadne. Perseus slew the Gorgon and later overcame the dragon that guarded Andromeda.

The Winnebago Indians of North America, divided the development of the psyche into phases or cycles, the transitions between which were marked by painful ritual ordeals symbolising death and regeneration. The adolescent cycle is represented by the mythological 'trickster' an individual whose behaviour is dominated by his physical appetites, who cannot relate successfully to others, who has no purpose beyond gratifying his primary needs and who lacks the maturity to recognise the limitations of fun and pleasure as sources of genuine fulfilment. He embarks on a dangerous quest, dies (symbolically) and reappears as 'Hare' the fully realised and mature hero.

Many of the gliders that I met in Austria corresponded closely to the 'trickster' archetype, nearly all were single males, mainly working in emasculating and isolating jobs in high technology industries and with limited social possibilities outside of their sport.

Unfortunately, because the significance of ritual and myth has been a casualty in the twentieth century struggle between logic and superstition, it is all too easy in today's society for such individuals to survive without religion, marriage, mythology, the medicine man and his totems and so on but in doing so they cut themselves off from the collective unconscious and risk arresting their development.

They may find themselves permanently trapped by their own rationalisations within the 'trickster' cycle, oblivious to the exhortations of the unconscious to elevate themselves into the 'Hare' cycle. Or indeed as in the case of paragliding, limited to the pedestrian logic of the ego they may even tragic-comically interpret literally the subconscious injunctions of which they are only dimly aware, and like Icarus borne on the idealism and over-confidence of immaturity, actually enact the metaphorical episode offered by the unconscious to represent their struggle to surmount the obstacles between adolescence and maturity.

Dear God! Thought I, as I digested this absolute floater of a thesis. What could be the meaning of such knavery? Picture my pique as I garnered this Whisted blighter's gist. Conceive of my chagrin. Clearly the man was precisely the type of dreadful, over intellectualising poop whose hooter it would be my singular pleasure to smite.

So nettled was I by the fellow's nerve, so chafed by his cheek, so stung by his slander not to say pipped by his pompous perfidy, that it was with a hand fairly trembling with indignation, that I penned an immediate and searing riposte.

12 06 1994

Dear Sir,

Having read your article in 'Skythings' I am inclined to conclude that you are utterly overstretching yourself. The framework of rationalisations that you construct around paragliding could equally be superimposed upon any area of human activity upon which you have not the least emotional purchase. It does more to expose your own attitudes than those of the pilots that you dismissively caricature.

Furthermore your claim that paraglider pilots are unwittingly enacting some species of questing behaviour as exhorted by their dislocated subconscious, is as insulting as it is baseless.

Yours

Nigel Jenkins BHPA P(H)*

*British Hangliding and Paragliding Association. Pilot rated (Hill Launch).

To my considerable surprise the fellow took this drubbing and came back for more.

21 06 1994

Dear Mr. Jenkins

My diagnosis of paragliding as a symptom of dissociation is not in the least controversial; indeed it is axiomatic within my profession, that dangerous sports generally are essentially a surrogation of the repressed 'heroic' masculine instinct.

Interestingly though, cross country paragliding, in common with a very small group of other activities, sharply differs from the adrenaline fuelled base jumping, skydiving white water rafting and their ilk. The reason for this, and, by extension, why it has become the focus of much of my work of late, is that paragliding, if pursued appropriately, seems to simultaneously offer the potential for ameliorating the personality problems of which it is an expression.

If you have difficulty in accepting the idea of your sport as symbolic ritual how do you feel about flying as a crude attempt at self medication? Similar in its motivation to drug abuse perhaps.

Yours

Bertrand Whisted M.Psy.

What fresh hell this? What libel? What bare faced poltroonery? Paragliding as self-medication similar to drug taking? I mean really.

And so it went on:

27 06 1994

Dear Professor Whisted

Propping up one speculative un-falsifiable hypothesis by grafting it onto another, is very poor science. Roughly equivalent to saying 'the reason that rap artists use overtly sexual lyrics in their music is to compensate for their personal insecurities, like men who drive big cars'.

I suspect that in your theory you are trying to find a basis to support what is essentially no more than your prejudice against people who take part in an activity simply because they happen to enjoy it.

Yours

Nigel Jenkins. B.H.P.A. p (h) (winch conversion)

And on.

4   0 7

1994

Dear Mr Jenkins,

There is nothing simple about happening to enjoy something. Drug users would doubtlessly claim to enjoy the effects of their drug and yet can we reasonably doubt that there is a hidden psychological explanation driving such self destructive behaviour? Hypothesis, I am sure you will agree is the engine of scientific discovery, and it is in this spirit that I propose the link between my model of the purpose of flying in the lives of the individuals to whom I refer in my article, with the role of drug taking in the lives of many users.

Both activities are recognisably ritualistic both cause measurable physical and metabolic changes both produce striking alterations in mood and both ultimately are an attempt to offset emotional deficiencies.

The hyper manic user generally uses cannabis or prescription antidepressants to bring his temperament within a functional range, the depressive indulges in stimulants to bring him up to speed.

I believe paragliding to be analogous to the use of hallucinogens which is also widespread amongst individuals struggling to come to terms with the dissociation caused by repressed trauma. To become 'centred' and to 'get in touch with oneself' are frequently cited justifications for this behaviour among the chronic users with whom I have worked.

I suspect that the myth that the drug l.s.d. is a causal factor in mental illness and in particular schizophrenia, probably arises from its popularity with individuals who at an unconscious level know themselves to be dissociated and seek to unite their conscious and unconscious mind.

With paragliding we have a similar duality, in that the activity is both a symptom of the problem of dissociation and an attempt at a therapy. The folly however is that it neglects to include the vital interpretive role which at different times and in different cultures would have been filled by the shaman the priest the witch doctor or the therapist.

yours

Bertrand Whisted Psy

Now then: If there's one thing that I have learned in life, then it is, 'never use 'Deep Heat' as a lubricant', (what a night that was)[15] and if there are two things I have learned, then I suppose the second would have to be: 'don't allow a chinchilla to play near a waste disposal unit.' But if there are three things that I have learned in life, then the third is that the really vital thing that any agent of persuasion will always seek to do in the early stages of a pitch is to attempt to establish a dialogue.

For example:

'What do you think about the national lottery?' Asked the luminescently attractive Marxist who accosted me in a shopping mall a few years ago. It turned out that what she really wanted to know was whether I would like to subscribe to 'Communism Now', a reasonable question to which the answer naturally was a cheerful

'No fear.'

The point is that from the professional manipulator's perspective, once you are engaged in conversation with the person, their natural politeness does most of your work for you. If you can achieve a couple of points of agreement, for instance:

'Yes you're so right the lottery is really a tax on having a limited understanding of statistics...' and without pausing for breath, tack on your own two cents

---

[15] *The Triumph Herald never ran the same again.*

worth, '... and as such is exploitative and should be banned.' Then you can make it seem as though you share a point of view and the rest is plain sailing.

At a particularly extreme stage of my obsession with this type of thing I submitted as my entry to a photography competition, fifty pairs of pictures, each depicting a man in the street or 'the mark' as they are known to hustlers and assassins. The first shows the delight and scarcely concealed hope as they are engaged by the cheerful positive, appealing stranger of the opposite s. The second depicts the shutters coming down as the realisation dawns that the stimulating and spontaneous encounter which looked to be in the offing, is simply a ruse to steer them where they have no wish to go.

One of these chaps, a young Canadian fellow, paid seventy pounds for, of all things, a hair and facial makeover voucher, from a particularly pulchritudinous saleswoman in a Brighton street. I know that that was the amount because I fished it out of the bin, into which he had angrily thrown it, just around the corner. I know that he was Canadian from his dress sense.

But I'm repeating myself. Something that I am constantly telling myself not to do. The point is, that back in '94, I was a callow youth and guilelessly rose to Whisted's bait. Like a fish on a hook, the more I struggled the more it became impossible to get away.

Our correspondence continued throughout the summer whilst he patiently turned me to his way of thinking. Gradually I began to see that my reasons for flying were not entirely, as I had always stated when asked; 'because it's a bit of a lark,' but were indeed an outlet for something else. Something deeper, something elemental. I began to accept that the conscious and unconscious parts of my mind were like two distant relatives who got along for form's sake but, each of whom, secretly regarded the other as 'a bit wrong in the head.'

Moreover I began to accept too that flying was not merely a futile substitute for the dangerous challenges of prehistory to which generations of young men were genetically programmed to rise but something else too. And once I'd seen it, I couldn't believe that I hadn't seen it before.

9 I'M CRAZY! ROMPS RESTRICT HUNT

At seven p.m. or thereabouts, I ankled downstairs to the hotel bar for a spot of lubrication and a bit of a sniff around. Paraglider pilots tend not to be overly bibulous as a rule, since flying for hours in the desert sun is quite dehydrating enough in itself, without compounding the effect with alcohol. Nevertheless the Imperial Hotel was packed with air-persons indulging in a bit of après-sky, sporting patch-work suntans and re-enacting at inordinate length, key moments from the day's adventures.

The appalling Babylon Zoo's insufferable 1996 hit 'Spaceman' was playing on the jukebox as I smoothly attached myself to a pair of pilots who had rented a house in the town for the season. I announced myself as Peregrin Axlerod as before.

My fellows (and I had rarely seen two more polarised examples of the skygod/skytwerp duality that is a feature of the flying fraternity generally) were an English expat and an Australian. They were both in their late forties but had that unmistakable air of having become a shade indifferent to each other's company that is common in elderly married couples. They were only too pleased, therefore, to have someone new to the scene in whom to impart their local knowledge. Duly I acquired the requisite intelligence for independent flying in the area: Where to stand for a hitch to the hill, how to get to launch, who to speak to, what to do. In the spirit of quid pro quo, I treated them to a round of schooners and continued to probe in the hopes of hearing mention of Professor Whisted.

'There's only four people you need to know in this town.' Opined J.J. the disarmingly laid back, local fellow. That this chap had never married was readily apparent in his buoyant and youthful air, and to the discerning eye he was clearly of that select breed who fly a paraglider simply because they happen to be really good at it. Had he been born on the coast, he would most probably have been a surfer instead. Pilots of J.J.'s ilk seldom have anything to prove but they can generally fly everybody else into a cocked hat, which is all the more galling for the pilots who do.

'Colleen who you've already met,' interrupted Bill Philby, a twitchy, highly strung specimen. 'Vic and Tom who run the diner and petrol station' he prattled on, alternately switching his beady gaze between each of my eyes with a rapidity that bordered on the freakish. Crazy teeth jutted from his slitty mouth in a rictus of sardonic glee. 'And Godfrey Wenness, the king of the hill.' I backed off a trifle in an effort to avoid those curiously dead eyes.

'Actually the mayor's a pretty good bloke too.' Added J.J. indicating the huge avuncular cove busy winning an arm wrestle at the other side of the room.

'John the Scatman,' surely one of the most fantastically bad tunes of all time, suddenly burst forth from the antediluvian jukebox in the adjacent pool bar with an entirely unjustified air of enthusiasm. Strangely, short of vaulting over the bar itself, this area could be reached only through the gentlemen's lavatory or through the back yard which was ruthlessly patrolled by Bastard, a formidable hound whose lineage clearly contained at least one dingo and if his physiognomy was reliable, possibly a crocodile as well. Bastard was famed for having bitten Clint the barman on the scrotum, a story for which he would provide visual corroboration with the minimum of encouragement.

Peering in the direction of the offending din, I spotted Otto, a schooner in his hand, engaged in conversation with a brace of local girls. One of them looked exceedingly bored and the other looked gigantic but subsequently turned out to be merely enormous. Both were displaying a great deal of skin and both were smoking with an enthusiasm that knew no bounds.

'Interestingly, there have been more flights of over a hundred kilometres logged in Manilla this season, than in the previous two combined,' said Bill suddenly.

Privately I inclined to the view that the word 'interestingly' had no place in a sentence such as this but rather than ventilate this opinion, I quaffed another neckfull of fizzy lager and contemplated my companions further. The rather extreme contrast in personality between Bill and J.J. appeared to be having the unsettling result that each of them was subconsciously trying to compensate for the other and in doing so were creating a positive feedback loop. The more excitable and frenetic Bill became, the more irresistibly JJ's demeanour approached catatonia in an effort to exert a soothing influence upon his associate.

The skytwerp is not to be soothed however. His approach to flying is a starkly rational one. Applying the tools of science and logic to optimise his flying, he waxes lyrical on the paralysingly dull esoteria of meteorology: lapse rates, katebatic flow, the Coriolis effect and what have you. Indeed if he is a truly representative specimen of the species then in all probability he downloads his g.p.s. trace too, and reconstructs the entire flight in his computer. He is, in short, a poop.

The skygod differs substantially from this outright knave. He is a feeling pilot, the kind that everybody wants to be but which, rather irritatingly, you absolutely cannot become simply by trying. He is a natural. An intuitive pilot who regards the sky as does a soaring eagle.

Now you might be inclined to infer from all of this, that the prospects for the unholy alliance between Bill and J.J. were consequently pretty doubtful. But if you so infer, then you err. Oh yes!

Let me assure you that such coves are as Yin to Yang. They are locked together in a sort of weird symbiosis.

Before long, Bill's interminably tedious technical twaddle was well and truly boring the arse off me. And in addition, the fraught internal dynamics of the pair's relationship were beginning to chafe badly on my sensibilities. Duly, I determined to explore the possibilities that Otto's new acquaintances might present, and to this end I excused myself on the pretext of answering natures call and, by way of the privy, repaired to the other bar. This was an expedient I was to deploy fairly frequently throughout my stay at the Imperial.

Towering a foot above the girls and their tobacco miasma, Otto Resembled nothing so much as mount Kilimanjaro with its upper slopes wreathed in cloud.

'Ah zis my friend Pregrin' quoth he as I approached. Friend was putting it a bit strongly, I thought but I let it go, 'Pregrin zis Colleen's coosin Ellie' he said, gesturing hopefully towards the larger and almost infinitely the second most attractive of the two women.

'Elle.' She snapped over-hastily, thus drawing attention too, rather than away from, any unfortunate associations that Ellie might conjure to mind. 'pleased to meet you Pregrin.' We shook hands.

'And zis Melanie.' Melanie was definitely very cute indeed with big dark eyes peeping from behind her fringe and a distinctly naughty smile. Despite the seeming inevitability that in the fullness of time, junk food, cigarettes and the almost total inactivity of the outback town lifestyle would be writ large about her person, she remained, for now, a flower. 'Bless my soul,' I thought to myself, registering the firm steady grip of her handshake, 'that is firm and steady.'

'How ya goin' Pregrin?' she asked, perking up a few notches and fiddling with her hair.

'Pleased to meet you Melanie.' I pipped.

'Are you one of them paragliders too Pregrin?' she asked folding her arms in such a way as to hoist more prominently into view a pair of breasts which had never been precisely inconspicuous. The question was actually pretty redundant really since no-one but a pilot would spend any longer in Manilla than it takes to execute a hasty three point turn. I confirmed this and proposed a frame of pool to take the strain off the conversation.

While Otto racked them up, I bought a gallon or so of froth from Colleen at the bar. In the course of the transaction I caught Bill and J.J. sharing a knowing look like a couple of schoolboys. I passed the beers around and enrolled Melanie in my team by wordlessly proffering the one cue in the rack which was neither split, nor missing its tip. She accepted this in exchange for a look clearly intended to be freighted with meaning. The girls went through the motions of playing pool in rather the same way that men dance in discotheques, which is to say with little skill or enthusiasm and more or less as a means to an end.

Presently we repaired to the plastic patio furniture beside the jukebox where the girls could concentrate on their smoking without the inconvenience of having to desultorily bash the balls at random around the table. It began to play Falco's execrable 'Rock me Amadeus'.

Elle's personality, as it turned out, contrasted rather sharply with the sophisticated femininity that her name implied. She would abruptly start speaking whenever she got bored of listening to whoever was talking (which was instantly) invariably to moan about what a dag somebody called Pete was. Naturally, the level of dagitude or indeed the personal qualities generally of this unknown wretch was not a subject Otto and I felt we could run with, and so typically the conversational sally would prove fairly abortive.

For example:

Mel	Is that in London Pregrin?
Z-H	No, Brighton's on the south coast about fifty miles from London, it's famous for its two piers and it's Royal Pavili...
Elle	...Jeez Pete's a dag!
Z-H	Er. Pete you say?
Mel	Ah Pete's this guy Elle used to go with.
Z-H	Bit of a dag eh?

Elle   Guess what he said to me at Vic and Toms last night.

Otto   Vot did he say?

Elle   He said he was glad Myra Macdonald lost her baby cause now she knows what he went through.

Z-H   Nice fellow.

Otto   Vot did he go srew?

Mel   His brother Darren drowned in a car Myra drove into the river.

Elle   Stupid drunk bitch!

Such Wildean badinage cannot be sustained indefinitely of course and, in the fullness of time, the girls stocked up with cigarettes and 'stubbies' of beer and announced that we were going swimming in the river. The same river in point of fact into which the s.d.b. Myra Macdonald had driven her car, whilst being extremely s. and completely d. the previous year. And the means by which we were going to weave the half mile to the swimming hole, was in Elle's crummy old Toyota.

At length we arrived at the blue hole, which, one couldn't help noticing almost immediately, was rather dominated by a semi submerged, yellow, hand-painted Renault 9. Thankfully Elle made no moves to disrobe as the rest of us stripped off to our smalls and instead

119

planted herself on the river bank where she proceeded to smoke and complain loudly about how lame it all was.

With some muted reservations about the wisdom of the undertaking I wobbled uncomfortably across the pebbles on the shore and into the water, in the manner of a drunk transvestite wearing stilettos on a ship in high seas[16]. Melanie skipped past me in her sandals and pants before executing a neat shallow dive, and surfacing to laugh gleefully at my pommie awkwardness.

Like Hylas, lured, by the naiads to enter the stream of Bithnyia, I toddled after her into the cool waters. Everybody has their element of course and suddenly Melanie was in hers. Mine, naturally, is the air, whereas Elle, pending the invention of waterproof cigarettes, never leaves dry land.

There was an almighty whooping yell of the type popularised by 'The Dukes of Hazzard,' and we turned to see Otto launch himself from a huge rock, shaped unsettlingly like Maurice Chevaliers nose, plummet into the water with a painful sounding splat and then surface with a curtain of water raining from his facial topiary and wearing an expression of studied inscrutability, as though defying us to find anything remotely funny in the occurrence.

'You gotta watch out for water snakes Pregrin.' Melanie said, suddenly serious, moving very close to me

---

[16] See 'Zinctrumpet-Harris and the Bangkok Beagle Brouhaha.'

so that her bare breasts lightly touched my chest. 'only kidding.' she laughed, feeling me stiffen slightly.

'Come on.' She cried, moving away but taking my hand, 'let's get under the waterfall.'

And so we did. Giggling like children in the refreshing spray. And when we'd had enough of that, we drifted slowly downstream on our backs sometimes touching, sometimes not. Gazing at the infinity of stars.

'I want your life Pregrin.' she told me with a sigh once I'd recounted my recent past. About Brazil and Mexico and Africa. 'Don't reckon I'll ever get out of Manilla.'

'You could go to Sydney' I ventured, 'Its only forty dollars on the train Move into a flatshare, get a job, save up for an air ticket and work your way around the world.'

'It's not that easy' she said 'my mum needs me to help look after my dad. He's dying of lung cancer.' I sought her hand and gave it a squeeze.

When, a little while later and still trembling a little, we re-joined the others, Otto was building a huge and elaborate reefer in the shape of a tulip, painstakingly constructed from twelve separate cigarette papers.

'Designed to be smoked vertically.' he told us, in fluent Manglish 'zats why ze petals to catch ze ash.' He passed it around as the four of us lay on our backs, arranged as a cross with our heads close together. Soon we were off on the usual round of cosmic conversations about how far away the stars were, whether astrology was true, if there was life on other planets, and what a dag Pete was.

There's definitely something about gazing at a starlit night sky that connects you across time and space with similar experiences from your past. I found myself being transported to the French Alps. It was 1995.

'Try to find a star that's too dim to see.' Whisted had told me as we reclined in adjacent deck chairs whilst sharing a bottle of brandy on the balcony of our ski chalet.

'Right.' I'd replied uncertainly. 'Although, I'd have to say, there is one difficulty that immediately suggests itself to me.'

'Which is?'

'A star that's too dim to see is too dim to see Bertrand.'

'Try not looking for it.' He'd suggested gently. I tried this. I tried it again.

'The act of looking directly at the star prevents you from seeing it Mostyn.' He had said. 'Like the face of god, you can only see it indirectly.' Suddenly I saw what he meant. A glimmering light which vanished when I stared at it but which softly blinked into life when I averted my gaze. I have subsequently discovered that this effect has something to do with the distribution of cells on the retina or something. Whisted's point though, had little to do with rods and cones, foveas and blind spots. What he was getting at, was something altogether other.

At about two a.m. a battered Toyota pulled up outside the Imperial Hotel. From within it, and at a deeply inconsiderate volume emerged the strains of the mind corrodingly horrendous 'Dr. Worm' by the pop combo 'They Might be Giants' followed by two tired men in the throes of trying to extract themselves from what was developing into an increasingly circular conversation about the relative merits of getting some quality sleep in order to be fresh for flying in the morning, versus the case for not being 'a pair of boring wankers. Eventually, and with some difficulty, the exponents of the former viewpoint managed to disengage themselves, declining offers of alternative accommodation at Elle's house and the car drove off. As the sound of it's dragging exhaust faded away the b.w.s belatedly realised that the front door had long ago been locked up for the night and the only way into the hotel was through the yard and led past the hellhound Bastard.

10 LOVELY ONCE YOU'RE IN

'They just sort of hang there don't they? I saw them at Beachy Head'

Everyone

Consider just for a moment, if you can bear it, that ludicrous popinjay, the stage hypnotist. Night after night, this uniquely oily tick struts out before a packed house, seemingly unashamed of his horrid spangly jacket and positively revelling in his vile mid-Atlantic accent. His aim? To bestow upon those there present, a dazzling demonstration of the mesmerist's art.

What, I suspect, you will almost certainly fail to detect through this vomit inducing display of swagger and smarm though, is the tiniest, weeniest scintilla of anxiety that lurks beneath. Because, believe it or not, despite his nauseatingly cocksure manner, this appalling excrescence is, at this point, undertaking a bit of a gamble. For he is absolutely counting on there being amongst the audience a few representatives of a select subset of society that are stupendously susceptible to hypnosis. It's a pretty safe bet. But a gamble nonetheless.

Consequently, the first part of a typical hypnosis show consists of an artfully disguised whittling down procedure. Firstly the entire audience is placed into a light trance and encouraged to believe that it cannot unclench its fists or some such trifle. Those who respond to this gambit are invited onto the stage where they are persuaded to forget their names etc. The process continues until the unresponsive and the fakers are weeded out and only the massively suggestible remain.

What entirely escaped me at the beginning of the Whisted affair, and in fact didn't come out until the police enquiry, was that he too had been playing just such a numbers game. Had he attempted to publish his article in a Professional journal, its speculative and unfalsifiable nature would have occasioned an avalanche of indifference. 'Your point being?' would have been the general retort. The cunning duality of Whisted's plan though, was that this premise was only a decoy. He launched 'The Icarus Complex' in every paragliding association magazine in Europe as a litmus test to flush out individuals likely to be suitable subjects for a rather elaborate and ingenious experiment that he had in mind. His fiendish logic was as follows:

Fifty thousand pilots would see the article.

Of whom some ten thousand would be aged between eighteen and about twenty three.

Of whom around a third would conform somewhat to the trickster archetype.

Of whom a few hundred would have at least a keen amateur's interest in and a measure of receptivity to, psychology.

Of whom half at least would respond feeling both pipped and at the same time, slightly rattled as though the article had been aimed expressly at them.

Which it had.

Up to this point the field had been self-deselecting. People's failure to react to the article identified them as ineligible for Whisted's purposes. Once we were in the open however, he engaged a selected group of us simultaneously in a protracted correspondence designed to weigh up each respondents cast of mind. To establish in each case who, in addition to being rather indignant and not a little offended, was also ultimately protesting too much. It was a scatter gun approach. A numbers game.

All that remained to be determined at this point, was the presence of the same quality that the stage hypnotist can detect by administering to his audience a series of progressively stronger transitions into trance, which, if successful, betray an almost preternatural vulnerability to hypnotism. To this end he drew up a shortlist and set about meeting us face to face.

30 07 1994

Dear Mr Jenkins,

I notice that you live in the South of England, I
am in the U.K. at present myself on a lecture tour
and will be at the Psychology Department of the
University of Brighton from August the ninth. If
you should care to I could easily make some time to
continue our discussion in person.

Additionally I have a proposal that you may wish
to consider.

Yours

Bertrand Whisted Psy.

P.S. bring your glider, it is forecast post cold
frontal with a 10 to 12k north westerly.

This was my first inkling that Whisted was himself a
pilot. I had naturally envisaged that some ghastly
specimen of sterile, turnip headed boffinry cowered
behind that preposterously judgemental attitude. The

127

notion that the fellow might be a fellow spirit of the air literally hadn't occurred to me.

I wondered at the character of a man who would be willing to turn on his fellows so. Or at least appear to. What were the ends that justified such means? Was he in fact projecting his own inadequacies onto us?

It wasn't until much later that I pondered also the easy fluency with the vocabulary of flying in the phrase,

'P.S. bring your glider, it is forecast post cold frontal with a 10 to 12k north westerly.'

And compared it to.

'…it was I believe rather insufficiently windy for really good gliding.'

The clumsy gaucheness of which, in the light of subsequent events, might be seen as a little contrived.

Intrigued I agreed to the meeting and duly, at the startlingly early hour stipulated, my venerable, open topped triumph herald, lurched into the car park of Brighton University's psychology faculty.

In a shaft of morning sunshine in one corner of the unlovely nineteen seventies quadrangle, the elegant figure of Bertrand Whisted, dressed in a white open necked cotton shirt and tan linen trousers, half leaned, half sat upon his glider bag, studying a folded air map; a pipe in his mouth.

He was a striking looking man in, I guessed, his late fifties, with a resolute bearing suggestive of the nineteen thirties, amateur, English gentleman, pioneer aviator. He had clearly been, in his youth at least, a specimen of rather extreme personal attractiveness, equipped with a shock of defiantly luxuriant hair, once blonde, now mainly silver and of the type that flops continually from one pleasing state of slight disarray to another. His hazel eyes spoke of great intelligence and smouldering intensity while endearingly higgledy piggledy teeth flashed in a smile that seemed almost to apologise for the plenitude of roguish charm with which he had been endowed.

'I know,' it seemed to say, 'but hey, what can I do?'

'Nigel,' He cried, as though greeting an old friend. He waited for me to climb from the car before clasping my hand warmly. 'Bertrand. He beamed, 'how perfectly splendid to finally meet you.'

That he was English was a surprise, without really giving it a lot of thought I had just assumed that he was Austrian. And that he was *so* English, rather than say, just a little bit, was not just a surprise but rather a pleasant one too.

'Well I think we should take your car, since it's such a smashing day?' he suggested.

'Fine.' I said, a little flattered, opening the boot for him to stow his wing next to mine.

My Tatty 1959 Triumph Herald, won in a game of steam iron roulette from Pedro Weinstein, a Jewish matador I met in Piedrahita[17], had been built in the era when cars still had a chassis and so I had been able to convert it to an open top by the simple expedient of unbolting the roof. A five minute operation which, aside from a propensity for the doors to fly open on tight bends, appeared to cause the vehicle no ill effects.

'Where too?' I enquired, crunching the car into first with the wooden handled screwdriver that served as a gear-stick.

'Why Devils Dyke by crikey!' he grinned, a gleam of excitement in his eye, 'It's a bally 50k day and no error!'

And he was dead right. It is a happy coincidence that the kind of day which offers the best cross country potential, is just exactly the kind of day upon which it would seem heinously poor form to languish indoors. The ninth of August 1994 truly was one of those zinging bright cold mornings with a fabulous blue sky and glorious golden light abounding.

As we bowled along the country lanes towards the South Downs, Professor Whisted, in the well modulated voice of a professional lecturer that carried above the

---

[17] See, 'Zinctrumpet-Harris and the Andulucian Affenpinscher Altercation .'

engine and the wind, began, perhaps from force of habit, to expand further upon his theory.

'It is my belief Nigel,' he boomed into the wind, the lights in his eyes suggestive of a scarcely contained dam of excitement welling up within him, 'that prayer, meditation, hypnosis, chanting, ritual and whatnot are all to a lesser or greater extent aimed at achieving the same thing,' He paused, watching me closely until I shot him an affirmatory glance   in return. 'which is to manoeuvre the mind into a state of egolessness that is favourable to communion with the unconscious.'

I too was savouring the electric tingle of the anticipation of a flight and was grinning like a loon.

'Drug taking,' he went on, 'is an attempt to shortcut the process in answer to an unconscious sense of the same need, felt in secular life where the framework for facilitating such communion is absent. It fails though, because it lacks the essential ingredients of discipline and guidance.'

'I'm with you so far Professor.' I cried and in fact it was only a sense of wanting to indulge the chap that prevented me from saying, 'Yeah we covered that already.' as I dare say Reeves would have done in my stead.

'Furthermore, ' he continued, 'I believe that self hypnosis, is the underlying aim of many of the more absorbing activities that people undertake ostensibly in the name of recreation. Paragliding, dancing, surfing, skiing, the plastic arts, indeed pretty well any activity in which the participant could be said, in that too telling phrase, to lose their self.'

I made a thoughtful face suggestive of assent to this view.

'Ergo they too address the resolution of dislocation' I chipped in.

'Neurologically the mental state produced by all of these activities is the same and is quite measurable. The brain as you will no doubt be aware, emits electrical waves at different frequencies, mainly beta waves during normal consciousness, alpha waves whilst resting, delta waves in deep sleep and so on. Under hypnosis, during meditation, in r.e.m. sleep and whilst engaged in activities such as paragliding, the brain emits mostly theta brain-waves which are consistent with the greatest accessibility to the subconscious.'

'I wonder if you could fish my sunglasses out of the glove compartment Bertrand.' I interjected, perhaps for the pleasure of addressing him by his Christian name as much as anything. After some rummaging around he located my excitingly hi-tech mirror shades inside the short length of bamboo within which I stored them at that time. This was the latest in a long line of receptacles to be pressed into service in this capacity, glasses cases being so infuriatingly easy to lose. Whisted ploughed on.

'Typically, paragliding appears to attract a participant whose mind is disproportionately dominated by the linear logical processes associated with the left brain. This is an individual who's rational and analytical mindset will not allow the leap of faith involved in embracing one of the many ideologies whose aim ultimately is to access the subconscious and yet he still feels that need. His conscious mind has such a tight grip on his mental life, he is so literal minded if you like, that it takes the dimension of danger, the mortal danger of death at any moment, in a situation of such blatant symbolism, as to be literally flying inescapably is, for the subject to silence the inner monologue and gain any respite whatsoever from the relentless serial cognition of the ego.'

Whisted, I noticed as I glanced across, had turned completely around in his seat. He was drinking in the sky. Inspecting the cumulus clouds that were building to the North of us in a long snaking street. Pointing the way East for a really epic flight along the coast.

'And up to a point it is effective,' He continued, 'the pilot, having undertaken a testing and prolonged cross country flight is measurably relaxed, buzzing with theta waves. He describes himself as 'centred', feels, if you like, at one with himself. The conflicting parts of his mind reconciled, he finds himself in very much the same state as the Buddhist who has spent the same period of time meditating.'

I fought to keep my eyes on the road, even at that time no less than three pilots known to me had been responsible for rear end shunts as a result of scouring the sky and not the road whilst driving to flying sites.

'The difference is that whilst the Buddhist, under the tutelage of his Bodhisattva, is engaged in a systematic program of guided lessons aimed at reaching Nirvana; for the pilot the effect is only temporary. He hasn't gained any actual insight or made any progress, because the exploration is purposeless. Indeed it is an exploration he is not even aware he is undertaking.

He has opened the door of his subconscious and faltered on the threshold. It is the equivalent of the hypnotherapist placing the subject into trance and then proceeding directly to bringing him out of hypnosis without placing any suggestions in his mind. The only benefit is the placebo effect arising from the sense of doing something rather than nothing about the problem. An effect which will diminish over time.'

We lapsed into a companionable silence for the rest of the journey as he left me to digest this angle. I realised later that it was Whisted's practice always to engage his subjects in this way. Never face to face as in an interview but side by side as a therapist and patient or a father and son fishing from a riverbank. No eye contact, no confrontation, no body language.

I continued to ponder this new slant on Whisted's position. To an extent, some of the pilots I knew conformed to the profile that he described. Stronger in logic than in self-knowledge; more intelligent than wise. I thought too about the intensity of my first few flights and how they had indeed displaced any articulated conscious thoughts. How I could fly for hours and upon landing, glowing with exhilaration I would realise how focused I had been in the air, to the exclusion of the usual carousel of linear mental narrative.

We arrived at the Dyke, a six hundred foot hill on the Sussex Downs, facing North-West. It was still early but already it was time to launch, the sky was perfect. Gliders were climbing out and within the hour the cold sea breeze would probably blow in and close down the thermals. We needed to get up and away before the wind switched direction.

We found a good spot and laid our equipment out on the grass. A paraglider unlike its cousin the hanglider, has no frame, no aluminium tubes, instead it has hundreds of Kevlar lines by means of which the pilot in his harness is suspended from the canopy. The lines are gathered at the bottom and joined to two sets of webbing straps collectively known as the risers and these in turn are semi permanently attached to the harness, one set to each side, by two 'G' shaped aluminium clips or karabiners.

The wing itself is an evolution of the square type parachute design but greatly optimised for gliding efficiency. It consists of a row of sixty or so aerofoil shaped interconnected hollow pockets each of which is open at the leading edge and closed at the trailing edge. Being made from nylon it is also a delicate child, so I squinted into each of its cells to check that all was well.

I checked the reserve parachute too. Unlike it's skydiving equivalent which is constructed of a porous fabric and packed in such a way as to draw out the deceleration from free fall, the paragliding reserve is a small non porous affair designed to snap open very quickly at low altitude and lowish speed and to rapidly decelerate the pilot to a rate of descent at which his ankles can withstand a landing. This is because most deployments take place fairly close to the ground following a mid air collision with another glider, in which case the pilot, still attached to his canopy, is normally descending relatively slowly due to drag.

I was clipping myself into the harness when Whisted, toddled over and handed me a rather unpleasant vinyl sports bag sporting a selection of thrilling stripes, plus the word Reebok (elk? Oryx?) and which contained a rather spiffing crash helmet.

'I have a friend at Oxford who builds robots for satellites,' said the professor, 'he knocks these up for me.'

It was of precisely the same type, I noticed, as his own. I inspected the item, which was an absolute thing of joy. It was of carbon fibre construction and had been modified to accommodate a pair of headphones which fitted snugly against my ears as I wedged it onto the old bean. It also had a small microphone on a little stalk and a trailing lead which he connected to a two channel radio. This he stowed in the front pocket of my flying suit. The helmet also featured an eerily effective noise cancellation system whereby the output of the microphone was fed to the earphones with its phase reversed, thus cancelling out almost all of the extraneous noise, including that of my own voice.

At this point Whisted placed his hands on either side of the helmet, over my ears as it were, and after fixing me with a long look, said in a calm but positive tone that almost seemed to come from within my head.

'Close your eyes Nigel. Now allow your mind to visualise a chair.'

A trifle bemused, I did as he asked and found to my surprise that I almost couldn't prevent myself from picturing this really rather vividly.

'What colour is the chair?'

'White,' I said silently. And was immediately annoyed with myself. Now I came to think of it, the chair I had conjured to mind had not in fact been white, it had had no colour at all. It was merely the concept of a chair onto which any colour could be projected. I was simply at a loss to know why I had said it.

'Here comes a cycle now.' he said.

I passed my hands through the brake handles and gathered up the risers, building the glider into a curved wall in front of me supported by the light north westerly breeze, its row of open cell mouths pantingly sought the air that would make the wing surge forward.

He gestured skywards, 'I'll see you at base.' he replied.

I made a last check all around me for other gliders, kites and other obvious dangers. I stiffened the sinews, and with a firm pull on the 'A' risers that join the front row of lines to the harness, I inflated the glider. I stepped towards it as it swiftly rose above my head, braking it slightly to prevent it overflying me. It all looked good, sitting above me like a kite, no tangles no tucks, I turned to the right (always to the right) and facing forward now balanced the wing above my head for a moment before powering forwards and striding into the air.

As I flew straight out from launch, the hill sloped away below me. I eased myself back into the supine position, turned the volume of my vario right up and almost immediately entered a thermal. The glider pitched back and an excited series of bleeping noises from the vario announced the presence of rising air.

I applied the right brake and by crossing my left leg over the right I shifted my weight the same way to put the glider into a turn. The effect of lift makes the wing want to fly straight so it can take a bit of doing to bring it around but soon it was established in a circle and I applied a bit of outside brake too, so as to fly slowly in the thermal.

The vario's frantic beeping reduced in pitch as I flew out of the strongest lift and by braking less on the right I widened the circle to try and locate the core. As I flew I could make out Whisted still on the ground, clipped in but lying down on his back with his legs crossed, puffing on his pipe, watching me climb.

The middle section of a thermal is normally the strongest and the vario continued to chirp encouragingly as the world circled around me, my climb was averaging one point five metres per second and in a few more turns the hill began to look small. I looked up to see a wispy cumulus forming above and behind me marking the top of the thermal and showing the angle at which it tracked back from its base in front of the Dyke.

The air, noticeably cooler, was rising more slowly as I passed one thousand metres above sea level and I began to ponder my options. In paragliding, altitude is money in the bank and thus it was with a little frisson of delight that I noted that from my present height I could, if I chose, cash it in by turning downwind and gliding for five kilometres, clear over Brighton to the beach.

Now, there is a widely held notion, the wrongheadedness of which it is almost impossible to exaggerate, that the whole business of paragliding consists chiefly of 'just hanging there'. The J.H.T. misconception tends to prevail amongst the gen. pub. for the perfectly adequate reason, that the spectacle of gliders apparently 'just hanging there,' is not uncommon, at scenic spots the length and breadth of the country. But I would invite you to be aware, that this pervasive fallacy contains precisely the same category of misunderstanding that one detects lurking within, for example, the statement, 'most gay women have short hair,' in the sense that you tend to notice the ones who do, and not the ones who do not.

Therefore if you have hitherto laboured under the misapprehension that the potential of paragliding extends no further than the doubtful accomplishment of hovering a few feet above the ground, or perhaps of wafting up and down beside a ridge in a futile game of follow the leader or even of loafing around on the hill wearing day-glo nylon and conducting tedious and interminable flying conversations in what amounts to an extremely elaborate and expensive picnic, then allow me to disabuse you forthwith by directing your attention toward the paraglider pilot's holy grail, that most estimable of enterprises: cross country.

The general idea of cross country paragliding or x.c. is pretty straightforward. One aims to get very high above take off and then glide downwind until by luck or judgement one encounters another thermal, whereupon the process is repeated until one runs out of lift, daylight or land. The thermal business though, it should be said, is very much a seller's market. As such, if your approach to x.c. depends heavily upon luck rather than j. - if you are, in short, a punter; then you are likely to end up gliding to a landing fairly early in the flight. The cognoscenti however, are supremely alive to the presence of thermals and can read the sky as does a soaring eagle. For these skygods, great distances are possible.

There are of course variations on the 'downwind dash' theme. For example there are those who make 'out and return' flights, and for a certain type of aviator the 'triangle' holds a fascination. The Achilles heel of these pretenders to the crown though is that the paraglider is not fleet. It is the tortoise of the aircraft kingdom, biffing along through the air at perhaps 35kph. In consequence, progress into or across wind tends to be rather depressingly funereal, whereas by flying downwind one can easily clock up a healthy 60kph over the ground and actually get somewhere.

The other respect in which the 'open distance' approach scores over it's poor relations is that shrugging off the bonds of gravity and charging thither without a backwards glance, to ultimately finish up in a wholly different part of the country or indeed another country altogether, is simply more psychologically satisfying. It positively bulges with the vital elements of adventure and escapism.

I think so anyway.

Way below me, I saw the top of Whisted's wing as he took off and headed directly into the bottom of my thermal. He hooked straight into the core and in an almost unbelievably short space of time, corkscrewed straight up to base.

'Good work Nigel' he said into my ear a few minutes later as he caught me up and positioned himself on the opposite side of the thermal. We continued to orbit for a few more turns, wingtip to wingtip, until we reached the first cold tendrils of the cloud. Whisted, I noted, had a most distinct flying style. Rather than holding the brake handles, the better to steer and govern the speed and pitch of the glider, he instead held the brake lines themselves, lightly betwixt finger and thumb, controlling the wing with the dexterity of a puppeteer.

'Time to go on a glide.' His voice was icily calm and lucid. 'Bear East North East.'

We allowed ourselves to be sucked into the cloud on its downwind edge to gain a bit more height and to avoid the worst of the rapidly sinking air that surrounds a thermal, then with Whisted on my left and ever so slightly behind me, we glided straight out fifteen hundred metres above the Sussex countryside.

'Right then Nigel, we are going to do a little exercise,' said Whisted inside my head, 'First I want you to let go of the controls.'

Now, I think it must have been in Turkey in 1993, whilst undergoing my emergency training under the tutelage of Rocky Bjarnderson, that I first realised the potency of an unambiguous instruction, positively suggested by a charismatic teacher, under circumstances of powerful emotion.

Albeit a figure of whom I had previously barely heard, Bjarnderson was apparently widely thought to be the best in the business and he was definitely a fellow who inspired confidence. Good looking, self assured, charming and totally decisive.

Each morning around a long table by the beach, my fellows and I assembled and listened intently to his briefings before labouring up the mountain in a jeep, lobbing off and gliding out over the bay to await his word.

The general idea at this point is to deliberately induce a mildly catastrophic problem such as a spin, a stall, or a deflation and then to recover the situation by providing the appropriate control inputs, before resuming normal flight. The principle is that when (rather than if) the same thing happens when you are jaunting along, near to a cliff face for instance or whilst flying low over trees, then you will be mentally prepared to react quickly and effectively. It is, in a sense, an exercise in mind programming.

When our group arrived on launch there was the usual display of pusillanimity, among the shilly shallying element and duly I took off first and manoeuvred myself into position a mile or so above the glittering Mediterranean. Bjarnderson's voice, positive, precise and relaxed, appeared in my radio headset and calmly instructed me to initiate a stall.

Now make no mistake, a deliberate stall is a radical enterprise to contemplate. Besides deploying your reserve parachute there is precious little you can do in paragliding that so completely and utterly throws open the door to misadventure. If you imagine putting a motor car into first gear whilst driving flat out on an icy carriageway then you may get some idea of the deleterious effect it is likely to have on your smooth progress. Indeed to instigate a stall voluntarily whilst over dry land is described in the robustly forthright 'Skythings' *{The Indispensable Monthly Companion to Life's Up Tiddly Up Upness}* as: 'The action of a stark staring imbecile!'

So naturally, in order to perform a manoeuvre that will reduce a normally flying glider to a plummeting, out of control, bag of washing, a pilot must first overcome a degree psychological resistance. Resistance which is, in practice, almost insuperable at the first attempt, without the benefit of a guide in whom you place complete trust.

And yet when Bjarnderson, who I had met only hours before and whom I had never even seen fly, ordered me so to do, I unhesitatingly obeyed. I watched numbly as my hands applied the brakes, slowing the glider below the stall point and entering the inevitable deeply unsettling and utterly disorientating backwards plunge that it involves.

Happy days!

Back in the present, I complied with Whisted's instruction and let go of the brakes. A paraglider will fly perfectly well with hands off on a glide through smooth air, and only tiny inputs of weight shift are required to keep it on course.

'Now make yourself comfortable in your harness,' continued Whisted, 'release the tension in the muscles of your neck and shoulders.' He was right, I was tense. A paragliding harness is actually very comfortable and supportive, you could sleep in it easily but during the climb without noticing it I had become clenched and knotted.

'Take a deep breath. And slowly release it again and as you breathe out send away all the tension in your muscles. Keep breathing slowly and deeply, becoming more relaxed with every breath.

Focus on the sound of my voice and let all other thoughts melt away as you continue to become more and more relaxed.'

I did - and I did.

Whisted banged on in this way for some time repeating and reinforcing his theme until I felt like a baby in a pram, swaddled in cosy blankets, content to simply stay put and be aware. I was feeling sublimely tranquil and enthusiastically receptive to his instructions.

At length and in a lighter more positive tone, he moved on to his pitch.

'There are three stages' he began 'in the development of a pilot. Each separated from the next by a significant psychological barrier. You can overcome these barriers and you will. And in doing so you will progress and realise your potential.

Many pilots fail to overcome the first barrier, of these most will drop out of flying in the first year. Those who do make it through, go on to become good pilots but very few are able to transcend the second barrier and become a master.

At your stage of learning to fly, you are barely flying the glider at all, you are merely struggling with the controls.

You want to turn right so you pull the right brake and wait for something to happen.

The glider hits some turbulence, your tense body gets tossed about in the harness sending all sorts of incoherent signals back to the wing, exaggerating the turbulence and so creating greater tension.

You are trapped in a samsaric cycle of overreaction and overcorrection. To overcome this you must learn to listen with complete honesty to everything the glider tells you about the air and learn to transcend the illusory distinction between you and your wing.

There must be no interface between you and the glider, any more than there is between a bird and its wings. It must become part of you, an indivisible extension of your body.

When you want to turn you simply turn, when you encounter turbulence your body rolls with it, absorbs it, interprets it and responds to it'

Whisted paused and then continued in a different tone, lighter with an upward lilt in the manner of someone winding up a telephone call.

'In a few moments you will hear the sound of your vario and you will take this as a signal to fly as though the glider was part of your body. You will be keenly alive to the signals it sends to you and you will find that you are able to control the glider without effort. You will be calm, receptive and completely relaxed.

For now simply enjoy the sensation of flying, and of being deeply and wonderfully relaxed.'

We were, by now, about five kilometres from take off and had descended about halfway to the ground. My frame of mind was a mixture of almost soporiferous calm and combined with an urgent rushing euphoria. These may not at first glance strike you as tenably coexistent mental states, in which case I urge you to cast your mind back to your childhood and contemplate, as a frozen moment in time, the precise instant of waking on Christmas day.

And bless me if the scales didn't jolly well fall from my eyes. The incoherent babble of feedback with which the glider had always assaulted me as we coasted through the air together, which I had taken for just so many jolts and bumps and shimmies (not to mention the occasional sickening plunge) was suddenly revealed to me in perfect clarity as one half of a dialogue in which I was able to engage.

And now with, as it were, the pupil of the minds eye fully dilated, I realised with a rush that the arcane and foreign tongue of the glider, once so opaque to me, was one in which I was suddenly, completely fluent.

Like the infinitely sensitive spiders web which transmits the vibrations of the struggling fly, the glider spoke eloquently to me, of the air. I listened and found I could reply, taking up the brakes into my hands once more I marvelled at how little I had to do to swoop and soar and how little I had to think about what to do.

I sensed a sudden change in the air through which I was travelling, the glide had been as smooth as silk but here the air was mixing, The glider slowed and climbed a little, coaxing one solitary blip out of the vario, then regained speed into an area of sink before gliding as I knew it would, into the tower of warm rising air that awaited beyond.

I dove into the thermal, hooked the glider round and pinged back up to the clouds.

I found to my delight that whereas previously thermalling had always been a bit of a hit or miss affair, flying in and out of bits of air moving at different speeds and generally getting buffeted about a good deal, I was now able to perfectly visualise the thermal and with an effort of will similar to balancing on a bicycle at traffic lights, spiral up in the strongest, purest core of lift.

'Tell me what you are thinking Nigel.' Whisted's voice intoned 'but don't think about what you are saying just about what you are doing.'

Hardly pausing to draw breath, I started to speak. Because of the noise-cancelling headphones, all I could hear of my words was a faint mumble. And whenever the mumbling stopped, I took it as a cue to start speaking again.

We flew a long way that day, most of the way to Hastings, *'The city that wakes but never really recovers from its little snooze just before tea time.'* and most of the way back. At the top of each climb Whisted would talk to me about flying and transcending and a good deal about relaxing. And at the bottom of the next thermal I would start to talk to him about, I knew not what. At about five in the afternoon we came in to land lightly on Brighton beach.

'I think you would agree Mostyn,' Beamed Whisted as he pumped my hand - my eyes were brimming with the tears of profound emotional release - 'We are definitely onto something here.'

We stayed and talked until the sun turned orange and an old hippy walked up and tried to sell us some ganja.

What Whisted was proposing, he told me, was a field trial of his technique and he was looking for volunteers. Trained pilots who were new enough to cross country flying to still experience its powerful rapture and were also across the basics of psychodynamic therapy.

Funding for the research, he said, would be forthcoming subject to observing strict standards of methodology and the research data would be available to all contributors and as such when written up it would count as my final year research project.

Naturally I didn't think twice. Actually, I barely thought once. In fact if you had asked the young Nigel Jenkins to outline his most outré fantasy for the circumstances in which he would ideally spend his final year, he would have probably mentioned living in a penthouse in Amsterdam in a ménage a trois with the Swedish Ladies Olympic beach volleyball team. But in a close second place would have been a scenario combining paragliding with altered states of consciousness, his other two favourite obsessions.

11 UP TIDDLY UP UP

The next day was Sunday and I awoke to the tumultuous squawking of the sulphur crested cockatoos who live in the eucalyptus trees along the banks of the Namoi river and who are unanimously of the opinion that seven a.m. is the perfect moment for a seemingly pointless flap along the river to an identically incommodious tree, whilst squawking like all hell.

As further sleep was seemingly impossible, I swung my legs out of bed and sat for a moment, gazing blearily into space, blinking away the sleep and piecing together my muddled recollections of the events of the previous night. Gradually it all came back to me. The business with the drainpipe, the whole episode with the knotted bed-sheet. Otto trying to lasso the dog while I distracted it with a hamburger on a bit of string. When I'd finished doing that, and as the room had settled down a bit, I began speculating on what further events might have followed the events of the night before and in particular what might have been the cause of the various noises to emerge from the room next door in the early hours of the morning. I was on the point of going on to speculate upon what events might in turn be precipitated by those events when, with a twinge, I found myself staring at a slightly nasty and highly whimsical watercolour print which hung on the wall opposite the bed. I had barely registered it the night before but realised now and with a rising sense of bewilderment that it was the exact facsimile of the picture which for as long as I could remember had hung opposite the bed in my old room in the east wing at Futwold.

Originally the property of my late father, this dreadful daub depicted a precarious looking mountaintop monastery at Montsegeur in South-Western France. Apparently in the fourteenth century, five hundred Cathar monks, disillusioned by what they saw as the corrupt decadence of the Catholic church, had holed up in this frightful dump to pursue a life of contemplative asceticism, shunning the shallow consolations of the unexamined life. That this high-minded behaviour would attract the opprobrium of Rome was in hindsight, rather foreseeable. As predictable in fact, as the denouement of *'Zinctrumpet-Harris And The Case Of The Man Who Bludgeoned His Butler To Death With A Frozen Salami And Then Fed It To His Basset Hound' (2003)*. Sure enough, the pope duly ordered in the militia and following a long siege, the hapless fools were slaughtered to a man.

Shaking my head I wandered out onto the upper terrace of the hotel to make a quick appraisal of the day. Conditions looked promising, the sky was as blue as the bottom of a blue-bottomed baboon, save for a few ragged husks of yesterdays clouds and one tiny nascent cumulus which formed over Borah and dissipated again as I watched.

A loud crash from the bedroom next to mine made me turn. There were a few muffled oaths, a lot of immoderate and unmistakeably female laughter and Otto, the acme of mortal hugeness, stumbled through a door further along the veranda. The hotel being virtually empty of guests Coleen had given us a dormitory each.

Otto grunted sheepishly and explained that he had forgotten he was sleeping on the top bunk, he then launched into an explosive fit of coughing interspersed with German profanities, the combined effect of which sounded uncannily like Welsh.

I had a shower and ankled downstairs. Colleen was pottering about in the bar.

'Hello Pregrin' she beamed. 'Make yourself a cup of tea in the kitchen if you want one love.' She said this in a hushed, conspiratorial tone to make it plain that this indulgence was only extended to her particularly favoured guests. Thanking her I toddled off so to do. I dug out the cache of vittles she had kindly permitted me to store in her fridge and was already munching toast and honey as I ventured out onto the lower veranda adjacent to the street.

'Morning chaps.' I pipped, eliciting a grunt of acknowledgement from Les and Derek. They were occupying the exact same position as when last we had met and looked about as likely to move as a philosophy student with a hydroponic dope farm in his basement.

Colleen reappeared to sweep up the previous nights broken glass and cigarette ends.

'So Elle's your cousin Colleen?' I ventured whilst sunning my feet. I'd been wondering how it was possible to have a cousin fifty years younger than oneself.

'People in Manilla have lots of cousins love.' She explained, and I realised to my horror that I'd been crassly indelicate. 'She's a lovely girl.' She added. And I don't mind telling you I felt like a perfect heel. But only for a moment. 'Pity she's so fat.' Colleen sighed. I inhaled a toast crumb and coughed furiously. My hostess paused to mop her brow.

'Gees it's hot enough to kill a black fella.' She continued.

Otto appeared, disappointingly carless, eating a banana and wearing a layer of opaque white sunscreen and a cap with French Foreign Legion style neck protection. We surveyed the hitching prospects without much conviction. Manilla is not noted for its hustle and b. at the best of times but on a Sunday morning it is actually comatose. A state of affairs to which the presence of a small brown dog, fast asleep in the middle of the town's high street, seemed to testify.

In order to advertise our liftlessness, we prominently positioned our glider bags at the corner of the pavement, leaning drunkenly, one against the other. We then retreated to the shade, taking it in turns to biff over to the kerb and anxiously squint down the street for any approaching traffic. It was eight thirty and Bill and J.J. had assured me that I'd get a lift by nine.

We were a little restive. What's more, encouraging signs of early thermic activity were in evidence, little cumulus clouds forming above the hill and along the spine-back ridge that ran north up the edge of the valley. A light south-east wind was setting up. Perfect, I thought, for a cross-country to the Bingara valley.

By eight fifty eight our plight was well and truly casting a pall over a conversation that had never been precisely bouncing with sparkle, when abruptly the sleeping dog awoke, sneezed, scratched its ear and trotted off towards the petrol station. Not a moment to soon either, as at that moment, seemingly out of nowhere, a convoy of assorted four wheel drive vehicles thundered up the main street and slewed to a halt right in front of us. A genial looking cove with surprising hair and downright disconcerting teeth gestured with his thumb toward the rear of his blue pickup truck.

Naturally, to fling our bags into the back and leap in after them, was, for we intrepid men of the air, the work of an instant.

The drive out to the flying club only took about ten minutes but nevertheless I got thoroughly sunburnt en route. The place, when we arrived, would have been easy to mistake for any one of the dozen or so impoverished looking farms along the road, except that at the end of the drive was a rather large and inexpertly hand-painted sign, featuring, at least at first glance, a squashed shark on a surfboard. If looked at for long enough with half closed eyes the picture would eventually resolve itself into a paraglider viewed from, as it were, underneath. Frozen at the climax of a particularly radical bit of acro.

I was shown inside and Introduced to the club president Godfrey Wenness, a middle aged Austrian who had moved to Australia from Europe, he told me, 'under the influence of a strange gravity', having first made a healthy stack in the second-hand rollerblade business. He was the outright owner of Mount Borah itself and by a mile the most happening man in Manilla.

He introduced me in turn to the club vice president, his seventeen year old Australian girlfriend Suzy, who had moved in from an unhealthy shack just down the road under the influence of Godfrey. She was the outright owner of a range of prominently displayed bootilicious bodily bits which were strangely uninfluenced by gravity and by a mile the slinkiest female in Manilla.

Suzy signed me up to the club and pointed me towards the dangerously dilapidated looking Toyota truck outside, whose trailer was rapidly being filled with gliders.

The best seats had all gone, which is to say that all the seats had gone in fact but apparently it was the general form that three likely punters could be accommodated on the roof of the 'Borah Basher,' if they were up to the physical challenge of clinging on. I positioned myself between JJ and Otto who was kindly programming the local flying frequency into my radio whilst munching an apple. Our legs were now dangerously obstructing the Pete the drivers view. At one minute past ten Godfrey strode from the house waving the ten a.m. weather fax from Sydney.

'It's a two hundred k. day fellas!' he cried, jumping into the front seat, 'It's on like a train! Lets go Pete.' And we were off.

12 THE FLYING DREAM

Throughout much of my third year at University, my erstwhile housemates Stig, Jizzer and Spunky, industriously swotted away, crafting their dissertations with an air of industry that was nothing short of disturbing. They paused only for the occasional bowl of cereal or total nervous collapse, oblivious to the crisp, vivid, heavenly days of early autumn passing them by, outside their window.

I, by comparison, was having a generally more wholesome time of it, rising at eight and joshing gamely up whichever Sussex hill was facing the wind that day. Before lobbing off and catching a feisty little thermal, by means of which to explore the day's possibilities.

After two terms of this I was fit and sharp and, by my accommodating standards, focussed and motivated, with the complexion of a farmer and the rangy appearance of the mountain man.

I would return from a day in the sky with a faraway look, a contented smile and a warm glow of triumph from the personal best, cross country distance I had flown that day, or the tricky triangle route that I had finally nailed. I would halloo my chums who were for the most part jittery with caffeine addiction and sallow from the long hours spent painstakingly composing ground non-breaking theses which would be read twice by an indifferent professor and then consigned forever to posterity.

I had, with some difficulty, persuaded my course tutor Dr. Ludwig Cillit-Bang, that the Whisted shindig represented a genuine research opportunity under the general umbrella of sports psychology. I pointed out that it was less obvious than colour therapy and less risable than laughter therapy. He inspected the, to be honest, extremely misleading preliminary proposal with which I had presented him and signed me off for the three weeks in the summer term that Whisted had earmarked for the field work.

Duly then, early in May 1995, and in accordance with Whisted's detailed instructions, I boarded a plane to Switzerland. And in the arrivals lounge at Geneva Airport - a surgically clean, stylishly austere, stainless steel monument to the core Swiss values of uncompromising efficiency and being absolutely loaded - I met up with the eleven other members of the team.

Paraglider pilots aren't hard to spot in a public place. This owes to them having a rucksack about the size and shape of a bale of straw, plus a small sports bag, not infrequently named after a quadruped of the family

Cervidae. This last has been carefully selected for being tacky and inexpensive and looking as though it might easily contain a walkman an autobiography of Eric Cantona, a bottle of Sangria and a collapsible sombrero, rather than fifteen kilos of radios, satellite navigation and flight instruments.

Another giveaway is their dress sense. This is bad. Not as bad as that of Canadians admittedly but definitely bad. It is true that pilots dress for function rather than for fashion but then again so do soldiers, and apart from Canadian ones they don't look like dorks.

Most pilots own but one pair of trousers, usually highly technical, breathable, u.v. proof and of the type which, with a fair amount of fiddling, can be converted into a pair of shorts. They always own two sets of footwear, huge chunky but also somehow slightly effete flying boots and a pair of highly technical sandals festooned with quick release buckles and Velcro in an effort to distance themselves from the woodwork teacher feel from which sandals on men will never quite be immune.

Most tellingly of all though, pilots nearly always sport some species of ghastly shapeless un-ironed t-shirt of the type that you get free with a new harness or a pair of sunglasses based around the principle of the two way mirror or indeed a holiday at the 'Peidrahita Skyfun Adventure Ranch,' where you can apparently 'Fly With the Condors,' as presumably had Alexander, an osteopathy student from Hamburg who sauntered into the lounge a few moments after myself.

'American?' He asked after we had exchanged introductions.

'Better still,' I retorted. 'I'm from England.' The pair of us stationed ourselves opposite the entrance and in due course we spotted Serge, an electrician from Rouen. A physically well appointed specimen, positively festooned with the attributes of the alpha male and with a countenance of sufficient cragginess to support a colony of seagulls. He also sported the kind of wide lopsided smile that gingers up the fairer sex no end.

One by one, throughout the afternoon, likely looking characters flew in from around the world. The next suspect, a way-cool, dreadlock festooned type, drooped into the lounge, his every gesture redolent of dope smoking, counter culture, hippy ideology. He was rigged out in tie dyed, ethnic looking trousers, a surfing 'hoodie' and a snowboarding jacket. His eyes spoke of the immoderate use of ganja that had cumulatively floated him through life to this point.

'Zane.' he drawled in a strange Scando-American accent as he took my proffered paw in that weird offset handshake reminiscent of an arm wrestle. He evinced about as much warmth and enthusiasm on the occasion of our meeting as one might feel upon realising that the traffic warden tucking a ticket under the wiper of one's motorcar is none other than the smelly kid from school who used to wet himself in assembly. 'Wassup?' he added, pointlessly.

'Pleased to meet you Zane, I'm Nigel Jenkins.'

'Yemen.' he said laconically, gazing beyond me, over my shoulder, at some distant but evidently more interesting object, in an attitude of studied ennui.

'No no, dear me no!' I retorted. 'I'm from England.'

Now the church of Zinctrumpet-Harris is a broad one. Heterodoxy is our watchword and tolerance our philosophy. But as a breed we are united, in the unalloyed and unequivocal enmity with which we view unconscionable poops of this ilk. They nettle us like all hell.

The Zanes of this world, with their irritating straggly beards, their annoying floppy body language, and their precious and logically contradictory dietary injunctions, are universally described by the credulous element as 'laid back'. This wrongheaded assessment fails though, to distinguish between genuine spiritual peace and smug inert complacency.

The truth of the matter is that coves of Zane's complexion are at best passive and feeble and at worst they are self deluding spiritual poseurs. Having misread just enough Buddhism to absorb the idea that 'doing' is an evil western idea and that 'being' is 'where it's at' they proceed as though it follows from this that they can (in the way, for example, that a paperweight can) draw an entire sense of identity from the bare requirement of 'being'.

They affect an enervated and self satisfied demeanour that passes for Zen serenity in the same way that a suntan will pass for healthy vitality but this camouflage invariably conceals a furnace of raging anger and self loathing, that can only be quietened by inducing the almost constant state of torpor provided by cannabis.

They are annoyingly detached. Not in the way that a bank managers house is detached but in the way that a boxer's retina is detached.

Happily, there is one tactic that is as kryptonite to such conceit. The way to fatally undermine this infuriating faux insouciance, in my experience, is to discover, by any means necessary, the fellow's real name. The name that he went by before he went to university and reinvented himself as the spiritual everyman with the single digit resting heartbeat. And it's generally something like Crispin or Toby or Sebastian. Because within every super-cool trustafarian there is a self-involved public-schoolboy, in denial about his class roots but comfortable with his private income, who has stumbled upon a great way of getting laid.

Incredibly there are those who have interpreted my antipathy towards this particularly odious species of tick as concealing a certain jealousy on my part. Jealousy of their worldliness perhaps? their self assuredness? their looks (and in particular that they don't look as though they have been dressed by their mothers.) But mainly jealousy of that aloof distain for the ignoble business of coin, available only to the very rich. All the serenity, in fact, that money can buy.

It's incredibly obtuse I know but there it is. The fact must be faced.

Eventually Whisted appeared, looking healthy and tanned and dressed, in rather sharp contradistinction to his acolytes, in a nicely pressed tan linen suit. He was animated by a tremendous air of confidence and stylish élan. He hailed each of us warmly in our various native tongues and ushered us to the Mercedes sprinter minibus parked outside. He then drove us across the border into the French Alps where we were installed in a rather picturesque ski chalet overlooking Lake Annecy.

Excluding Whisted we were twelve.

I was given quarters at the front of the building with a world beating view of the general Alpine charm. As it was early evening and there was to be no flying that first day, ventured out onto the balcony where Serge was trying to learn *'Somewhere Across the Seine'* on a tiny yellow stylophone. I busied myself in hollowing out a section of baguette as a new home for my sunglasses, having realised with a sense of mild irritation that I had left the twin Havana cigar tube that they had formally occupied, on the plane.

By the time the dinner gong went, I was dozing lightly in a chair on the balcony, a Rosie Cheeks novel forgotten in my lap, dreaming about a nude pillow fight with the Swedish Ladies Olympic beach volleyball team. I duly repaired to the dining room where Gaston the cook had prepared a feast of confit du bouef in a terrine de l'Arch de Triomphe sauce.

'Welcome,' beamed Whisted when we were all seated around the table, there was a wicked glint in his eye, 'to the best country in the world. The best food, the best wine, the best architecture. Three coastlines, a great climate, two ranges of mountains for skiing and flying, a rich tradition of art and literature and the most poetically beautiful language in existence.'

Inwardly eleven minds simultaneously pondered the Achilles heel of this glowing appraisal of our host country, against which these considerable qualities must surely be weighed.

'La Belle France!' cried Serge on cue, raising his glass and beaming his wicked grin.

Whilst we ate, Whisted briefed us for the weeks ahead. There was a buzz in the room. The whole hoohah was starting to gather momentum.

The idea apparently was to fly cross country as a group, searching for thermals like a flock of birds. Whisted planned to focus on one member of the group each day, placing them into a trance during the first glide and then, under deep hypnosis, gradually regressing them back through their life. He would invite them to re-experience their feelings as a child, pausing regularly at different stages before encouraging them to continue into infancy and then the moment of their birth. According to Whisted, subjects who were regressed beyond this point often displayed startling past life personalities.

'Now as you will doubtless be aware,' Whisted ventured, when he reached this point in his discourse, 'people under very deep hypnosis are able to recall past incarnations.' We all tried to look as though we knew this. 'Since the phenomenon originally surfaced in 1956 with the sensational Bridey Murphy case, a wealth of supporting evidence has accumulated, powerfully suggesting that a vast realm of inaccessible memory exists within the mind, which can only be retrieved whilst in a hypnotic state.' He sloshed back a big draught of the good stuff. 'The point as far as we are concerned is that whilst the subject is talking with, a voice not his own, we can be assured that we are communicating directly with the subconscious. The opportunity with which this presents us therefore, is nothing less than a conduit through which we shall pass into the subconscious mind. The eyes, they say, are the windows of the soul.' He beamed at our rapt faces 'The minds eye then, is verily a portal to the sublime.'

The aim, it seemed, was to breach the scleral membrane that protects the conscious mind from its unconscious. To allow the obscured attitudes and traumas buried in the subconscious to surface into the light of day and in doing so unlock the potential for progress from the state of dislocation.

'For someone who finds himself strongly compelled towards an irrational act such as flying,' Whisted reasoned aloud, 'then it is whilst flying that he is most reachable by the therapist, as he is then most in the thrall of his subconscious.'

Upon landing Whisted planned to put the day's victim straight on a plane home so as not to pollute the remaining subjects in the experiment with expectations and preconceptions.

As we finished what was to be our first and last supper together as a complete group, Whisted charged our glasses, sparked up his pipe and began what I later realised had been a sort of cognitive softening up process.

'The American philosopher John Searle,' He began, 'inspired by the meditations of the computer pioneer Alan Turing, designed a thought experiment called "The Chinese Room". An experiment by means of which he sought to demonstrate the ambiguous nature of consciousness.' As I tucked into my ninth glass of Burgundy there was definitely something slightly ambiguous about the nature of my consciousness.

'The scenario to be imagined' he continued, 'is that of a locked room in China in which, at a desk, sits a non Chinese-speaking fellow. Lets say his name is...' he paused.

'Reevsh.' I volunteered, thinking of an American film that I had recently seen and which had made something of an impression upon me.

'Reeves then,' he continued, 'and into the room, every once in a while a piece of paper is thrust through the letter box. The said item features a Chinese ideogram, which means nothing to Reeves of course and he is obliged to consult a look-up table thoughtfully provided on the desk in order to determine the designated response. This, another Chinese symbol, he copies onto another piece of paper which he pops back out through the letter box.' Whisted paused to survey our reactions as the import of all of this sank in. Or not.

'The insight here,' he went on 'is that viewed from the outside, the occupant of the room appears to be communicating in Chinese. However, as Reeves does not in fact understand the questions he is being asked or the responses he is giving, he is actually behaving rather like a computer.' There was much nodding of heads around the table.

'The implications of this are pretty considerable,' he continued 'not least for animals, which have always been considered ineligible for human rights on the strength of supposedly lacking that defining human quality of consciousness. Rene Descartes for instance, considered animals to be mere mechanisms, lacking a soul, lacking his famous duality of body and immaterial mind. Something which he reserved for humans alone. Darwin's discovery however, forces us to recognise that we and they are simply at different points on the same continuum.'

'Nah man' Objected Zane shaking his head with the unfortunate consequence that a festering dreadlock plonked itself into Ginko Biloba's glass of port, 'I mean, like, animals wouldn't be able to have this conversation yeah? Even if they could speak, they couldn't get their head round this shit.'

'Quite so,' agreed Whisted. 'Our cognitive abilities are an order of magnitude greater than even our closest relations in nature. But that doesn't mean that they have none; they do. There is no sharp distinction to be made on such grounds. The difference is one of degree – not category.' Zane looked less than convinced. 'When you tell a person that they resemble someone else,' the professor persevered, 'someone famous for instance, nine times out of ten they will dispute that there is any similarity. They simply cannot see it. Perhaps this is because, confined by the unique vantage point of our ego, we separate the world into 'me' and 'not me' perhaps because we place too much emphasis on the minor details which distinguish us. In any case, as it is with an individual, so it is with a species. It affronts our vanity to accept that we are animals too – witness the indignation occasioned by the advent of the theory of evolution – and yet virtually every part of our body, including our brains is homologous to systems found right across the animal kingdom.'

'Physically we are like them yeah but mentally we are different. Animals just follow their instincts,' drawled Zane 'but we can reason.'

'The Cartesian distinction between mind and body is an illusion.' Returned Whisted emphatically. 'The mind is generated in the brain and the brain is a physical organ with physical limitations. If you consider consciousness to be independent of biology I would invite you to spend some time in the company of a pregnant woman or a drunk person or to consider the effects upon temperament of adrenaline or testosterone or serotonin.'

'Yeah we're affected by those things, they make us want to do certain things, eat coal or hit people or get depressed or whatever but we don't have to. We can choose. But animals just have to do what's in their nature.'

'Don't allow the contrast between our society and the way that animals live, seduce you into assuming that a similar contrast exists between animals and humans. If you took a thousand babies from the maternity ward at Charing Cross hospital and put them on an island for a couple of generations you would return to find men who had been destined to be accountants and dentists, fighting each other to the death with rocks for the chance to mate with a reluctant female. Evolving from simple life forms has been a long journey, like Sisyphus pushing a big rock up a steep hill. We have passed a lot of significant milestones along the way, few of them absolutely unique to humans. Intelligence, sociality, communication even tool-making. But at some point, many millennia ago, we made it to the top of the hill. We reached the point beyond which our culture's propensity to develop outstripped that of our biology. The rock started to rush down the other side of the mountain experiencing acceleration due to gravity at ten metres per second per second, quickly putting us impossibly out of reach of all other species.' Zane wasn't finished.

'Yeah, I'm not saying we didn't get where we are by the same process animals did,' he began, 'but we have got something that never evolved in them. Free will.'

Whisted steepled his fingers 'Consider our man in the Chinese Room.' he began. 'Consider Reeves.' We did so 'Let us assume that the fellow is perfectly happy doing what he's doing. He has no plans to leave any time soon. But he could. He could if he chose, simply walk out of the door.' With the minimum of effort we conjured this scenario to mind. 'Now, suppose that someone comes along and quietly locks the door. Is Reeves still free?

'No.' said a few voices

'Yes' opined a few others.

'No.' Zane decided after a moment's thought.

'Surely he remains free to do what he wants, no?' Whisted enquired wryly.

'He's free to do what he wants but he's not actually free not to, so it's not a free choice.'

'Likewise you are free to become a homosexual if you want; but are you capable of wanting to?'

'Hell no!' snapped Zane. 'er I mean no.'

'So you have free will, within the confines that your nature will allow.'

'But that's not my nature man, its social conditioning. We are taught that.'

'Ah the blank slate theory.' Smiled Whisted. 'But that it were true Zane.' Whisted rose and moved to the fireplace. 'The idea that minds are born like empty vessels of equal potential just waiting to be filled with attitudes and subsumed into stifling social roles is the standard social science model. It is a beguiling idea but it's a myth. It prospered in the egalitarian atmosphere of the post enlightenment era, promising as it does the potential of true equality, of an even playing field and all of that. 'He stoked the fire a little. 'Inconveniently for socialism though, it simply doesn't persuade. Equality is a principle - and an important one - but it is not a fact. Can we really accept that social conditioning and industrious practice equipped Mozart to compose symphonies at the age of four, whilst young Serge here can barely carry a tune on his stylophone?' Serge aped an exaggerated Gallic shrug in a 'hey what can I tell ya' kind of way. In the process accidentally tipping a whole glass of wine into Neil Dupres' Isle flotante. 'Are we genuinely persuaded that a ten year old mathematics prodigy at Oxford who has revolutionised his field is separated only by attitude and parental encouragement from Nigel here who can barely covert feet to metres without getting a headache?' I pulled a face of the "ho hum" variety. 'Do we honestly believe that any amount of gender role reinforcement can completely account for the differences in behaviour between men and women?

The brain has evolved to be able to think in certain ways. Ways which have been critical to our survival in the past but which may not be today. It generates impulses which may be difficult to interpret outside of the context for which they evolved. The impulse to fly for example.' He tapped out his pipe and placed it on the mantelpiece. 'The challenge facing us now, good people, is to expose those ancient drives and put them to work on your behalf. To master them.

I have flown with each of you and, I hope, helped each of you to transcend the psychological barrier between simply operating the controls of the glider and really flying the wing. You were, each of you,' he said looking around the table, his eyes coming to rest on Mike Stands, a sound recordist from Strandfontein who blushed uncontrollably and began furiously inspecting his wineglass, 'trapped in your own Chinese room. You were decoding the feedback that the glider delivered, comparing it against the reservoir of stored experience that you had each recorded in your memory and generating the appropriate response. Interacting with the gliders controls on the strength of what you knew, rather than really understanding what it was telling you. The next time we fly, we shall go much deeper. The next time we fly your objective is to reach the next stage. To overcome the next barrier. In a few short months you have gained proficiency in flying your gliders equivalent to ten years of patient practice. Now it is time to learn to leave behind the glider itself and simply to fly the sky.' Whisted was on his feet, glass in hand now. 'Let us drink,' he declared, smiling at a room of people who had, in all probability, never read Jack Kerouac 'for tomorrow we lean forward to our next crazy venture beneath the sky.'

13 THE ZONE

One of the splendid things about flying the Annecy valley, besides the fact that it is about the most thrillingly scenic place on earth, is that everything tends to happen in the early p.m. Generally there is no point in taking off terribly early, since there is no wind in the morning to sustain a soaring flight and, as yet, insufficient thermal activity in which to climb out.

Duly we all arose at a highly civilised hour, enjoyed a pre-prandial dip in the lake and then caught the local shuttle bus up the Col de Plein Fei, a fifteen hundred metre mountain at the tail end of a range leading northwards into the Alps.

Pausing at the rather splendid café immediately adjacent to the take-off area, the terrace of which affords a ringside view of the more entertainingly catastrophic launch attempts, we indulged in an unhurried bruncheon and then, in a leisurely fashion, laid out the gliders, donned the splendid carbon fibre crash helmets with which Whisted had equipped each of us, clipped in and lobbed off.

It was to be Serge up first, with Stands in line after him. I was chosen to bring up the rear after Neil O'Gism, a linguistics student from Derry. This prospect occasioned in me no small anxiety since, especially in Europe, to get twelve solidly cross countryable days out of twenty is no inconsiderable thing. Luckily, as it turned out, all was tinkerty tonk and one by one we each had our turn as perfect day followed perfect day.

On the third of may 1995 our party sailed off across the sky for the first time, describing a shallow vee, the search formation favoured by migrating snow geese and Lancaster bombers, spaced a thermals width apart. With Stands at the side and Serge forward we hunted as a pack and divided the spoils. As one of us found lift, the others would join him in the thermal and thus by cooperation we each improved our chances of making our way around Lake Annecy in a series of glides from cloud base.

The course that we took is a well established route in the area known among local pilots as 'le petit tour.' It involves gaining a bit of height at launch and then gliding along the range to the next peak and really climbing out before dropping back one valley away from the lake to the mighty 'la Tournette' and on to 'les Dents' whose jagged summit resembles a set of truly third world teeth of the sort that your average American would rather die than live with.

From cloud base above les Dents, one can safely glide the two kilometres or so across the Lake at its narrowest point, to the Roc du Bouef. From there we soared along the sunny side of the R. du B. for a few kilometres before splitting into two groups. Whisted peeled off to continue south in company with Serge, the day's Isaac, whose immolation would continue above the flatlands towards Alp D'huez, whilst the remaining pilots hopped over the ridge at it's lowest point and biffed over the lake once more to burn off a few thousand metres in any manner pleasing to them.

For my part, so sublime was my frame of mind by this stage, so centred were my chakras, so restored was my chi energy, so tranquil my javatma, so manifold my good vibes and so plenitudinous my theta waves, that I wished for nothing more than a meditative waft about in the silky smooth restitution air, rejoicing in the general spiffingness of everything.

Predictably, and by way of contrast, Zane, the man who put the penis into happiness, responded to the exquisite poignancy of the moment by: 'getting ugly with the acro.'

It emerged fairly quickly that this awful tick had a bit of a bent for looping and helicoptering his glider and some of the others in trying to match this performance descended in a more erratic and haphazard fashion. Such vulgarity forms no part of my philosophy of flying however, that type of thing is all a bit 'Pepsi Max' for my taste. A quality incidentally, that it shares with that beverage.

In the fullness of time and beneath a setting sun we came in to land, be it soulful and sanguine or fizzing with adrenaline, in the main landing field on the South-East shore of the lake.

Day after day, we continued in this style whilst our little party dwindled, until finally only Whisted and I remained. Finally on May 29th, having fortified ourselves with coffee, croissants a small pastis and a Gaulloise at the mountain top café, we laid our canopies out on the grass amongst a patchwork quilt of gliders, and went through the ritual of adjusting and checking our kit whilst we inwardly thought our way into the flying mindset.

For the first time since we had arrived in France the sky was building early and it looked as though it might overdevelop before the day was out. When this happens the cumulus clouds formed by the rising warm air as it condenses out at the dew point or cloud base, continue to grow, fuelled by the strong convection, into towering and threatening cumulo nimbi. These monolithic, death dealing blighters, their shape a little reminiscent of Marge Simpson's surreal hairdo, are endowed with formidable cloud suck. They are also harbingers of thunderstorms and as such are regarded by fliers with a jaundiced eye.

If it did storm in the valley, then this would probably wash out the flying for a week or so, since the moisture in the ground would lead to even greater overdevelopment on each successive day, it was imperative therefore that we took our opportunity.

Timing our launch to coincide with a thermic cycle, we took off into a swarm of other gliders circling in the sky like brightly coloured butterflies. We immediately began to climb and shortly arrived at cloud base whereupon we set off on a glide.

Whisted's voice, measured and positive, appeared in my headphones.

'Righto Nigel, first I want you to let go of the controls.'

As before, he took me down through a routine of relaxation into a deep, delicious, almost opiated trance before regressing me gradually back through my life, pausing occasionally to illicit a response. A description of my surroundings perhaps, or of my feelings at progressively earlier stages of my life.

'How old are you now?'

'I am six years old.'

'Look around you, what do you see.'

'I'm in my bedroom in the East Wing; building a model of a Sopwith Camel out of toothpicks.'

At the point of my birth he continued the regression, leading me back into other lives, some of them quite surprising, to a point that he judged to be suitably primal. He then progressed to the following sequence.

'Imagine that you are floating on your back in a pool of warm water, you feel supported and at ease and you find that you can breath deeply and easily even though you are now a little way below the surface. You feel wonderfully free and safe and relaxed and all that you want to do is sink more deeply into the pool. Take a deep breath and slowly exhale and as you release the breath, feel yourself sinking deeper into relaxation. Deeper and deeper into the pool of your mind.'

This, I discovered later, was a deepener; a sequence usually concentrating strongly on imagery suggestive of descent. A staircase, an elevator, the deepener is delivered after the subject is in trance to intensify the state.

And by crikey, it worked like the blazes.

I passed behind the curtain.

At this point, as I receded deep within myself, losing all sense of my body and my surroundings. I could still see but only vaguely. As though I was watching a screen, connected to a security camera. Then two things happened almost at once: firstly I found that I was suddenly able to hear my own voice once more, although rather disconcertingly it sounded really rather unlike me, and it faltered slightly at the instant in which I became aware of it. And then it stopped.

The second thing that happened was a realisation. And a realisation of a fairly jarring variety. It was the realisation in fact that the semi-permeable membrane dividing the conscious from the unconscious is in fact there for a pretty good reason.

It is there to protect you from the ghastly truth, that the mind is meat.

I gasped as I apprehended the breadth of my entire sensory experience since conception. Everything I had ever done or seen or said or thought. The best sex I had ever had, the most embarrassing social solecism I had ever committed. The whereabouts of all the things that I had absent-mindedly lost over the years. The telephone number of the Thai restaurant in Exeter, in which I once had a disastrous blind date with a girl called Hayley.

All of it.

'Horrid isn't it.'

I jumped like a stung badger and wrenched myself away from the perusal of a highly graphic recollection of the night of my eighteenth birthday which had arrested my attention.

Whisted?

'Don't worry Nigel, I was a bit deflated when I first saw mine but one gets over that.'

Whisted's voice had lost its soothing hypnotic tenor and assumed a didactic tone.

'As you will now be aware Nigel, the mind is just the brain. No more and no less. And the brain is modular in structure, composed of distinct and separate areas of specialised cognitive function.'

He was right, suddenly I was aware of this. In the same sort of way that you are aware of the exact position of your body even in the dark.

'These modules have evolved to deal with the various problems faced by homo sapiens hundreds of thousands years ago. Evolution is much too slow to have made any perceptible progress in the time that has elapsed since.'

I thought of the phrenological heads offered by the nineteenth century scientists as models of the mind.

'like a computer?'

'Not *like* a computer Nigel. The brain *is* a computer. The mind is the software that runs in the mainframe of the brain.'

As experiences go, exposure to the limitless limitedness of ones own subconscious is a highly unsettling one. It was similar in a sense to the experience of visiting the set of a television period drama that had enchanted one in one's youth, and seeing how cheaply stitched together the illusion suddenly seems without the mediation of the camera and how readily the viewer conspires in the deception by not looking to closely for the flaws.

It also brought rather sharply into focus one of the more telling dualities for which the English language provides: That between *'to see,'* as in *'to see an object,'* and *'to see,'* as in *'to see what it is that someone is saying.'*

'But surely there must be something that is intrinsic to me to account for the difference between my personality and someone else's' I protested.

'Everything about you is completely unique Nigel.'

I felt a little better

'It's just that everything about you is as similar to other people as makes no difference.'

I felt a little worse.

'But people are so different.'

'Are they.'

'Certainly. They have character, personality individuality.'

'That depends very much on your frame of reference I'm afraid dear boy. In your eyes people seem very different because the human's strategy for survival is entirely predicated upon making meaningful distinctions between one individual and another. As a consequence of this, everything about a person is pregnant with clues about their social status their ancestry their intelligence their health. Whether they are friend or foe, perfect mate or genetic dead end.'

'Yes quite.'

'The thing is you could say the same about most sentient life forms.'

'But a person has more personality than, I don't know, a mouse. Even me?'

'That's just your own-species bias Nigel. Mere anthropocentricity. What seems like personality to you is really just a function of complexity.' He paused 'Take a simple system, a lightswitch for instance, it can be on or off, no ambiguities just a binary opposition.'

'Alright.'

Now consider that old car of yours. Still a machine, or rather a composite of several machines, much more complex, more variables. Over time it develops a few traits. A cantankerous dislike for cold mornings, a whining noise above forty. A wooden handled screwdriver for a gear-stick, a tendency to pull to the right. Erratic and unpredictable behaviour, it develops...'

'Character.' I said doubtfully.

'Of course, the reality is that we are simply projecting character onto it but equally that is what we do to each other.' He continued. 'Every system conforms to simple laws Nigel. A pendulum for instance is a very simple system that is so predictable that it can be used as the basis for a clock. Add another smaller pendulum to the bottom of the larger one however, and suddenly you have a system whose behaviour, whilst still governed by the same physical laws, is virtually impossible to predict due to the practical impossibility of measuring its exact speed and position at any precise moment. Add another one and you are well and truly into the realm of chaos. The tiniest error will immediately lead to huge deviations from your predictions, and yet it is, in theory, totally explicable and by the standards of anything organic it is an extremely simple system.

It's actually our failings, and the strategies that we adopt to conceal or compensate for them, which lend us our individuality. Our personality is just the way our consciousness expresses our drives. To other life forms, humans must seem as uniform as a flock of seagulls. To a greatly more intelligent life form we would seem completely predictable'

'But where is my soul. My me?'

'It is riven in the very architecture of the brain Nigel.' He returned, 'Consciousness is an emergent property, arising from a synthesis between inherited hard-wired programming in the structure of your brain and the moderating influence of conscious experience. This character expresses itself in the way that the physical structure of the terrain affects the character of a river running through it.'

At that moment something rather unexpected happened. And from deep within my subconscious, I could only watch helplessly through eyes like back to front binoculars, as my right hand, which had been gripping the risers with every evidence of aroused passion, suddenly snatched up the right brake and yanked it hard, initiating a tight banking turn.

The world spun around as the glider established a new course. My heart froze. Dead ahead of me, and a thousand metres or so above, loomed a gigantic cumulonimbus. A four mile high cloud, too dense for the sunlight to penetrate, its dark base boiled menacingly.

In the paragliding world, the cu-nim is the stuff of legend. Think of it as whirlpool in the sky, draughting air between cloud-base and the stratosphere. A portal between the domain of the mortal and the kingdom of the gods. It stands in the same relation to a paraglider pilot as a rip-tide does to a surfer or an avalanche to an off-piste skier. And, rather inconveniently, I appeared to be flying directly towards one.

'Why am I doing that?' I asked in sudden panic.

'Because your subconscious is inhabiting your body in the way that your conscious normally does, whilst your conscious mind is trapped in here, behind the two way mirror.'

'Its going to get me killed!' I squawked.

'Why do you think your subconscious drives are telling you to fly into the cloud Nigel?'

'I don't know.'

'Think of Icarus.'

'What?'

'His need to rise to a man's estate and gain the respect of his father...'

'Yes, well actually Whisted, this situation is getting a bit urgent in case you haven't noticed.'

'What year is it?'

'What?'

'What year is it?'

It seemed a bit of an odd question considering the circs. But I let it go.

'1794 of course.' I shrieked impatiently.

'And who are you now?' Whisted asked.

'I am Lord Frobisher 'Stiffy' Nutcutlet Harris of his majesty's Sussex Rifles, Sir.'

'You are gaining height very rapidly now,' The hypnotic tone was back, 'you can feel the air rushing past your face.'

He wasn't kidding, I was positively hoofing up to cloud base. The colossal dark bulk of the cloud lurked above me in a highly intimidating manner. My vario must surely have been screaming as my climb rate exceeded ten metres per second but I could hear nothing except Whisted's calm and well modulated voice. Let's be clear. If drawn into the Cu-nim, then my chances of survival were about ten percent at best.

'What year is it?'

'1840.'

'And who are you?

'Brigadier Cecil Zinctrumpet-Harris at your service, Sir.'

'You are rising even faster now, up and up through the cool air,' This was the opposite of a deepener, he was bringing me to the surface. 'you can feel the brake handles in your hands, In a moment you are going to come out of trance and take control of the glider.'

Beneath every cumulo-nimbus cloud, exists a theoretical entity known as 'the cone of death'. It's a bit like the stopping distance that exists in front of a motor car. An inverted virtual cone, the same width as the cloud, its depth determined by the strength of the up-draught and the glider's maximum speed. The c. of d. represents the 'too late now' zone for paraglider pilots. Once you enter the cone it doesn't matter how fast you try to fly away, it is mathematically impossible to escape the cloud's pull.

'Who are you now?'

'I am Sir Mostyn Zinctrumpet-Harris, 1930s English gentleman aviator, adventurer, blageur and a damned useful chap in a tight corner.'

It was too late. With crushing g-force the glider was plucked like a dandelion seed into the hurricane of air surging upwards into the cloud and everything became a swirling white then an ominous grey and finally it became completely and terrifyingly dark.

'You are now wide awake and fully in control.' came Whisted's voice in my ears. A little inaccurately it seemed to me on the face of things but sure enough, with a Herculean effort of will, I found now that I was able to regain the use of my arms and grab wildly for the brakes.

I was back! I could hear once more. The screaming of the vario. The roar of the wind.

The glider, wearying of the vicissitudes of the whole enterprise, chose this moment to collapse asymmetrically and plunge into the most sickening cascade of spins and total deflations.

Once I had tumbled into the wing a couple of times and frantically struggled free of its ensnaring lines, it started to become evident that I wasn't plunging downwards as fast as the air was rushing upwards past me, and thus no matter how un-glider-shaped the glider became, I was still gaining altitude at a hell of a lick. The vario was off the scale and the air was rapidly becoming extremely cold. I was desperately fighting for breath, and only moments away from a highly unpleasant end.

Amidst the chaos, a course of action occurred to me. Granted it was rather an extreme one but then again the situation seemed to call for something fairly radical. Duly I proceeded, subject to the limitations of being tossed about like a fat schoolboy's pencil case, to put the project through without delay.

With hands, violently shaking from freezing cold and mortal terror I fought to unscrew the barrel of the karabiner that joins the right hand risers to the harness and effortfully I slid the gate across. I wouldn't have the strength to lift the riser clear of the G shaped karabiner under positive loading but since the glider was continuing to collapse all over the place, like a rugby team on a pub crawl, I only had to wait a few moments for a spot of momentary weightlessness to do it for me.

Suddenly the risers came free and were instantly wrenched from my hands. The glider, now only attached by one side, immediately whipped off into the gloom. I started, seriously to plummet. The relatively nearby planet earth and I began to approach each other at a rate of acceleration roughly equal to ten metres per second squared.

As I plunged at a fearful velocity through the swirling cloud, it was as though Phobos and Deimos, the twin gods of fear and panic, were each taking it in turns to distract my attention whilst the other sneaked around behind and cried boo! into my ear.

At this point the implications of my rather extreme course of action began to press themselves upon my attention with some urgency. It seemed to me, as perhaps the more percipient reader may already intuited, that the situation was in danger of acquiring that dreadful, frying pan/fire quality that attends so many of ones more hastily taken decisions. To wit the emergency parachute used in paragliding, whilst a splendid item in many ways, is emphatically not designed to address the circumstances in which I currently found myself. These were, as far as I knew, pretty much without precedent, since to interfere in any way with the connections between glider and harness whilst actually airborne, is widely considered to be highly unwise among the flying fraternity in general. And in particular the sport's refreshingly forthright organ 'Skythings' *{The Indispensable Monthly Companion to Life's Up Tiddly Up Upness}* describes such behaviour as: 'The action of a certifiable loon!'

The practical upshot of this was that at nearly freefall velocity, my non porous rescue chute would very likely crack open with such a jolt as to either explode and destroy itself, or alternatively it might open and not explode, in which case I was likely to be badly mangled, nay garrotted, in the resulting terrific deceleration.

I located the reserve handle with my right hand and pondered the matter furiously. The likely results of throwing the reserve were either negligible if it ruptured or pretty disastrous if it opened intact, on the other hand it was hard to imagine an outcome resulting from not throwing it that fell in any sense short of utterly catastrophic. Another factor was that if I deployed before I had fallen clear of both the cloud and the cone of death, then I would abruptly change direction and once again hurtle upwards towards the upper atmosphere and certain death.

This was clearly going to take a bit of thinking about.

And then, just as I was resolving to keep my options open in the hopes that things might look up, there was a development which swept aside the whole issue. Rocks! Big hard sharp rocks! And trees! Dense coniferous forest a hundred metres below me! Where there had been a ghastly swirling misty greyness engulfing my senses, suddenly there was a mountain. The Cu-nim, drifting with the wind must have tracked back towards La Tournette, the huge peak behind take-off whose upper slopes were above cloud base.

Within a split second I had pulled the reserve handle, sending the tightly packed parachute and hurtling upwards into the air. There wouldn't be time for it to open but I did it anyway.

When you are flying, and especially when you are falling, you start to develop a keen awareness of the spot at which you are going to hit the ground. It is the one clear still point amid a scene which swims and grows. I could see it now, vividly, fifty metres below me, through a tunnel of green. A couple of really big and jagged rocks, jammed in amongst the trees.

Between the rocks in fact, was where I was about to impact at a hundred and fifty kilometres per hour.

In the last hundred metres before, what was looking increasingly like being a rather messy accident, I found myself numbly registering a crashing ripping sound accompanied by a spasmodic, snatching, face stretching deceleration. The trailing glider, snaking about above me was thrashing through the treetops, tearing against the branches snagging, snapping. 'hmm' I said to myself whilst, at a greatly reduced but still deadly speed, I continued to head for the gap between the rocks, 'now that could be significant.' Next the half open reserve neatly hooked itself over a twenty metre conifer, which immediately bent double rapidly slowing my fall. 'Bless my soul' I remember thinking as, about one metre off the ground, the tree, which had bowed to the limit of it's elasticity absorbing most of the energy of my descent, obligingly cracked sharply in half, depositing me neatly onto the tolerably comfortable cushion thoughtfully placed upon the white cantilever chair.

The chair was a simple wooden affair of the type originally developed within the Bauhaus school of design. It went rather nicely with the folding table immediately adjacent to it. Upon the table sat a brandy balloon, into which a rather good cognac was being decanted by a slim elegant figure in black with white gloves.

'Sir, I unnerstand you may be in need of a gen'l'men's gen'l'man.' He growled in a rasping American drawl, 'The name's Reeves.

14 CRAZY MOTHER PRINTS IN SMUT

In the third term of my second year at university, Trinny, my flatmate, and I had been sleeping together on and off for a couple of months. It was nothing serious, Trinny was not the type to restrict herself to just one lover, and it was an unspoken understanding between us that neither would ask the other any difficult questions. In my case this was because I knew I wouldn't be getting any answers. For Trinny's part, it was because she wasn't really interested.

Trinny was a whole lot of woman. She liked to talk during sex, explicitly detailing exactly what she wanted to do and to have done. She kept a pair of furry handcuffs locked to the top of her bed like a trophy and she loved to keep herself shaven absolutely smooth.

In the main, it was just good clean, dirty sex.

One evening when I was hard at work in the college library, Trinny, sounding a little mysterious, called from the pub at the corner of our road having locked herself out of the flat that we shared with three of our friends.

'I lost my purse so I've got no money either,' she said, 'but I've bumped into Reece and he keeps buying me drinks, so don't be too long.' Reece had been Trinny's boyfriend back in the first year and since splitting up with him she had been more or less working her way through his friends, myself included.

It took me half an hour to ride my motorcycle across Worthing, during which time I fantasized about what might be finally about to happen, only half believing that it really might. I knew she still wanted Reece and part of me was a bit jealous at the idea of someone else having her but, somewhat to my surprise I was finding the idea of Trinny swapping between lovers and generally getting a really good seeing to by two men, strangely exciting.

It was almost last orders at the pub when I arrived. Reece seemed a little embarrassed as we shook hands, probably thinking I wouldn't be too pleased to find another man trying to move in on my girlfriend. I just thanked him for taking care of her and headed to the bar.

Trinny, her eyes sparkly after a few drinks, was on top form, flirting like crazy with both of us, she looked really gorgeous in a light summer dress that made the most of her curvatious body. More than once I caught Reece glancing admiringly at her full breasts.

At closing time, Reece offered to walk Trinny up the road to our place while I took the bike. She shot me a meaningful look at this before accepting. I was in the kitchen fixing drinks when they tumbled through the front door giggling and I could tell from the way they were looking at each other that Trinny had already got things under way with Reece.

She passed round the drinks and led us both into the lounge, then came up and kissed me hard on the mouth before turning away and giving me a mischievous look over her shoulder, invited me to unzip her dress.

As she slowly and seductively peeled it off our eyes were all over her curvy body and in a moment she was standing there in her underwear with a wanton look on her face. Without taking anything else off, Trinny sat on the sofa and watched, her hand finding its way between her legs, as Reece and I quickly got out of out our clothes. I felt myself becoming quickly excited and so was Reece, Trinny told me later that the sight of our arousal drove her crazy with anticipation.

No.

This isn't working. I'm not in the mood.

With a smile, I save the story in a file marked 'The University of Life by Rosie Cheeks,' in a directory named 'The Cad Magazine, erotica circa 3000words.' Next to this is another folder called 'The Occasionally Diverting Adventures of Mostyn Zinctrumpet-Harris,' and below that, one entitled 'e-mails, Melanie.'

As I shut-down my stylish aluminium portable computer, a distant rumble of thunder, presage of the approaching monsoon, reaches me across the paddies that stretch to the foothills of the Western Ghats. It prompts me to consider whether the rooftop restaurant of the Mumbai Raffles Hotel may, after all, prove an ill-chosen venue for my thirtieth birthday party. It has been a terrific season, my third since I was in Manilla but it is just about over now. In a day or two it will be time to move on once again.

A swarthy indigene decants a pre-prandial cocktail into my glass as I extinguish the hooka and pop my sunglasses into the shellac Darjeeling tea caddy in which they live these days, (glasses cases being, as they are, so easy to lose). I head into the crowd, acknowledging the Swedish ambassador with an airy wave of my hand.

One of the most precipitous pitfalls with which the career path of professional writers of erotic fiction such as myself is beset, besides that of developing an unhealthily depraved cast of mind and generally shocking the bejesus out of people, is that eventually you tend to run out of stuff to write.

To begin with you pillage your own sexual history for useably vivid material, then you ransack your fantasy life for its strongest images and finally you either call it a day or you set out to get inside the minds of others.

What you absolutely cannot do, no matter what you may think, is simply make it up. It lacks that ring of authenticity, you see? They can tell.   It's like a joke translated into English by a German or a piece of abstract art created by one of those people who say, 'I could have done that.' It may superficially resemble the thing that it apes but it would only fool someone with, respectively no sense of humour or aesthetics. Pornography, like comedy, has to do more than seem the part, it has to actually work. It has to produce an actual physical response in the audience or it has failed and ergo it isn't porn.

I think it was in about 1997, whilst in search of grist to my sordid mill, that I inevitably strayed into that vast stratum of subterranean sleaze which in those days was still occasionally referred to as the information super-highway. Following this, and for years afterwards, I lounged around my dimly lit Brighton retreat, which was at that time furnished like a Bedouin tent, reclining upon cushions, a hooka smouldering by my side, my stylish aluminium portable computer nestled in my lap, idly tickling the velvet ears of my no-legged chinchilla Stumpy, whilst stalking the labyrinthine sewers of the internet.

I formed creepy voyeuristic relationships with other net prowlers: swinging couples, bored housewives, webcam exhibitionists. I indulged them in their need to tell me their experiences and fantasies and then I wrote them down, wrote them up, changed the names and sold them.

It must have been early in '99, whilst in the course of one such scavenging sortie, that I first made the acquaintance of the Tyrolean termagant, Trinity. I had embarked upon the enterprise of locating and contacting my perfect fantasy woman and to this end I subscribed to a number of databases of varying degrees of seediness.

Of course the process of sifting through the huge number of profiles stored in these outfits is actually one of straightforward number crunching. One fills in a questionnaire detailing ones requirements and the degree of weight to be attached to each stipulation and the computer discards the profiles with any characteristics that amount to what salespersons call, a dealbreaker and comes up with the best match.

Strangely though, when actually filling in one's wish list, the procedure seems rather other than passive, or at least it did to me. It felt like a form of freakishly accelerated evolution. As though I was selectively breeding the f. like a thoroughbred racehorse, intervening to ensure the inheritance of certain characteristics and exclude certain others. The difference is that digital information unlike genetic information doesn't take generations to permeate the gene pool. You can and I did, produce the ultimate specimen of the non-chap element, entirely from scratch, in half a day.

Now I know what you're thinking. 'That's not the same thing at all,' you say. 'You didn't invent the woman, you merely discovered her.'

And yet didn't nature similarly invent her by the non-random selection of randomly occurring genetic change? Didn't nature merely discover the genetic code required to produce her, just as Mandlebrot discovered the algorithm for producing fractal landscapes? What, after all, actually is the difference between an invention and a discovery? Show me an invention that wasn't lying dormant as a potentiality waiting to be discovered. I merely reverse-engineered things to arrive at the same result without all the hanging around.

You do need a large sample to start with of course, otherwise even the most undiscriminating of criteria will quickly eliminate the entire field. For example, imagine that you are a man contemplating the mainstream dating scene in Brighton, a city with half a million people. A quarter of a million will be women, of whom fifty thousand will be within five years either side of one's age, of whom twelve thousand will be single, of whom ten thousand will be heterosexual.

This of course is the total market, so even supposing that website membership runs at a generous one percent amongst this group then only a hundred f.s are actually in the game. Of these only about forty will have ticked any of the five boxes other than 'definitely,' (for which, read: 'without delay,') in answer to the question 'Want children?' Assuming that three in four of these are rejected on the strength of physical specifications and that one swerves the tory voters, bubbly blondes, those whose lives are ruled by astrology, born again Christians, free spirits with g.s.o.h who are 'happy in their own skin', and Capricorns, then one is statistically left with 0.025 remaining candidates. Or in round numbers: none! From a possible five hundred thousand.

So, to be in with a chance you really have to spin your web world-wide, and when the computer disgorged its findings, the only 100% match that it found was with a twenty five year old Austrian woman. The photograph was from an angle from which surely only her most intimate acquaintances would have recognised her, and the profile made it plain that she and I were very much reading from the same page in terms of our tastes and peccadilloes. I crafted for myself a dating profile spiel of suitably platitudinous banality and forwarded a copy of my own details:

I'm a fun-hating kinda guy. The type who is only happy when he's unhappy. This is a bit awkward actually as for years now I've been absolutely on cloud nine. My ideal partner would not be able to make me laugh, as I've been giggling like a loon for ages and it's starting to affect my work (I'm a funeral director).

I'm a socially versatile chap, feeling equally uncomfortable and awkward having a wild night out on the tiles as I am curling up under the duvet on a Sunday afternoon with a dvd and a bottle of Verve Cliché. I love pubs and clubs, also tubs rubs and hubs.

Don't be fooled by appearances. Within my passionately romantic exterior beats the heart of a self absorbed grouch. I never miss an opportunity to miss an opportunity to make a touching gesture like remembering an anniversary, writing a love poem, turning up for a wedding in long trousers etc. I believe that the single most important element of a relationship is mutual respect and so is having your own space and so is communication.

Being an un-materialistic soul I don't set great store in possessions, I prefer money. My absolutely favourite place in the world, bar none with no exceptions whatsoever is Venice. And Thailand.

I believe that it's not what's inside a person that counts, it's what they look like. I think it's better to regret what you did in life than what you didn't do. Except for in the rather large number of cases where the reverse is true. I believe that we should always take life for granted and live each day as if there were a never ending supply of the wretched things. If there's one thing I've learned in life it's an abiding suspicion of homespun philosophy.

I value honesty (or do I?)

I'm looking for a girl without any baggage or bitterness, who can approach a relationship with an open mind, free from preconceptions, and won't turn out to be just another deceitful whore who runs off with my mate Gavin.

Possessing the ability to read between the lines would also be an advantage. Or, come to that, a 1959 Triumph Herald gear-stick.

Naturally my quarry responded immediately and a sizzling dialogue was opened. A dialogue which had endured for six months or so and contributed substantially to supporting the Z-H household, when we finally, and from my point of view, rather unexpectedly, met.

For what it's worth it is my personal belief, admittedly based pretty much entirely on my observations of the travails of others, that there are three threshold values which must be met if a pairing between two people is to have any kind of a future.

These are the permanent members of the United Nations security council of love, in the sense that the absence of any one of them constitutes a veto. These qualities reveal themselves progressively and at different rates and it is this time lag that accounts for the much of the anguish with which so many fellows of my acquaintance seem to contend.

In reverse order of becoming evident then, a prospective mate ought to rule the heart, the head and of course, that other place as well. Or to put it another way you have to be able to love the person, like them and desire them. The last criterion of the three is the most immediately apparent of course. One squint at a photograph will pretty well clear the matter up. The second takes a while to determine as a rapport builds and common ground emerges, whilst the first, emotional compatibility, is a nebulous shape shifting fiend and the stuff of nightmares.

They are though, each of them, absolutely indispensable and cannot be ranked in order of importance any more than can the links of a chain.

Many are they that respond to my perennially single status with council of courage and compromise. The self appointed cognoscenti of love who, from within the sanctuary of a happy marriage reinvent their pasts in quixotic rose tinted hindsight, bandy such terms as 'unrealistic expectations' and 'give and take. 'I ,however, cling resolutely to the belief that one should not attempt to make a go of things with someone who is not, in your eyes, desirable and to your mind, captivating and in your heart, adorable any more than you would be prepared to live without a brain a heart or that other thing. And if you do - and I don't think I can make it any clearer than this - you will end up divorced.

They are imperatives.

The happy three.

They are the Trinity.

15 ZANY CRETIN TRIUMPHS STORM

'Is it possible for me not to be me? And being me can I wish to be another?'

Denis Diderot.

The immediate aftermath of the accident at Annecy, was all about stretchers and helicopters and the general drama of emergency medical repatriation. Everyone was very kind and very efficient, and asked me, in several languages, where it hurt and whether I could feel my toes, and in the main they were pretty good-humoured about receiving very little from me in return. By and large I was allowed, and indeed chemically encouraged, to sleep through the whole affair.

Back in England I was examined and evaluated by a range of specialists in white coats and there was much muttering about brain damage, magnetic resonance imaging, acute shock and so on.

It took quite a while for everyone to realise that there wasn't really anything wrong with me. I was not brain damaged, in fact physically I was virtually unmarked but the doctors assumed there had to be a good reason to account for the fact that, unless assertively stimulated by means of little lights being shone into my eyes and loud clear instructions being bellowed at me, I was seemingly oblivious to the outside world. In fact I would, given the chance, spend upwards of twenty hours a day sitting in a chair and gazing vacantly at my own slowly clenching and unclenching right hand.

And the doctors were right, there was a reason for this, and a reason which they were understandably unlikely to arrive at without knowing quite a bit more about the circumstances of my accident. And the reason was that I was still in my pool. Still floating, drowning really, in the warm baptismal pool in which Whisted had immersed me and administered the rites of initiation to his church of the mind. The waters had closed over my head and I couldn't tell, for the life of me, which way was up.

The thing is that whilst one can, with time, mentally adjust to the loss of many of those things of which life can suddenly divest one (a valued chum, a non-essential body-part, or a reputation as a good egg, to mention but a few) there is, nevertheless, at least something ancillary about such things. Their loss may be sorely felt but at least one's self remains intact to contemplate the situation.

Whereas, the reason that I was so completely and utterly at sea in the days following the accident, was that in a tragic and actually rather irritating paradox, the thing that I was trying to adjust to the loss of, was the very thing to which I would generally resort, in order to help me to get over the loss of something.

It was belief. Of a certain kind.

That abiding, optimistic, Panglossian, belief, that many of the worlds more spiritual souls, cherish in their hearts. The belief in fact, to which people are referring when they say things like:

'I don't believe in organised religion because it's caused so many wars but I do believe there's something out there.'

The belief, in other words, that a life as nasty, brutish and short as this one, simply cannot be all that there is. If you have it, then whatever else you lose, this faith alone will pull you through. If you lose it, then it is like contracting a retro-virus which attacks the immune system; you have no defence.

The persistence of this type of belief speaks of a huge difference in perspective between people, as regards that which constitutes a reason to believe.

People who believe in a God for instance, not infrequently offer as a reason for their belief, something along the lines of:

'I believe in God because if he didn't exist there would be no point to life.'

Or.

'I believe in God because if he didn't exist there would be no justice awaiting those who trespass against others.'

In contrast, non-believers and in particular, scientific rationalists, are likely to trot out something such as:

'I do not believe in god, any more than I believe that Basingstoke would make a charming place to spend your honeymoon, mainly because there is precious little (big word coming up) **evidence** to support the theory.'

Or.

'Anthropomorphism is simply a part of human nature. We project human qualities onto animals and hurricanes and even things that we ourselves invent like ships and cars and God. He is made in our image.'

Indeed, after a couple of beers, they may even offer up something like: 'The concept of God is an inevitable consequence of the fact that humans have a consciousness, in the sense that God represents an idealised and externalised version of the self. He is a personification of ones conscience and one's better moral judgement. The 'good,' in fact, that is as nearly God, as evil is nearly Devil.'

These two different approaches then (and there is no objective way to demonstrate that either of them [the second one for instance] is in any sense [miles] superior) are based on two different takes on the meaning of the word 'reason'.

The first viewpoint, embraces the word 'reason' in the sense of 'motive', as in: 'the reason I believe this is because it makes it easier to get through the day' or 'the reason to believe this, is because the implications of not believing it are simply too dreadful to contemplate.'

Whereas the rationalist view embodies the word reason in the sense of, a justifying reason, in that it is a provisional statement designed to account for observable phenomena, and fits the facts more squarely than other competing theories.

Or, to put it another way, the first is intended to console and the second to explain.

Both approaches have their advantages too. The open mindedness of the first view, it is argued[18], is the more hopeful vision, in that it introduces purpose and design into a tableau which might otherwise be seen as a bit thin on meaning. Conversely the scientific view, isn't terribly comforting but does have the advantage of not being piffle.

It all depends on what you want to get out of your beliefs, and of course whether, to believe something

---

[18] *Wrongly*

simply because you choose to, is ultimately really to believe it at all.

For example the Boston strangler's mother, was sustained to her last by an abiding belief in her son's innocence[19]. Perhaps this is entirely as it should be, she was his mother after all but it still, ultimately, betrays a reluctance to look reality in the face.

So.

Previously to the Annecy debacle, I too had played host to a vague and defocused belief in there being, 'something else out there' since it seemed the only way to account for the fact that I appeared to be in possession of that most splendid of items; a soul.

But of course this had been rather fatally undermined by the first-hand revelation that my mind was, in every way that counts, merely another highly evolved and highly specialised body part, just like the strangely unfamiliar right hand at which I gazed fixatedly throughout those dreamlike days.

It was an organ in fact, the anatomy of which I had been privileged to inspect at close quarters. A biological computer, the intricate complexity of which tends to deceive one into assuming that it is something more.

An organic thinking machine of more or less the same type that you would find installed in a chimpanzee, albeit with a bit more RAM and a better sound-card,

---

[19] I should imagine.

allowing for better cognitive function and speech. It had painstakingly adapted, over millennia of evolution, to the particular demands of life in the stone age. It was thus equipped to cope with avoiding predators, identifying nourishing food, forming social alliances, speculating accurately about the contents of other people's minds, and choosing a mate. Anything in fact which improved an individual's chances of passing on its genes.

Now this, in itself, did not present a problem. I had no trouble in accepting that our personalities are dominated by primal drives arising from evolutionary imperatives. The urges to breed for instance and to protect one's brood, with violence if necessary, are as meat and potatoes to the chap element. Indeed Dr. Ludwig Cillit-Bang used to waffle on endlessly in this vein, and he was certainly a proper old brain-box.

But I did have a powerful resistance to the idea of evolutionary psychology being *all* that there is. I was having difficulty locating the 'me' in all of this. Or at least accepting that what I had always thought of as my own, unique, personal, self, could, in fact, be no more than an epiphenomenon. An emergent property. A by-product of all of distinct mental modules within my mind, as they jostled and vied to express themselves.

The awe in which I had always regarded the ethereal, unknowable nature of consciousness, had been suddenly and brutally vanquished by knowledge. My own personal model of the nature of self, duly underwent a complete transformation. It went from being something rather magical and utterly wonderful, to being something distinctly explicable and entirely functional. A paradigm shift which led me to formulate the following analogy:

When viewed by a human eye, from the right distance and at a suitable angle, a television picture appears as, say, somebody reading the news. Of course we know that it is merely an illusion suggestive of this. Move closer and you realise that the screen is made up of tiny dots, slow it down and you see that the sense of motion is achieved by a series of frames succeeding each other at a rate that exceeds the eye's ability to differentiate them. The success of the illusion is hence dependent on the equipment with which and the conditions under which, it is perceived.

It seemed to me that, since the only perceptual equipment we have for examining our consciousness is our consciousness itself, we should hardly be surprised that it comes across as pretty authentic. The mistake is in thinking that there must be a 'me' having these thoughts, when in actual fact, 'I,' am the thoughts.

In short, as I languished in hospital, what I was trying to recover from was the realisation that consciousness, just like the television picture is merely an illusion but an illusion generated by the persistence of vision of the minds eye.

And I did recover too.

Each day that passed, found me more able to cope with the new me. Me, the robot, as it were. After a while I was able to look in the mirror and recognise myself.

Like a crash victim trapped in the wreckage, afraid to try his legs in case they don't work, I tentatively explored my mind until satisfied that I still had everything intact.

The only difference, was that everything was different.

Because what Whisted had shown me amounted to the difference between metaphorically seeing something, and actually seeing it. Between comprehending something and apprehending it.

Eventually, after fourteen days or so of total obmutescence I felt ready to break my silence. The second most disconcerting effect of this, was that, as quick as a flash, the white coats surrounding me were replaced by grey suits as other people came, to put other questions. Identification was produced. Special Branch. The state. The establishment. I found myself being reflexively evasive. They wanted to know about the accident. About what we had been doing in France, about Whisted and his technique. They were particularly interested in finding out what had been said on the radio. They were polite and sympathetic but very insistent. Pressure was applied, they brandished a copy of my psychology project proposal. They even wheeled out my course tutor Dr, Ludwig Cillit-Bang to talk some sense into me. I named the other pilots but denied that

Whisted was culpable for my accident. As far as I was concerned what had happened was between the professor and myself.

When it became clear that I wasn't giving them the whole story, they played the card which they had been holding back. They showed me missing person's reports filed by frantic relatives, details of search and rescue operations, photographs of the crash scenes, of shredded gliders, blood. The blankly staring eyes of Neil O'Gism his face a deathly white. Death certificates in seven languages. Letters from the families exhorting me to assist the police in any way I could. They told me that in a series of accidents on successive days between the third and the thirteenth of May, eleven paraglider pilots had died in the Chamonix valley having flown, apparently deliberately, into cumulo nimbus clouds. That I was the only survivor of the Annecy twelve.

My faith was shaken but not destroyed. The strength of the impression Whisted had made on me was such that even this struck me as inconclusive. It seemed to me that it was all completely consistent with the nature of a conspiracy. If Special Branch had wanted to trace Whisted. To silence him and suppress his technique, what would they have done but this?

So I asked for a telephone and dialled a number.

'Hello, is this the River Kwai Restaurant, Harbour Road, Exeter?' I asked and held my breath.

'No,' Replied a thick Welsh accent 'this is Lewis and Lewis sewing machine and telescope repairs Merthyr Tydfil.'

Now I was really confused. Nothing checked out. I had been tricked and I didn't know how to feel. I was deluged simultaneously by extreme dismay and acute relief. Two waves of emotion exactly out of phase, each canceling out the other. I felt nothing.

Numbly I told the police everything I knew. As much as I could remember of what Whisted had said to me under hypnosis. I divulged my e-mail password and by extension all of the communications that had passed between us, and the article that had started the whole thing off.

It quickly transpired that Whisted had never been heard of at Sussex University's Psychology department, where (although, when I came to think about, it not actually within which) we had met for the first time. Also his e-mail address had been suspended and the string of letters after his name proved to be bogus. The police did some trawling through a computer or two and built up a biography of the man. It turned out that he had had careers in marketing, public relations and advertising, the holy trinity of turd polishing. He had been deported from America in 1991 amid allegations of fraud, whereafter he had turned his hand to stage hypnosis and close up magic.

All of which was a ghastly jolt certainly, and yet for me it was, as reported, decidedly the second most immediately striking development to be precipitated by my re-emergence into society.

There was something else too. And it rather knocked me sideways:

Typing these words now on my stylish, if rather world weary, aluminium portable computer, you find me luxuriating in a commodious, first class airline seat some 35000ft over the Alps, nursing still the extravagant hang-over resulting from my thirtieth birthday party at the Mumbai Raffles Hotel. And whilst a rather adorable air hostess named Chantal skilfully decants a pre-prandial cocktail into my glass I find myself conjuring to mind a, no doubt rose tinted, picture of the young Nigel Jenkins.

The chap bashfully grinning back at me now from the pages of the Zinctrumpet-Harris memory album, is a retiring, fresh-air-loving, woolly-jumpered, countryside-rambling sort of a fellow. He is pausing for a breather in mid-hike, his cheeks rosy, his boots caked in mud, savouring a cup of the old restorative, decanted from a thermos flask, as he perches on the steps of the war memorial by the cricket field in a Sussex market town.

A wholesome type then, hearty, a bit of a loner and of course an orphan, brought up by the state. He was also rather a classless young chap. No cut glass accent. No upper crust pretensions.

This was to change.

After Annecy, to my great surprise, I found that when I opened my mouth to speak, it felt entirely natural to do so in an extremely posh accent. And not a particularly authentic sounding posh accent either. More of a caricature really. A caricature of larky, caddish, joshing, bally poshness you might say. Indeed to adopt the neutral, received pronunciation, of my speech before the Annecy episode required a conscious effort of will that amounted virtually to histrionics.

And it wasn't just my accent either. When I sought a bon mot with which to express a thought or illustrate a point, my vocabulary would offer up some daft anachronism reminiscent of the inter war period. Ditto my delivery, was rather antediluvian too, longwinded, circumloquatious, endlessly parenthetical and really a bit silly.

In an absurdly short space of time I had assumed the mien of the feckless nineteen thirties bachelor aristocrat. And furthermore, if it marked me out for ridicule amongst the hoi polloi, then I cared not one jot.

'Ho hum!' was my attitude, since it was not, when all is said and done, actually my voice that occasioned their levity, and hence it was no reflection upon myself.

It was however the same voice that I had fleetingly heard myself using as Whisted led me over the threshold into my subconscious a fortnight or so before. And more or less the same voice that I have used every day since.

As a compulsive rationalist, I immediately botched together a theory to account for all of this, based upon the following observation:

The English, I would say, are pretty largely of the mind that our national taste for self-parody is symptomatic of a really first class sense of humour. Universally renowned for it, we fondly think. The envy of the world, just like the B.B.C, the health service, the monarchy and of course the British sense of fair play.

Well I've biffed about the five continents a good deal, and I have to tell you that not once in all of that time has a non Englishman seen fit to volunteer such an opinion unprompted.

In fact the prevailing view among the non English element would seem to be that a good sense of humour is generally indicated by a person's willingness to be laughed at by others, whilst a propensity to laugh at one's self is more likely to betoken insecurity and self absorption and a desire to gain attention.

Such was certainly the interpretation that I placed upon the startling transformation in my outward self in the weeks after the accident. This was surely a protective layer, a pre-emptive self mockery designed to deflect the slings and arrows, that kind of thing. Something, perhaps, which would fade with time.

Whether I would, in due course, have reason to revise this analysis, only time would tell.

In any case, I definitely found that I couldn't really take other humans seriously any longer. I envied, to the point of bitterness, their blissful ignorance. Their total failure to appreciate how little their precious individuality may in fact amount to. How the richness of life's tapestry masks the simplicity of the pattern from which it arises. I wished only to avoid them like the plague.

In the pursuit of this end I enjoyed the complicity of no lesser agency of justice than Special Branch itself. Upon my discharge from hospital, working on the theory that my Svengali would attempt to track me down and attempt to reassert his hypnotic grip, they proposed that I undergo a complete change of identity, to render myself untraceable.

Their logic was that for any type of ideological fanatic to exercise total radio control over an airborne automaton represented an unacceptable potential for, not to put too fine a point on it, terrorism.

As far as I could recall, all that Whisted actually had on me in the way of details was my e-mail address but I had definitely mentioned to him on at least one occasion that I lived in a home for developmentally challenged orphans, and since my accent suggested the south of England, this was a disclosure which, from his point of view, would have tended to have narrowed the field somewhat.

Everything would be arranged and paid for by Her Majesty's government. I could even choose my own name.

They provided the little flat in Brighton and an allowance, by means of which, I surrounded myself with objets sleaze. I rigged myself out in bespoke raiment of the professional idler, cultivated a suitably sensational pencil moustache and shortly I legally became Sir Mostyn Zinctrumpet-Harris: waster, freelance pornographer, borderline junkie and earthbound skybum, which is of course to say, bum.

What better place after all, to take refuge from the stigma of idle unemployment than within the aristocracy.

I dosed myself up on opium, the religion of the atheist, and life generally started to go back to as normal as life can be, when you have a thoroughly blown mind and a Bertie Wooster fixation.

At about this time I noticed, to my irritation, that I no longer enjoyed music. The deepest of the arts, once capable of wheeling out the whole bally rainbow of emotions, seemed suddenly not in the least opaque or mysterious. My new twenty twenty introspection exposed it for the grubby acoustic trickery that it is. The frequencies and patterns of sound that the brain recognises as corresponding to certain environmental stimuli and to which it responds by producing appropriate mental states. It simply failed to register with me any longer. Like so much wallpaper.

In fact the only tunes that filtered through to my consciousness were those occasional, howlingly awful musical abberations of which examples include Paul Hardcastle's execrable '19', Nena Hagen's decidedly grating '99 Luftballoons' and the brilliantly terrible 'Bankok, (Oriental City)' by Murray Head. Gimmick records to be precise, notable chiefly for the sense in which they differ from music at large rather than the sense in which they add to it. Musical taste that dares not speak its name.

I also developed a peculiar horror of television, the make-believe quality of which I had come to find enchanting during my university life. It quite disgusted me that people's emotions could be bought so cheaply. I was in no mood to cooperate with the peddlers of illusion.

And, strangely, I had seemingly fallen victim to a systematic campaign of persecution by seagulls. The blighters appeared to regard me as a seafarer regards a landlubber and for five years they pelted me with guano from every angle.

A more general and rather overwhelming effect of the accident was an absolutely galloping fear of being duped, tricked, conned and generally taken for a ride. A consuming agoraphobic distrust of any approach made to me, which led me to shrink away from the world and immerse myself in sleazy, nihilistic bohemianism.

For nearly five years, amid an opiated miasma, I drifted with the tide, back and forth across the dividing line between functionality and psychosis. Although there were times when I was seized with a mania for activity, for long periods I was unable to summon up the impetus to face the world. Days on end were spent in lounging around my seedy Brighton garret, clad in silk pyjamas, a brocade dressing gown and Turkish slippers, tapping away desultorily on my computer. I contemplated writing a book, detailing the whole sorry saga but ultimately decided that the world didn't need another confessional first novel by a tortured emotional husk.[20] Besides, something told me that the story had a few chapters left to run. Five in all probability, if you count number seventeen.

All the while I was silently doing battle with the creeping paranoiac suspicion that Whisted would eventually make contact by whatever means and reclaim me. At one particularly delusional stage I even became convinced that he was attempting to communicate with my subconscious via the anagrams in the day time television quiz show 'Countdown.'

In his haste to abort the session in Annecy, Whisted had brought me to the surface too fast. The sudden decompression had caused me to develop the bends.

Throughout this timeless fugue, when I did emerge, blinking, from my den, it was mainly to conduct obsessional field research sorties into the arcane crafts

---

[20] *See, 'The Skybum, (The occasionally Diverting Adventures of Mostyn Zinctrumpet Harris)'*

of mentalism, manipulation and persuasion. The only people I felt I could trust were those that I actually knew were trying to control me. I had been used most shabbily you see. Cheated, in fact, of my very soul.

During these excursions I posed as a gullible mark for persuaders and mountebanks of every complexion, mediums and psychics, clairvoyants and astrologers. I consulted Herbalists, Homeopaths, hypnotists even financial advisors.

On Wednesday August 11 1999 for instance, a few weeks before my encounter with Trinity, I was, not atypically, up in London shiftily sidling up to some followers of Hare Krishna as they dined in their restaurant and recruitment centre in Soho Square. I was anxious to have something explained to me.

I suggested to them that if, as they claimed, a persons wrong deeds would be visited upon them in a subsequent incarnation, then surely the remarks for which a certain England football manager had paid with his career in a storm of protest the previous winter: remarks to the effect that disabled people were reaping what they had sown in a previous life – contained, if not a terribly sunny outlook, then at least a certain haphazard logic.

The monks seemed shocked and appalled that I could suggest such a hateful idea and said so.

'Disabled people have done nothing wrong and are not being punished,' I was told. 'they have a condition,'

I carefully explained that I couldn't be more in accord with this view. I added though, that as someone who didn't believe in Karma for a moment, it wasn't incumbent upon me to reconcile the cause and effect relationship that they proposed between crime and punishment, with it's inescapably implied (if repugnant) obverse: that, if it were true, then evidence of punishment would logically be suggestive of crime. The Krishnas smiled and shook their heads, marvelling at my superficial understanding of karma. They went back to eating their cake (and having it) and I left unedified, lamenting my spiritually impoverished Western outlook but mollified by the lesson that most of the time in life, what you say is less important than the attitude people assume lies behind it. Or as Glen Hoddell would doubtless tell you - don't stick your neck out.

Mid afternoon that very same day saw me outside in the summer sunshine, lying on my back on the grass in Soho Square whilst Reeves served me Pimm's and shielded me from seagull excrement with his copy of Nietzsche's Ecce Homo. We were waiting, along with millions of others, for the first total solar eclipse for four hundred years.

As the moons penumbral shadow passed across the earth, a hush descended upon the assembled throng. The birdsong ceased. Even the unselfconsciously fatuous prattle of the spiky haired media nincompoops who infest the area was momentarily suspended as we all beheld a spectacle only ever afforded to a slice of a slice of humanity.

Of course what you take away from such an experience, entirely depends on the type of person that you are. For me, the greatest insight of the event was the abrupt realisation that the stars are, of course, still there during the day. During that brief hiatus of semi night the whole universe suddenly blinked into view and with it the realisation that it had been there all along.

If I had stopped to think about it I suppose I would have been able to anticipate this, after all it is the same sky, save for the presence of the sun whose brightness prevents the human eye from seeing the stars. If the pupil were to dilate sufficiently to see them as it does when gazing at the night sky, then the brightness of the sun would blind us. The fact remained though, that I didn't figure it out.

I didn't see it until I was allowed to see it for myself.

16 TRANSPORTS OF DELIGHT

Godfrey had been absolutely right! It was a 200k day and it was indeed 'on like a train' (although that exact simile would be unlikely to occur to an Englishman for obvious reasons). There was do doubt about it, in the spirit of the Millennium, the same God that had bestowed upon us Auschwitz and reality television, had reached down into his celestial boots to ensure that December 30th 1999, in New South Wales Australia at least, was to be a positive riot of paragliding potential.

The dreadful jalopy that was the Borah basher, continued to grind its way up the mountain with glacial slowness. The stuttering note of its engine suggesting that it was about as likely to keep going, as a straight man who inadvertently enrols at a gay samba-dancing school. JJ told me that the truck had been repaired so many times that all that remained of the original vehicle was the license plate. Even the bits that had been welded onto it, had had bits welded onto them.

'Can't kill them Toyotas.' He said. I didn't contest his point, it seemed to me that a discussion of whether a vehicle which had had all of it's components replaced was actually metaphysically the same machine, might find a more receptive ear in Pete the basher driver; a man who clearly liked to contemplate reality from every angle.

Pete was yet another Austrian, wanted by the law for drug dealing and currently lying low in a shed in Godfrey's garden. He tended to invest most of his leisure time in getting 'off his tits,' on homemade amphetamines. The fellow had a heart of gold of course but unfortunately a brain of marmalade. He muscled the truck around the vertiginous turns gripping the non power assisted steering wheel in the manner of a castanet player, his thumbs priapic lest they should be badly wrenched in the event that the front wheels were suddenly grabbed by a pothole. According to Melanie, Pete had had a short relationship with Elle the tobacco enthusiast which she had broken off in disgust after he accidentally set fire to his hair, whilst sniffing glue, in the back of Myra MacDonald's yellow hand-painted Renault 11.

As we neared the top of the mountain, the gradient lessened and the Basher gained a little speed, affording us a welcome breeze. Here and there in the dense bush that lined the dirt track, kangaroos shyly watched our progress, one of them with a tiny joey peering out of her pouch, which only the most leaden hearted soul would fail to find inexpressibly adorable.

At length the basher wheezed to a standstill at the South East take-off and we hopped down and massaged some life back into the more numb areas before reclaiming our dusty glider bags from the trailer and dispersing around the area.

Once a pilot has prepared his equipment, laid his canopy out on the ground and clipped in to his harness, he is to all intents and purposes ready to go. One firm tug on the risers, a bit of brake and a few powerful driving strides will see him airborne. Typically though he doesn't do this. He doesn't take off for another fifteen minutes during which time he stands in the sun, scanning the area for signs of an approaching thermal. Trees thrashing about further down the slope, birds circling, a swarm of insects suddenly wafting up in front of launch.

What they are also doing, perhaps without being conscious of it, is thinking their way into the flying zone. Subtly optimising the mind for the particular demands of free flight. The adjustment will happen naturally of course once you have been airborne for a while but take off is a pretty abrupt and radical change of circumstances for an ex-caveman and since the actions of the first few minutes of a flight are critical to it's success, a bit of mental preparation can make the difference between climbing out and bombing out.

The kind of pilots who launch first, launched first and went straight down to the 'short East,' an emergency landing paddock at the foot of the hill. Other 'wind dummies' followed them like lemmings, maintaining their take off height for a time, before gradually losing the battle and sinking out over the main landing by Godfrey's house. I wondered if they had really seen anything to suggest that a cycle was about to kick off or merely that their fifteen minutes had elapsed.

By about eleven o'clock though, people were beginning to climb out in reliable lift and the whole atmosphere of suppressed excitement on take-off began to intensify. Within an hour there would be no-one left on the mountain but Pete the basher driver.

I ate a Satsuma, still pleasantly cold from Colleens fridge at the Imperial, applied a layer of sunblock, liberally nitrated some parched looking thistles, zipped up my flying suit, retrieved my mirror sunglasses from the metal cylinder within which I stored them at that time, installed them upon the beak and with my bunched up glider slung over my shoulder I toddled across to the big sheet of Astroturf stapled to the ground on Borah's East face.

Now paragliding is not an 'adrenaline sport', certainly it is not that most unsavoury of things an 'extreme sport', likewise paraglider pilots are far from being fearless people. Their comparative sanguinity in a

229

situation that would give many of the right-thinking element the galloping heebie jeebies, corresponds to something altogether other:

For the committed skybum, flying is life. All time is lost that is not spent flying. For this reason, to be fearful of flying because of the attendant risk of losing one's life, makes no sense at all. There is no possible outcome that could result from flying that is worse than the idea of not flying. Nothing that one could lose, that one would not lose by ceasing to fly. That said, as I kicked off my obligatory fifteen minutes of standing on launch contemplating the conditions, there was definitely a thrill of nervous excitement and a certain unsteadiness of hand.

I watched the shadows of the clouds as they tracked across the fields from the southeast. As a reference I picked a particularly large one, shaped a little like Serge Gainsbourgs nose, which was just passing directly over Godfrey's place and heading my way. I started the timer on the excitingly technical watch that I had won in a game of revolving door roulette against Chang Evans, a Welsh Sumo wrestler that I met in Burkina Faso.[21]

An hour earlier, whilst waiting at the farm in the shade of a Eucalyptus tree, I had fished out my g.p.s. and prevailed upon Bill Philby to set it up for Australia, they

---

[21] See, 'Zinctrumpet-Harris and the Ougadougou Kudu Voodoo.'

are amazing gadgets of course, and can tell you just where you are anywhere on the planet to within a few metres but strangely only once you tell them which country they are in. He had marked a waypoint on my g.p.s. pinpointing the position of the farm which the device now appeared to be telling me was a trifle under three kilometres distant.

Conditions on launch were fairly breathless, with perhaps the suggestion of a light south easterly but every twelve minutes for the past hour an explosive thermic cycle had ripped through, causing a brief and deeply encouraging interlude of comparatively hectic wind. Rather too strong and gusty to safely launch in fact.

My plan therefore, was to lob off thirty seconds or so before the next thermal kicked off, and I could see it already swirling through the cornfield next to the bottom landing whipping up dust into a Lilliputian tornado.

Consulting my satisfyingly over engineered watch I noted that the cloud, at present directly overhead, casting its shadow across take-off and perhaps more reminiscent now of the proboscis of Sascha Distel, had taken six minutes to cover the three kilometres from chez Godfrey making the wind speed at cloud base exactly 30k.p.h. It was blowing a hoolie at altitude, whilst down at launch you could have blown smoke rings.

As the trees at the foot of the hill began to thrash around, I judged that the thermal was less than a minute away and shortly it would be too strong to take off. I therefore arranged the lines and risers for a forward launch, made a last check of my leg straps and karabiners, and with the frisson of joy that attends any irreversible action requiring total commitment, I charged off the side of the mountain and into the air.

As soon as I took off I knew it was going to be touch and go. I was 'bombing out' in a big way. The sink alarm on my vario groaned wildly in protest as my descent exceeded four metres per second. The powerful updraught of the thermal was sucking in air from every direction causing the wind to blow down the slope. The glider surged and pitched as I strove to control it, my eyes fixed grimly on the emergency landing field, the one still, clear point amid a scene which swam and grew.

Suddenly, with barely a hundred metres to go before a landing in which trees seemed destined to feature fairly prominently, I connected with the lift. An audible moan involuntarily escaped me as the deceleration forced the air from my lungs and I immediately cranked the glider round into a tight turn. The vario shrieked as four down became four up. Five up. Six. A stalk of corn lodged momentarily in my lines as I climbed up past take-off, still turning very tightly in the narrow core of the thermal.

As the mountain began to look small, I relaxed enough to recall to mind Whisted's words on the subject of flying, as I had every time I had flown since Annecy. They came back to me like a faint echo and I started to think, not about the glider, or the bubble of air in which I was flying but about the whole sky. I started to fly as a bird flies. The wing immediately reacted as I ceased to fight it. The angle at which the thermal was tracking back with the wind was taking me downwind as I circled up, presenting me with a decision. I would soon be too far downwind to have any hopes of getting back to the hill if the lift ran out or if I lost the thermal, but it felt steady and I was happy to commit early. The day looked strong and there were a couple of gliders ahead of me, including Godfrey, whom, I assumed, could be depended upon to know when and where to go.

My audacity was rewarded. I arrived at cloud base and went on a glide. Everything was absolutely wizard. I was cock-a-hoop!

For the first thirty kilometres of the flight, I didn't lose more than a thousand metres of altitude between thermals. I steered a course that kept me within glide of the gravel road that ran due West across an arid plain from Borah through the Boggabri Gap and on to the town of Boggabri.

Ahead of me a long broken sharks-tooth ridge marked the prehistoric collision of two vast continental plates. I followed the road slightly across wind until an hour after launch I approached 'the gap'. I had been warned that the place was a notorious sink hole so I stopped to turn in any lift I could find, in order to be sure of having the height to glide clear.

As it turned out though I passed over the highest peak with no less than three thousand metres to spare and so with my heart in my mouth I decided to abandon the road to Boggabri which the other gliders were sensibly following, in favour of a straight track to the next and last town directly downwind. Narrabri was 50 kilometres due North-West, a course which took me over the vast, dense and highly intimidating Pilligra Scrub.

On the glide I pushed the speed bar half way out with my feet, accelerating the glider to, according to my gps, a ground speed of one hundred kilometres per hour at base, which reduced to about seventy once I had descended a thousand metres or so.

I took a slurp of water through the nifty hydration system with which the harness is equipped, popped a Pontefract cake into my mouth to maintain my sugar levels, and tried not to worry.

Cross country paragliding in the long run is all about headology. It is the solid decisions that you make which keep you up there, and your lapses in concentration which see you sinking out and landing or, as the Australians say, 'taking a sleddie'. You are, in this sense, remaining aloft entirely by the power of the mind and to this extent you could say that the whole enterprise depends upon something not unlike belief. The attitude one aims for therefore is one of informed optimism, without which it very easy to think oneself onto the ground. And having taken the decision to go directly downwind, meant that I absolutely couldn't afford to sink out for another fifty kilometres at least. Landing out in the snake infested, all but impassable boonies would mean a five hour walkout to the road in the desert sun; a prospect that was withering to contemplate.

For those with eyes to see it, the sky is as pregnant with possibilities and pitfalls as a poker hand. In five card stud one has no control over the hand one is dealt but there follow two chances to swap up to four cards with the pack. By this means an accomplished player will frequently extract a victory from the most un-promising draw. He will review his prospects with a view to improving then. He will examine the fortunes of the other players, ponder the odds, confer with his instincts and then weigh in with a healthy stack. He will, in short, seek to benefit from the non random selection of randomly occurring change.

Mystifyingly, a certain breed of pilot when faced, as on this day, with a truly unstable and active sky; resolves to sit it out. He inspects the hand that he has been dealt and, perhaps mindful of friends who have been dashed against rocks and the time when he was dragged through a fence by a dust-devil, he responds by folding with as much dignity as he can muster. He will mumble something about likely over-development. He will mutter about cu-nims and gust fronts. In all probability he will waste no time in high-tailing it to the pub and setting about a glass of the cold stuff, leaving others to run the gauntlet.

The skybum though does not quail. Not for him such poltroonism. Having made the effort to get to take-off amounts to having staked his 'blind' and assuming that it is at least launchable then the S.B. is jiggered if he'll leave the table without making a go of things. Having seen his hand he seeks to develop it to his advantage. If he climbs successfully to base, then, suddenly he has accomplished something. Money in the bank. Something upon which he can gamble (should I stay or should I go?) He finds himself at a decision point equivalent to having drawn, say, a pair of sixes. He can hang onto his pair, and change the other three cards, reasoning that he may get lucky with a three of a kind. Or he can show a bit of chutzpah and change his four lowest cards in the hope of obtaining a really commanding hand.

Having grasped the nettle above Mount Borah and committed myself to leaving the only obvious source of lift in view, I was presented at the Boggabri Gap with, as it were, my second chance to change of up to four of my cards. At this point my outlook was roughly equivalent to having drawn the queen, king and ace of spades plus the king of hearts and the queen of diamonds. Two good pairs then. Kings and queens. A solid hand but not one in which one would have complete confidence of success. Pairs and threes do not an epic cross country make. The dilemma therefore had been whether to follow the conservative course and capitalise on the progress I had made in a westerly direction with the prospect of a ninety kilometre x.c. to Coonabarabran, or to opt for the downwind dash with a higher ground speed and hence greater distance potential, by throwing away the king of hearts and queen of diamonds in the hope of being dealt either the missing components of a straight (ten and jack) or a flush (any two spades.) A statistically doubtful outcome then, but one which, if obtained, could secure me membership of the exclusive 161 club (restricted to pilots who have flown one hundred miles). A gamble then.

Electing to implement sanctions of this sort are, to put it mildly, a bit controversial within the flying world as they represent a clear breach of the I.F.R. rule.[22] Indeed, to put oneself in a situation where there is no safe landing within glide is described in the splendidly forthright 'Skythings' *{The Indispensable Monthly Companion to Life's Up Tiddly Up Upness}* as: 'The action of an unconscionable cretin!'

To further concentrate the mind, I was now getting rather uncomfortably low and it is a lamentable and little understood feature of flying, that the probability of locating a thermal is governed by a variant of the well known 'married man principle,' This dictates that just as the blissfully betrothed chap exerts a magnetic

---

[22] *(I follow Roads)*

fascination over the female element,[23] so the chances of happening upon a thermal are at their maximum when you are least in need of one. And vice versa.

The air was beginning to become distinctly warm around me and I was sufficiently close to the fierce looking scrub that I could hear birdsong again for the first time in the flight. A herd of kangaroos scattered as my shadow passed over them and I found myself anxiously leaning forward in my harness, scouring the area for possible sources of lift. Dry mouthed I turned into wind to set up for a dicey looking landing and a retrieve that seemed destined to be memorable for, at best, extreme dehydration and severely perforated shins; at worst, vultures and bleached bones.

Then, mercifully, on the downwind edge of a field of thistles, with a mere one hundred metres above the ground, I got a low save. Just when it was almost too late, I found what I was looking for. I was tipped off by a wedgetailed eagle lazily patrolling his territory. Not beating his wings but gliding in rising air. The thermal was weak and after eyeing each other from opposite sides of a big slow circle he left for richer pickings. Feeling for the core, I searched upwind a little and connected with stronger lift, hooking into a tighter turn, my confidence growing as I climbed. I began to plan my next move, flying the sky.

---

[23] *Although this may be because his wife has bought him some decent clothes.*

And what a sky! The view to the North was like a picture. A picture of the sky at any rate. Obviously not a picture of a man on a horse or a couple of kittens playing with a ball of wool or some such thing[24]. No this was a glorious skyscape by an old master. Bruegel's 'The Fall of Icarus,' maybe, or something by Piero Della Francesca.

It was very heaven.

Incandescent in the mid afternoon sunshine, perfectly formed cumuli, promising strong, well-defined thermals called to me like the sirens, tempting me yet further off course and deeper into tiger country.

'Hey ho!' I cried aloud with the sunny optimism of a pilot who is going up, rather than down, and I coasted on into the glory. The day grew in strength, as the earth began to give up its heat.

Eventually I saw Narrabri in the distance ahead of me, the last town down track, glittering like Eldorado in the early evening sun. Two thermals away, then one and then at last I was afforded one of the most delicious sensations that cross country paragliding is able to deliver. The realisation that one's goal is within glide. That one has done enough. Any more lift at this point would be superfluous and so naturally in accordance with the aforementioned 'M.M. principle,' I found bags of the stuff. I was still at base when I had well and truly arrived at Narrabri. I overflew the place, a low rise grid even smaller than Manilla, scoping out the best hitching

---

[24] *Or some fruit.*

point for the journey home. The road simply ran fifty kilometres south to Boggabri and then forty k. east back to Manilla. There was no other road leading out of town. This was the end of civilisation. From here it was two thousand kilometres northwest to Uluru and Alice Springs.

I drank in the endless desert that was Australia. I had the strongest urge to carry straight on into nowhere. It was five o'clock. There were three hours of light left to me. The day had a hundred k.s left in it for the taking. My heart was singing. I was in the zone. I could have boated around over the town for an hour or two, spiralled down and landed by the road home or next to the pub for a schooner of froth and a comfortable bed. But I am a cross country pilot. A nomad. What I do, is what I am. The decision made itself. I headed on into the red centre, into the sun. Setting a course towards the only visible geographical feature in view. A barely perceptible shape on the horizon. The start of another sharks tooth ridge perhaps? My map didn't go that far. A goal at any rate.

For the first two thermals I had to contend with the odd pang of anxiety as I moved steadily away from safety, towards uncertainty. Thirty clicks downwind though and a glorious sense of calm descended upon me as I passed the point of total commitment. Whatever happened now, I wouldn't be getting back there tonight. Where I landed I would sleep, wrapped in my heat reflective survival blanket and an exquisite glow of satisfaction.

It just kept on working. The lift acquired a smoother, mellower quality as the restitution effect began to build. The air was no longer rising in tight cores but in much larger, less-defined areas of buoyancy. I held the brakes with one finger of each hand, steering with the slightest inclination of my weight, two miles high now, Narrabri small in the distance behind me, the rocky outcrop that was my goal starting to look possible. But it was too soon yet to think about that. Experience had taught me that to become fixated on goal was to fall short. The furthest I would be able to hope for on my present glide was about twenty kilometres. Say to that white glider to the West...

Well there's a thing. Thought I.

For a glider to be out here it would have had to have flown the 120km from Borah without me spotting it, which was inconceivable. Unless of course it had flown 60km into wind from the rocky promontory that was my goal - not actually impossible but extremely difficult. There literally wasn't another physical feature anywhere around here capable of serving as a launch.

Half an hour later we converged in a thermal, circling around one another like duellists sizing each other up. I immediately recognised Whisted's flying style. Rather than holding the brake handles, he always flew with his bare hands directly on the brake lines like a puppeteer. Also the helmet, a space age carbon fibre affair, was identical to the one I myself was wearing.

And then, abruptly, his voice appeared in my headphones.

'Congratulations Nigel. Or rather Mostyn. This must be a personal best distance for you.'

I was determined to equal his insouciant cool.

'Actually no but it will be when I make it to that rock to the west.'

'Lead the way dear boy.'

We covered the distance fast, each of us striving to best the other, suddenly it wasn't about staying up any longer or even making it to goal. It was about getting there first. Out-thermalling each other. We flew like two eagles fledged from the same brood.

One half of the sky was already lit by stars, the other smouldered in a glorious sunset. The largest grin spread across my face, the glee, the sheer euphoria of the thing made me giggle like a child.

And suddenly we were there. In the dying moments of the day the promontory was within glide at last. The two hundred metre sheer-sided eminence honed by the wind and sand, seemed to draw us in.

Its summit would make for a critical landing and what vortices of air might be generated by its residual heat, I knew not. So I chose to hang back and to watch the other glider go in first. In the event though it sailed reassuringly smoothly into land and I turned in to follow.

Because the wind had dropped to nothing, my landing approach was pretty fast, I flared the glider hard but was nevertheless obliged to run flat out over uneven ground for the first few metres before slowing to a walk as the canopy collapsed behind me. The sudden exertion jarred a little with my epiphanic reverie and I busied myself with my lines for a moment to regain my composure.

When at length I did look up, it was to see a cascade of ebony hair tumble down as Trinity removed her crash helmet.

Holy Christ on a pogo stick!

You could have rendered me prostrate with a piece of plumage!

I gaped for a moment at the out and out wrongness of this development. The sheer incongruity of seeing Trinity's face, when I had worked myself up to finally confronting Whisted, was without a doubt a dramatic development. Indeed it belonged very firmly at the very opposite end of the scale of dramatic developments from the denouement of *'Zinctrumpet-Harris And The Case Of The Butler Who Was Ripped To Shreds By A Pack Of Otterhounds' (2003)*.

Having said that, she was still quite simply the most describably lovely looking woman upon whom my eyes have ever been clapped.

'Welcome to the Lyceum Mostyn.' She said.

In one fluid movement Trinity peeled off her flying suit beneath which she wore only skin tight black shorts and a lycra bra top.

'How did you find me Trinity?' I managed, still numb from the jolt, unclipping from my harness with trembling hands.

'An associate of ours programmed your radio to transmit a data burst for about a tenth of a second every four minutes.' She said. 'The data is decoded into text by any suitably equipped unit on the same frequency.' She held up her radio for my inspection. On its display was the message:

Jenkins t/o 11.20 bearing 300 degrees. using name pregrin axelrod.

Otto! You sneaky blighter - I thought. Whisted, it seemed, had agents everywhere. This is what comes of being the non instruction manual reading type, I told myself. Frankly it is as much as I can do to tell the time.

'I picked up the signal this morning at about eleven a.m.' continued Trinity 'fairly weak and coming from the direction of Manilla, so I waited for a few hours and set out to meet you.'

'And when you met up with me, you called up Whisted on another channel and he pretended to be you.'

'He didn't say he was me Mostyn.'

I thought back to the exchange on the radio.

'Alright he let me believe it was him.'

She smiled a little smile to herself, it was the first and the last time that I would see it.

'You wanted to believe it.'

Silently and separately we folded our gliders and I unpacked a few things from my harness. I was mildly surprised to see that there was a simple encampment here and signs of regular habitation, the remains of a fire contained within a ring of stones, a windsock and two 'swag bags', that Australian innovation, a simple camp bed that can be rolled up small and carried.

When I rejoined Trinity, much of my equanimity had returned. The motion of flying was still with me no matter how immovable the rock beneath us. Actually I was rather enchanted by the splendour of the sky. I was pretty captivated by the moon too and perhaps a little haunted by the desert's eerie sense of emptiness. She passed me a slice of mango.

'Actually what I meant,' I resumed, 'was how did you find me in England?'

'Whisted found you Mostyn. Through the internet. He knows a lot more about you than you may realise, more perhaps than you know yourself. Don't forget he heard you free-associating under hypnosis.' I shifted uncomfortably. 'Based on the knowledge that he had of you, he trawled the web registering with adult contacts databases until he found you.'

'But that's got to be millions of people.' I felt my face colouring slightly, 'And I used an assumed name.'

'Millions of people yes, of whom seventy percent are men, of whom sixty percent are heterosexual, of whom twenty percent were born close to 1975, of whom ten percent live within fifty kilometres of the Futwold and Grange Foundation for Developmentally Challenged Orphans, of which five percent have a thing about shaven...'

'Yes! Yes I get the idea.' I butted in testily.

'Once he had thinned down the field as far as possible he simply searched the few hundred profiles that remained for keywords that you habitually use. Words like 'jolly' and 'dashed' and 'fairer sex'. He found you in less than half a day.'

'Cripes!'

'Then having studied the requirements that you stipulated in the six or seven profiles that were almost definitely you...'

'He chose you to be the bait in a trap.' I finished.

'We created a slightly different profile for each of the websites you were registered with. On the adult swingers' website I was Nadia, an open minded bi-curious female in South London, physically and sexually tailored to your preferences and geographically close enough but not too close. On the love and romance site I was Hannah1977, an English teacher at a private girls' school in Wivelsfield, Sussex, who 'never seemed to meet nice men'. On the sex chat site I was Trinity, the raven haired exhibitionist with the graphic imagination and the thing about furry handcuffs.

Our assumption was that you would eventually propose to set up a meeting but since the site through which you made contact was strictly about e-mail sex and not for actually getting together, we had to wait nearly six months until you accidentally gave away your whereabouts.'

I thought back to our messenger conversation on the morning of Aunt A's summons.

- Whato Trinity. Just a line to say thanks awfully for the pictures.

- You enjoyed them I hope?

- Sensational! But I'm afraid I will not be able to join you online tomorrow night at our usual time as I must away to the family pile in Balcome, my Aunt Augusta has demanded my presence.

I'll drop you a line when I get back,

Tinkerty tonk,

Badboy1975.

'I was in Austria when I got your message Mostyn but by that evening I was in London and by midnight I was in the empty room above Doctor Futwolds office with chloroform and a climbing rope.'

'Did you give any thought to a less drastic course of action at all?' I enquired mildly, 'Standing by the B2114 the following day with a cardboard sign reading 'Brighton Please' for instance.'

'Taking into account your suspicious and reclusive nature, Whisted judged such an approach too unreliable. If I had told you directly what it was that I wanted of you, you wouldn't have cooperated. It was vitally important to have your undivided attention for at least twenty minutes in order to,' she paused picking her words with care, 'prepare the ground.'

I thought back to that day at Futwold, about the strange and stilted exchange. The unsubtle sexual misdirection, the computer with which her attention was partly occupied and also her unlikely familiarity with Vivian Stanshall and J.R. Hartley.

'It was Whisted wasn't it?' I asked, 'He was online on one of those messenger thingamajigs, telling you what to say. How to hypnotise me.'

'I didn't hypnotise you Mostyn, I activated you.'

'Oh my word!'

'He is not well, Mostyn,' she said, suddenly serious, 'he feels he owes you a debt. He is most anxious to set things straight. There might not have been another chance.'

A possibility occurred to me, 'Do you love him Trinity?'

She paused, weighing her response, 'Not in the way you mean.'

'Now, I know that I have asked this of you before Trinity,' I ventured stifling an unexpected yawn,' and whilst I am deeply sensible that this is the sort of question one normally asks at the very beginning of an acquaintance and all that, erm.'

'Who actually am I?'

'Who actually are you?'

'I am just somebody that Bertrand Whisted met whilst walking one afternoon in the mountains near Westerndorf in Austria.' she replied 'I was waiting for the wind to pick up. He introduced himself and asked me why I liked to fly a paraglider. I just laughed and told him that I was always asking myself that same question. So he told me the answer.'

'Ah righto,' I murmured, crept into my swag and slipped away into the most sublime slumber.

17 SEEING AND NOTHINGNESS

'When men stop believing in God, it isn't that they then believe in nothing: they believe in everything.'

Umberto Eco.

'Many a man has fallen in love with a girl in light so dim he would not have chosen a suit by it.' observed Maurice Chevalier, crooner, philosopher and the owner of a really first class nose. And as it is with love, so it is with the even bigger emotional commitment that people make in their lives. Their alignment to a world view. A paradigm. An ideology. A weltenschauung. A philosophy. A belief system.

Of course, few people settle down and raise a family with their first love, and likewise, by thirty years of age, few of us see the world as we did at seventeen. Our perspective broadens, certainties seem suddenly uncertain, our consciousness of our own subjectivity increases.

A bit.

But love is blind and in the main, when people form an attachment to an idea or a set of ideas, be it Christianity or scientific rationalism, they tend thenceforth to be oblivious to its shortcomings.

Consider this statement:

'Our soups are made with completely natural ingredients, unlike processed foods which contain added, synthetic chemicals, many of which have been proven to be toxic.' The belief that this positive compost heap of misinformation is seeking cynically to exploit, is the visceral rejection of scientific clever-dickery in favour of that thing called 'nature'. Now let me be the first to concede that processed foods do indeed contain added chemicals. This is because everything ultimately is made from chemicals. And the difference between a natural ingredient and an 'added, synthetic chemical' is like the difference between a mole, and a cancer. One of them sounds a lot scarier than the other but they might actually refer to precisely the same thing. Chemicals are compounds of elements and any atom of an element is identical to any other, whether it is found in a fresh summer meadow or an aerosol air-freshener designed to smell like one.

Ditto it is true that processed foods contain *toxic* chemicals - and are none the worse for it. For instance -

at this precise moment I am typing these words on a state-of-the-art, titanium, portable computer that I bought just an hour ago in the first class lounge at Schipol airport. I am seated at a café table in Frans Halsstraat in Amsterdam. And I am cheerfully munching on a rather splendid quail's liver pate, whilst fully in the knowledge that it is positively awash with toxic chemicals. Should I be concerned that my breakfast contains, sodium, a highly reactive and toxic metal? Ought I to fret that it also laced with chlorine, an agent used to gas soldiers in trench warfare? No, not especially, because fortunately these vile poisons have chemically combined to produce the compound, sodium chloride or table salt, which is as natural a substance as there is.

Soup, on the other hand, is not a naturally occurring substance. Soup is a processed food because soup-making is a process. In the malign logic of marketing spin it would be entirely reasonable therefore, to declaim soup as a synthetic processed food, composed of chemicals, and promote salt as a natural wholesome nutrient, vital to a healthy, happy life. Such is the nature of semantics.

Now I'm not saying that you would be better off eating junk food every day than something genuinely fresh and nutritious. Merely that rather a lot of things have sneaked into this second group which more properly belong in the first. And it goes a lot further than junk food posing as additive free nourishment. I have met people who would never even contemplate popping an aspirin on the grounds that it is a 'chemical' but who claim that smoking marijuana is harmless as it is an 'organic herb'. This is junk ideology posing as radical free thinking. The reality of course is that any form of smoking is un-natural and enormously deleterious to health, whereas aspirin is the refined and purified version of an age old natural remedy extracted from the bark of the white willow tree.

All of which wouldn't be that big a deal except that, like Sodium and Chlorine - credulity and alienation, when present in the same individual, also tend to combine to produce something which, like table salt, is pretty benign and can be put to a variety of uses. They produce a certain kind of mindset which will eagerly grasp at any notion as long as it isn't too orthodox. As a result, in instinctively shying away from the scientific and religious establishments, the credulous chap often uncritically places his confidence in people whose agenda is really very dubious indeed. People who understand that the manner in which an idea is presented is more important to its success than what it consists of. People who would claim to know more about him, than he knows himself.

To choose an example completely at random: most hypnotherapists will tell you, in that airy way that they have, that everything we see, hear or otherwise experience, is recorded and locked away deep within our minds. Naturally they cannot actually prove this, but they don't have to. They leave that type of sophistry to the scientists. It's just something that they happen to know. When asked to substantiate their claim, they tend to point to the cases in their experience in which buried memories have been teased out from the minds of their patients or initiates over the years. Ask to see instances of such retrievals which have been properly verified and they will favour you with a little smile which speaks eloquently of the gulf in understanding between you. The smile begins by saying 'if you'd seen what I've seen, you wouldn't doubt what I am telling you.' It then takes on a half-pitying, slightly condescending quality and adds in a half whisper 'but I will indulge your need to doubt everything, because I can see that you are threatened to the point of hostility by my freedom from the stiflingly rational mental incarceration in which you languish.'

Of course the freedom from the burden of evidence that would satisfy reason is no inconsiderable freedom to enjoy. It is the freedom to make unsupportable statements as though they were facts that brook no dispute. No less, in fact, than the freedom from accountability generally. An enviable freedom indeed then. Although, on balance, probably not one that you would want to extend to your mortgage advisor or your neurosurgeon.

So let's examine the basis on which they make this particular claim. In the 1950s a rash of sensational cases of past life regression appeared in the popular press.

People were suddenly assuming, under hypnosis, an entirely different identity, usually of somebody living long in the past.

With its implications of reincarnation, the phenomenon was hugely seductive to an emerging new mindset of secular spirituality. It has also been widely interpreted as suggesting that within the subconscious hard-drive of the brain, a full bandwidth recording of our sensory data streams is filed away to be retrieved by the skilful hypnotherapist. This idea appeals on a number of levels. Firstly it would seem to offer the potential to unlock the early life traumas which we quietly suspect have propagated our low self esteem and caused our relationships to fail. Secondly it provides an iceberg-like model of the human mind in which the greater part is assumed to lie below the surface. A beguiling vanity in which the truly self-involved can but indulge.

The trouble is that in the fullness of time, each and every case of p.l.r has been comprehensively debunked and displaced by a new syndrome with a new acronym. False memory syndrome. The stories simply didn't check out. As more and more cases came to light, it became unavoidably clear that patients were constructing their past-life identities from scraps and fragments of data and offering them up as memories for the simple reason that their hypnotherapist had, wittingly or otherwise, suggested that they do so.

The best guess amongst neurologists, meanwhile, is that the human capability for recall, differs pretty drastically from the simplistic computer analogy in which an exact clone of every frame of our visual experience is stored in the memory as though in a folder called 'my pictures'. Sophisticated experiments with memory seem to suggest that we remember having seen something rather than remember seeing it. We do not re-experience the situation, rather we consult our notes. We trust ourselves (If I say I saw it then that's good enough for me). It would appear too, that a memory will change considerably over time and is strongly subject to suggestion. When two witnesses to the same event discuss their impressions, for instance, they will dramatically adjust their own versions to produce a hybrid on which they can both agree.

But perhaps the most compelling reason to doubt the 'my pictures' fallacy is that it fails the 'Why?' Test. Evolution is very keen on efficiency. It doesn't equip wind pollinated plants with colourful petals because this uses energy and since they don't need to attract insects it would be wasteful to do so. Nature doesn't give humans the physical strength of our primate relatives because we live by our wits and do not need to branchiate hand over hand through the forest canopy. So why would it lash out on a memory equipped to record everything that we see hear and think? The hunter-gatherer lifestyle for which the brain evolved has no need of such a facility. It would be like fitting an estate agent with a soul.

We know that the eye discards most of what it sees and most neurologists believe that the brain also discards the overwhelming majority of the data that streams into it throughout our lives. But what would those losers know? They waste their time painstakingly establishing strict methodologies for eliminating error in the study of such things. They pointlessly compile detailed data to determine, empirically, whether the effect they are looking for exists and how great it is. Why! such poops are simply obsessed with patiently and systematically sifting the evidence before forming their hypotheses and even then they insist on testing and re-testing them on large samples of individuals in double blind trials before drawing their conclusions. If only they realised, like the hypnotherapists, that all you need is a bit of selective anecdotal evidence and a sense that it would be just so wonderful if it were true.

Of course none of this disproves the hypnotherapists' glib claim that 'it's all in there waiting to be unlocked'. Such a theory is, by its very nature, all but un-falsifiable. Merely demonstrating that subjects under hypnosis lie and invent, doesn't prove that the information isn't actually there. Only that there are no grounds to state dogmatically that it is.

And what of it? You ask.

Is this strictly germane? You enquire.

Is it entirely wise? You wonder, to plunge, once again, into meandering bromide on the nature of things and risk disrupting the flow of a narrative that is nothing short of a dramatic roller coaster? And the point is well taken. It's just that in one situation in particular, it *would* be just so wonderful to know for certain that the mind has, at least in principle, a bit-perfect facsimile of our entire sensory experience contained within it?

The scenario to be imagined, is as follows: Suppose that a man stood accused of a terrible act. The taking of a human life, no less. And the verdict hinged upon your testimony as an eye-witness. Would it not then be of the greatest imaginable comfort to you, to know that the mental photograph of the scene which you were inwardly perusing, was an actual, captured, digital still image. A binary artefact, unchanged since the moment that you apprehended it. To know that it was not merely a set of rough notes, hastily taken from an impression which melted long ago under the glare of scrutiny, and much modified since? Knowing that a mistake or an assumption on your part would have the direst consequences. That a man will be judged on the strength of just one frozen moment in time, lodged at some neural address, deep within your brain.

That, at any rate, is why it is so very important to me.

18 THE ACADEMY

' The dreadful martyrdom must run it's course.'
W H Auden 'The fall of Icarus.'

I awoke with the sun, my stiff body moving slowly at first like the pair of goannas basking on the bare rock nearby. The marginally less battered of the two creatures was eyeing me in a slightly freakish way and they reminded me of another pair of Australians I knew who liked to sit in the sun all day gazing into space. I duly dubbed them Les and Derek.

Trinity was already up and about, slicing a Guava into sections with a machete. Blearily I squinted about the immediate environs.

'The Lyceum you say?' I croaked.

'This is where we lived for the first year,' she said, not looking up from her task. 'Until there were too many of us. Now it serves as a stepping stone, a half way house.'

'Half way to where?'

She scanned the horizon to the West for a few moments, shielding her eyes with her hand, and then pointed.

'There,' she said at length. I looked and could just divine a distant shape, 'the Academy.' She added.

I dressed, rigged, slapped on some sunscreen, fished out the specs from the tubular receptacle serving as their container this week and parked them on the schnozz. By nine o'clock we were in the air heading West.

It was a stronger, more thermic, and altogether more boisterous day. The buoyant air, heaving like the swell of an invisible sea. There was a gentle headwind, which became rather stronger as we approached cloud-base. So we confined ourselves to the strong middle section of the thermals, hitting full speed-bar on the glides, until the speck on the horizon crept within glide.

If the Lyceum was an eminence, then the Academy was a monolith. An immense column of rock erupting vertically from the desert, unassailable except by air.

As we glided in, I began to make out more detail. There was a village of dome tents which rather resembled a herd of outsized grazing armadillos, also a large cultivated kitchen garden, and people. Dozens and dozens of people.

Landing in the middle of the day was always going to be rough. I hit some lift at the last moment and had to make another pass but I nailed it at the second attempt. A few fellows, each of them with closely cropped hair, rushed forwards to our assistance. Willing hands subdued my thrashing glider and bunched it up into a heap for me whilst I unclipped.

'Thanks awfully.' I beamed at the chap who passed me a most welcome bottle of mineral water. Cold too.

'Not at all.' He breezed.

They were a likable bunch, mostly young men, all of them apparently habitués of the same hairdresser and each with the look in their eyes common to many of the people I had approached in the street over the previous five years. These were people with a deep and abiding faith.

I was gently ushered through the village of tents, past a satellite dish, a wind-generator, a rain catcher, some solar panels. Through the vegetable garden and towards the rock strewn higher ground to the north of the plateau.

At the very Northernmost edge of the promontory, seated in splendid isolation upon the largest and most commodious rock, his face in profile, silhouetted against the sky, his entire demeanour a study of meditative reflection, was an old man.

If, as Trinity had suggested, he was anxious in any way, then it certainly didn't show.

As I approached, squinting at the sun I could nevertheless see that he had aged considerably. And badly. His sun ravaged skin was deeply lined, the jaunty foppishness for which his hair had been notable, had deserted it entirely.

'You Sir, are a difficult person, up with whom to catch.' I opened.

'Then you sir, are doubtless a person impelled by a powerful sense of purpose.' Whisted reasoned. Correctly as it happened. He continued gazing off into the distance. 'Am I to assume then, that you require me to justify myself Nigel? Or rather It's Mostyn now isn't it?' he enquired at length, in a tone that suggested that this prospect rather drained him of his will to live.

'It is. And I do.' I replied 'And with good reason I should say!'

Turning to look at me for the first time he arranged his features in such a way as to convey a sense that he recognised this point of view, but personally he was inclined in an altogether different direction. The kind of face an adult will sometimes pull when a teenager proposes abolishing the monarchy, or that all rich people are greedy.

I stopped a few feet away from him, standing with my arms folded and an air of petulance. Whisted's followers gathered around us many of them placing their glider bags on the ground as a seat, forming a simple amphitheatre. Trinity placed one for me, and I sat.

Having anticipated this moment for months I found to my frustration that I didn't know quite how to start.

'Look here Whisted!' I blustered 'we trusted you with our lives and you deceived us monstrously.'

'I did deceive you it is true.' He replied. 'But we did increase the sum of human understanding.'

He wasn't one to weasel out of things you had to give him that.

'And that justifies the sacrifice of eleven human lives?'

'Eleven human lives?' he said mildly as though eleven thousand would have been no impediment, 'Of course it does. How many human lives are sacrificed daily in laboratories in the pursuit of scientific progress?'

'Oh yes quite.' I retorted sarcastically 'That's absolutely the same thing isn't it?'

'Fertilized embryos are genetically human and biologically alive hence they are human lives.'

'It's completely different Whisted. They don't have the option of a normal life they cannot survive without support.'

'Nor can a three year old child.'

'For heaven's sake why are we even talking about this?' I demanded, my dander well and truly inflated. 'I haven't travelled to the end of the earth to be fobbed off with sophistry.'

'Because in judging me for placing your lives at hazard you choose not to acknowledge that you yourself do not hold human life to be sacred.'

'I don't?' I spluttered incredulously, the emphasis very much on the 'I'.

'You have just conceded as much but I shall amplify.' He took a few puffs on his pipe, 'There is a scenario to be imagined.' He began. Here we go I thought, 'A runaway train' he said, 'laden with, say, radioactive nuclear waste. Racing down the track towards a city centre terminus. If the train isn't prevented from crashing, then the resulting catastrophe will devastate a city at the cost of a million lives. You can however divert the train into a siding but a small child is playing there.'

To my irritation I found that I almost couldn't prevent myself from visualising this frightful impasse rather vividly.

'Do you pull the lever?'

'Of course. The needs of the many outweigh the needs of the few.'

'Well Mostyn, if you considered human life to be sacred you would be unable to perform an act which would lead to the death of a human, whatever the circumstances may be. That is the nature of an absolute belief it is not negotiable there are no exceptions.

In pulling the lever, however justified you may consider yourself to be, you are by implication offering up the child as a sacrifice. Placing a subordinate value upon its life. Once you cross that line, you disqualify yourself, now and forever, from holding the position that human life is sacred.'

'Alright,' I said, 'not sacred maybe but infinitely precious.'

'Take care with the word infinity Mostyn. If a human life is of infinite value, then the loss of the child's life is equivalent to that of the population of the city. A million times infinity is still infinity.'

'Good grief!' I ejaculated in exasperation. 'Alright, not infinitely valuable, merely,' I groped vainly for the word I wanted but had to settle for, 'very valuable.'

'Which is as relative as to be entirely meaningless.'

I sighed.

'As a declared utilitarian,' he continued, 'you will accept that the right course of action, is that which produces the greatest balance of happiness over unhappiness.'

I hastened to rebut this slur.

'As ever, I am delighted for you to tell me your views Whisted but kindly do not presume to tell me mine.' I said archly, 'I am not an adherent to any school or tradition I have my own ideas.'

'Name one.' He said without a moment's hesitation.

'I beg your pardon?'

'Name one idea that you consider your own, and I will tell you who said it first.' He said flatly. 'In fact if you can name one idea that cannot readily be fitted into the pantheon of thought, accumulated throughout history. One insight however minor that is truly, genuinely yours, then I shall willingly accept the blame for the deaths of the others.'

A yawning silence opened up. There was of course nothing I could say.

'It falls to very few people to contribute in this way.' he said in answer to my silence. He fixed me with a long look until his words found their mark. Until I realised that he was referring to himself.

'Mostyn, you are better placed than most to appreciate the overwhelming lack of genuine individuality in the human mind. It isn't pleasant to be told what ones beliefs are but if you coyly refuse to state your position in the hope of evading its internal contradictions, then it shall be done for you.

Since you were morally able to sacrifice the life of the unfortunate child in the runaway train scenario,' he went on, rising to his theme, 'you are clearly not an adherent to any absolute moral position such as 'thou shalt not kill'. You have conceded that life is negotiable and that lives are, in principle, interchangeable, can be weighed one against the other. This is utilitarianism, a relativist philosophy which, in practice, almost everybody exercises but to which very few people are willing to nail their colours because, as in the case of the child on the railway track, it throws up some pretty unsavoury consequences.'

Feeling thoroughly stung, I resolved to hear him out and my face said as much. Whisted re-lit his pipe before continuing.

'The utilitarian is obliged to evaluate an action, say, invading a country with a totalitarian regime, on the basis of its likely consequences. Will the benefits that accrue to all concerned, outweigh the combat deaths and civilian casualties which will almost certainly be incurred? If so then he is not only justified but actually morally obliged to support the invasion.'

'That doesn't amount to a mandate for unlimited unilateral action.' I protested.

'It empowers the individual to act according to his convictions if he believes it will lead to the greater balance of happiness over unhappiness.'

'So what greater happiness has arisen from the deaths that you allowed to occur?'

'True happiness is impossible without freedom Mostyn. And historically freedom has usually been won at a cost. The struggle for civil rights comes to mind in this regard,' He added, 'and freedom from the shackles of the biologically determined consciousness with which evolution has endowed the normal human mind, is a liberation, the potential of which could scarcely be exaggerated. The aim of the exercise was to free you from yourself. From the animal that you are.'

'But that's not what Annecy was supposed to be about.' I spluttered. 'It was meant to be an evaluation of hypnosis during flight as a tool for addressing dislocation. We had a programme of testing and research. Proper, respectable, scientific, research, leading to quantifiable results. Actual, measurable, empirical evidence. What was wrong with the plan?'

'That was never the plan Mostyn.' He said calmly. 'Correct me if I am wrong,' he continued, 'but is it not respectable scientific practice in human trials, for the subject to be, as far as possible, unaware of the nature of the experiment being carried out upon them?'

'Yes of course.'

'So a little deception was necessary to ensure that the experiment was a success.'

'A success? Given that the outcome at Annecy was a ninety percent casualty rate, how exactly was that a success?'

'The experiment proved that the subconscious can be confronted and subordinated.'

'It did?'

'You know it did Mostyn. Before Annecy you had only the dimmest awareness of your subconscious mind. Since that time you have become intimately acquainted with it and gained mastery over it to boot.'

'Even supposing I accept that, which I don't, the point stands that when a utilitarian evaluates a course of action, he must favour alternative ways of bringing about the same end with less risk. Nobody had to die.'

'As I believe I told you once before Mostyn. My technique absolutely hinges on the element of extreme physical danger, to coax out the inner man. It also requires a context of inescapable and blatant symbolism. Only in this way can a subject of the trickster type, silence their inner monologue and allow their subconscious to express itself.' He took a couple of puffs on his pipe, 'I dare say there are alternative ways of bringing about the same end. But at less risk? Probably not.'

That I was far from persuaded of this, must have been writ large upon my face as, barely pausing for breath, Whisted plunged into the following exegesis.

'The brain,' he began, and his voice had never sounded more donnish, 'like the body, of any creature whose survival strategy depends on activities such as hunting and fighting, is necessarily equipped to offer its greatest functional potential in circumstances of urgent and mortal need.

Faced with it's almost certain annihilation the brain is willing to offer any sanction. It will enthusiastically grant access to any mental resource, the implementation of which may deliver it from peril. Even those areas of function that are strictly off limits to the consciousness, the firmware of the brain, can be modified if the mind is sufficiently convinced that it has nothing to lose. This re-calibration is implemented by a part of the brain called the Amygdala. The fear centre. It is responsible for allocating the brain's resources, sidelining less critical considerations, to optimise it for the task in hand.

To a limited extent this mechanism can be accessed during surrogate activities such as flying, in which the competitor feels hyper alive as his body and mind enter a state that was originally evolved to present the best response to combat, or to a hunt upon which the individuals survival might depend. This state is called 'the zone'.

Flying involves the smooth co-ordination of several areas of the brain. The cerebellum monitors the orientation of your body, the position of your hands, your centre of gravity. The putamen contains the flying skills that you have accumulated through practice, the hippocampus helps with the ones that you must improvise. The motor areas instruct the actual muscle movements allowing the frontal cortex to think about the bigger picture. It is by not thinking about what you are doing that you enter 'the zone'

And the margin by which the level of function available to the brain in 'the zone', exceeds the pedestrian ontology of everyday mental life, is precisely the margin by which you were able to surmount the illusory barrier between your conscious mind and your almost limitless biological mental potential. During the Annecy experiment, your actions in the face of death showed extraordinary bravery and resourcefulness, and thus you liberated yourself from your narrow minded, self imposed limitations.'

It had to be said, that just at present I didn't feel very limitless.

'The beauty of the thing Mostyn, is that in the course of normal life the brain can consent to this, on the basis that when the adrenaline levels have returned to normal and the dust has died down, the conscious mind will have long forgotten that, for a critical moment, it was the mind of a god. The focus of my technique though, is to capture that moment. And make it permanent.'

This was the part with which I had a problem.

'But I don't have the mind of a god.' I pointed out.

'But you can Mostyn. The fundamental changes have been made. It's just a matter of training, discipline and the interpretative role of the therapist.'

'So presumably you would you claim to have brought about this transformation on your own mind?'

'Physically my brain is practically identical to everyone else's. The difference being that I have unrestricted access to all of its many and considerable resources.'

'Prove it.'

'Very well Mostyn,' he smiled, 'I invite you to devise a test which would satisfy you that, by an effort of conscious will, I can indeed re-calibrate my brain. A task that you know for a fact is physically possible but effectively impossible at the first attempt for someone with a normal mind. But' he raised a cautionary finger, 'let me first go on record as saying, that any task you devise to exclude the possibility that what I say is true, you will subsequently conclude was susceptible to error.'

This was all sounding a bit messianic to me and I decided to call his bluff. I perused the various objects scattered about the area, there was a machete, a small solar powered fridge filled with ice and fruit, and rather incongruously there was a little yellow stylophone. I rummaged about for one or two items in my Reebok attaché case (Vlad the Impala?) and in Trinity's too. Whisted regarded me wryly.

Eventually, and in a rush, a course of action occurred to me. With clumsy haste of a child, I concocted an exercise the successful completion of which, the normal human mind would be utterly incapable. A dauntingly difficult feat only possible once its arcane mechanics had been patiently explained and it's demanding technical proficiencies, painstakingly acquired. I assembled my apparatus out of Whisted's view, I explained the task to him, applied the blindfold, installed the handcuffs and then I whisked away my heat reflective survival blanket with a conjuror's flourish, whilst turning over the oversized egg timer.

Two, jaw-dropping minutes later, Whisted sat sipping a freshly shaken, ice-cold pineapple Daiquiri as the strains of 'Hey Jude,' reverberated yet about the rocks.

All those there present were much amazed.

Evidently the fellow could, just as he claimed, tweak the generalised settings of a mind configured for a prehistoric existence and optimise it for a single specialised purpose. He could enter the zone at will.

He was the uberman.

Not to mention the uber-barman.

'Alright, but finding a way to hack into the mind is just the start,' I protested weakly, 'you can't go fiddling with the interior of the subconscious just because you are able to. You'll send people barking mad.'

'That, Mostyn, is just the sort of feeble minded piffle with which the pioneers of conventional neuro-surgery had to contend.' Retorted Whisted, whilst removing the blindfold and slipping off the furry handcuffs, 'No good will come of it you mark my words.' He added in an exaggerated parody of the accent of a West Country churl and in doing so elicited a few sycophantic titters from amongst the assembled. 'Look here Mostyn, a person with a normally configured mind is little better than an animal. Yes the influences of his modular organic brain are more subtle and complex, mediated by experience and the needs and injunctions of wider society but he is nevertheless in essence merely an instinct-driven, higher primate, slavishly serving his primal evolutionary drives in pursuit of those elusive states of brain chemistry that correspond to happiness, contentment, fulfilment and pleasure. States, his brain will only grant to him as a reward for successfully advancing the chances for survival of his genes.' He was into his stride now.

'Supposing he identifies and attracts a female with compatible d.n.a.' Whisted ploughed on 'his brain rewards him by doping him up with chemicals. Pleasant and addictive chemicals. It's called falling in love.

If he mates with her, he experiences the incentive of intense physical pleasure. But actually the pleasure is in his brain, the sex is in his brain. His own subconscious brain is bribing his conscious with drugs. Incentivising him to propagate his genes.

This is not the life man is destined to lead Mostyn. To be controlled by the prehistoric survival agenda of his biology. If man is to continue ad infinitum obediently and unwittingly enacting the elaborate pantomime that is no more than our expression of the simple animal lusts common to all species, then how can we reasonably draw a distinction between us and them? Man must shrug off his bestial legacy and take control of his destiny at any cost. A new man must emerge from the husk of the old. A self- determined, rational man, the master of his own psyche, endowed with genuine freewill. The man that shall surpass man. It is his destiny. His nature.'

'Is that Nature, Whisted? Or Nietzsche?' I enquired tartly.

'The higher we soar, the smaller we seem to those who cannot fly.' Replied Whisted. 'That, is Nietzsche.'

'Hold on a mo, I countered, struggling to marshal my thoughts, I can just about accept the idea that all human behaviour is informed by their primal drives for food sex and shelter but what can you put in place of that? What can you do without creating robots of whose programming you are the author? You cannot cast yourself in the role of God unless you have something to offer people, better than the urge to breed and survive.'

'I can offer them free will, self-determination, freedom from the obsolete imperatives of animal survival.' He reiterated patiently. 'Imagine the liberating potential this offers to mankind.'

He was really playing to the gallery now.

'Consider how easily the instinct of the male to protect his family with aggression, has been co-opted by the powerful and put into service to fight their wars since the beginning of time. Can you imagine a world populated by women co-operating with this? The uberman whose behaviour is driven by reason would never be duped in this way, since he would be fully capable of subordinating his instincts.'

This sentiment met with considerable approval from all quarters.

'Consider the relations between the sexes.' He added 'Rows of mediocre specimens of masculinity toiling away in gymnasia, striving to acquire the physical attributes of the alpha-male, to whom the females he desires are genetically programmed to respond, and whom he can never be. Whose interests are served by such a system? Surely not the average person whose natural birthright of sexuality is commodified, synthesised and then sold back to him through the media as an unattainable fantasy.'

Again his point produced a general stir of assent, eliciting murmurs of 'quite right' and 'well said'. It was difficult not to notice however, that among the assembled throng, the alpha male type was not precisely over- represented. In fact from where I was sitting there was only one disciple who might realistically have attracted such a description.

What we are doing here,' He continued indicating the sea of rapt faces around us, 'is preparing suitable young minds to transcend their biological programming. The surrogated impulse that brings them to paragliding, brings them in turn to me. They come here looking to foreswear their animal legacy and to gain mastery over their mental life.

They study the hierarchy of inborn human needs, most eminent amongst which is self-actualization, learn the role of the peak experience in achieving this, and the importance of ritual and discipline. Then it is their turn to face the initiation as you did. To seize control of their potential in the face of death.

'Good grief, you don't mean you are doing that still?' I gasped incredulously, 'That folly! How many more have you killed?'

'We have had disappointments.' He tapped out his pipe on the sole of his flying boot and placed it with infinite care within a fissure in the rock, 'but no fatalities.'

'Well I like that Whisted!' I blurted, insensed with indignation.

'Have you met Quentin by the way?' he interrupted mildly, indicating a fellow seated a little way distant from me, perched on a glider bag and failing to run around, like a chicken with its head still on. It was the young man to whom I referred just now in connection with alpha maleness and he was smiling in a way that rang a distant bell. He looked a little different with his closely cropped hair but his handsome countenance was still endowed with sufficient cragginess to support a colony of seagulls. It was the electrician from Rouen.

'Holy moley!' I cried, springing to my feet, 'Serge, Is that you?'

'Whato Mostyn,' pipped the Frenchman, approaching with hand outstretched, I shook my head in disbelief as he wrung my paw, 'except it's Quentin these days.' He added in a clipped and plummy accent.

'What about the others, Mike and Neil and...'

'Absolutely tip top young bean,' came a voice from behind me. I turned to see the Lanky frame of Alexander, the osteopath from Hamburg, ankling across to where I stood. This was all most unexpected.

'Alexander!'

'Hugo if you would be so kind.' he smiled. One by one I spotted other members of the original line up too. Hidden in plain view. 'We are all here,' said Alexander ne. Hugo, vigorously pumping my hand, 'oh except for Zane. He crash landed into the Coonabarabran sewage treatment works a couple of years ago and drowned in a most unfortunate manner. Apparently the poor fellow choked to death on a...'

'Yes!' Whisted's tone brought Alexander up short.

I erupted into a fit of uncontrollable giggles. 'Thank you Hugo.' sighed Whisted. When I'd got my shadenfreuder under control, I turned to address him once more 'But Whisted, you told me...'

'Ah ah.' He held up a finger to silence me.

'Alright you led me to believe they were all dead.' Suddenly I was smiling with the dissipation of latent anger that I hadn't realised was there, and I wanted to sit down again.

'You allowed yourself believe it Mostyn.' Whisted soothed, 'I never said any such thing.'

'But you confirmed it.' I cried indignantly.

'I merely said that the breakthrough that we made in Annecy was worth the price of eleven human lives. It was the authorities who told you that that was what it had cost. Each of the other pilots survived their initiation unharmed, as you did, and one by one each of them slipped away and sought me out, to become the first generation of our movement. Only you remained sceptical.' He added, 'And now you too have returned to us.'

'Actually,' Mike Stands chipped in, 'I did get a shocking nosebleed, worse luck.

'Yes, and I was knocked absolutely silly for about half an hour.' Added Neil O'Gism ruefully. There really was no trace of his broad Irish brogue.

'But surely,' I said, struggling to formulate my thoughts, 'why would Special Branch...'

'Why would Special Branch, the government's agency for the suppression of subversion and insurgency, wish you to believe that I was a dangerous maniac?'

'Actually, when you put it like that I suppose.' I tailed off weakly.

'They have been looking for me for some time you see.' He said, 'They mean to stop me. They even sent an agent, an assassin to kill me.'

Abruptly there was a shocked silence. It wasn't only me to whom this was news.

'Oh Lordy!' I gulped, 'What happened?'

A suddenly change seemed to have overcome the man, 'It seems he was successful.' Whisted sighed.

After clambering muddy and breathless onto the shore of understanding, I felt myself slithering once more into the murky swamp of incomprehension.

'Erm, at the risk of seeming a bit dense.' I ventured, 'For an assassin to be truly successful, wouldn't he have to actually pop somebody off?' But no one was listening to me any longer. Whisted had turned to urgently address Serge who, it was evident, had become his lieutenant.

'Quentin old thing,' said he, grasping the Frenchman's sleeve, and looking distinctly stricken now, 'He must not be blamed. It is not his fault. He is merely the unwitting dupe of those who stand to lose everything by our philosophy.' Serge looked at me in a way that dispelled any doubt I might have had about the identity of the mystery dupe to whom he referred. The unwitting cove, whose fault, whatever it was, wasn't.

'Promise me.' Gasped Whisted.

But even as Serge turned back to face him, the old man's silver head was lolling drunkenly to one side. A thread of saliva trailing from his mouth.

He was in fact, quite dead.

A low moan escaped Serge's lips as, with great reverence, he lowered Whisted's frail form to the ground. It was more than clear from his face that he approved of this development not one jot.

The assembled too, were clearly as rattled as a woodpecker's eyeballs, giving voice to manifold explosions of dismay.

Serge snatched up the silver cocktail shaker and examined it with a fever. The thing was made in three parts, the cap, which sat on the ground nearby, the top half, which featured a built in strainer by means of which the contents were decanted, and the bottom half which sported an execrable engraving of Frank Sinatra in a tuxedo.

His hands trembling with desperate emotion, Serge separated the two halves and sloshed the contents onto the worn smooth, slightly dished surface of Whisted's recently vacated sitting rock. Clearly visible amongst the fast melting pebbles of ice were the broken glass pieces of the vial that had contained the poison.

The vial that had smashed amongst the ice whilst Whisted had shaken the pineapple daiquiri with his feet, whilst playing the left handed part of 'Hey Jude' on the stylophone.

'Where' Serge thundered 'did you get this?' His manner strongly suggested that a straight and unequivocal answer would be appreciated at this point.

'My cocktail shaker?' I replied, 'Why, Zanzibar I think it was. I won it in a game of cigar cutter roulette a few days ago.' Serge clapped his hand to his brow in a gesture of acute dejection. 'I was asking around in the hopes of hearing tell of Whisted's whereabouts,' I babbled, 'and I sort of fell into conversation with this chap you see.'

Serge moved over to where I was standing until his face was very close to mine. He looked searchingly into my eyes for a long moment.

'Mostyn this is very important.' He said. Rather unnecessarily I thought but I let it go. 'Was this man an Eastern looking fellow with an Italian accent?'

'Well I'm blessed, you're absolutely right. A Chinese gondolier. Name of Leonardo Ping if memory serves. He demonstrated the pineapple daiquiri trick in the piano bar of the Zanzibar Hilton. It takes simply ages to learn apparently, so I thought it would be the perfect...'

'Blast!' Serge groaned and turned away.

'Harold Chen.' Said Alexander ruefully.

'Commander Harold Chen.' Said Serge, 'Special Branch.' I was beginning to experience the worrying feeling that I might have done something spectacularly stupid. 'Whisted, Hugo and I were in Zanzibar two weeks ago, recruiting new members from amongst the pilots on the island.' He added.

'Harold Chen tried to infiltrate the group using the alias, Leonardo Ping,' continued Alexander, 'Whisted took him flying in the mountains but he was able to see through the chap and he cast him out. Chen must have fastened the vial to the inside of the cocktail shaker, gambling that you wouldn't look inside.

'No no.' I objected 'how could he know I'd ask Whisted to do the trick?'

'Because, old friend, people like you always have to witness a miracle at first hand.' He said sadly 'Chen knew that Whisted would invite you set a test of which the normal human mind would be totally incapable. As he always did to those who are incapable of faith.'

It must be said, I did feel a bit of a clot. And also a little annoyed with myself for falling for the pitch of a character who, with the benefit of hindsight, was perhaps not really so very plausible after all. Certainly the next time that I ran into a Chinese gondolier in Africa, It would be difficult to maintain an open mind.

Now I don't know if you have ever found yourself on the top of a huge rock in the middle of a desert, being gaped at in incredulous disbelief by a hundred profoundly devout cult members, each of whom is struggling to come to terms with the fact that you have apparently just ruthlessly slain their founding father. On the balance of probability, I would imagine not. In which case let me advise you that the experience is apt to bring on a certain sense of self-consciousness. There really is no way to live it down.

In struggling to affect an air of suitable gravity, I cast my eyes around the scene as though for inspiration. Gradually becoming aware as I did so, that beyond Serge and the rock around which Whisted's disciples clustered in their anguish, beyond the fireplace and the solar powered fridge and the little village of tents, a slim, figure, immaculately dressed in black, stood patiently waiting. He was holding my flying harness in his white gloved hands, proffering the shoulder straps in readiness to receive my arms, rather as though they were the sleeves of, for instance, a purple paisley smoking jacket.

18 THE ACADEMY

'Man is a credulous animal and must believe something. In the absence of good grounds for belief, he will be satisfied with bad ones.'

Bertrand Russell.

Actually, under the circs, the brethren of Whisted's holy order were pretty decent about the whole sorry business of their founder's annihilation at my hands. Indeed Serge, stoic and wearing the look of a man whose moment had arrived, even made a show of trying to persuade me to join them and play my part in the 'mind revolution'.

And a part of me actually rather fancied the idea too. To dwell amongst these happy folk, to embrace their rarefied monastic ways, would be for the first time in my life to be something other than a misfit.

In fact, short of living in a penthouse in Amsterdam in a ménage a trios with the Swedish ladies Olympic beach-volleyball team, I could think of no lifestyle more seductive than one of ascetic skybummery. It is a really first rate existence, splendidly in tune with the rhythms of nature. Its emphasis is on hope and optimism and the cultivation of a meditative and contemplative cast of mind.

Ultimately though, it seemed to me, that to have had the arsewitted heel who was responsible for accidentally slaughtering the movement's spiritual leader, cluttering up the place as a permanent reminder of the tragedy, would have been in the most monstrously poor taste. I suspected that secretly everybody was rather hoping that I would simply hoof off. Having arrived out of the blue, it seemed that I was fated to leave under a cloud.

Besides which, the spectacle of a hundred men and women languishing in the thrall of their charismatic guru, to the point of affecting his speech and mannerisms, losing their identity to his, had told me everything I needed to know. Had put into perspective the extent of the self knowledge that Whisted was offering.

But, as reported, there was definitely a part of me that wanted to stay. Wanted to believe. A part of me in fact that would prefer to be happy, than to be right. It was the more instinctive, intuitive, elemental part of me which had been surgically spliced from the architecture of my personality by Whisted's psychological scalpel and which, having nowhere else to go, had thereafter always loitered in close attendance like a disembodied ghost.

'Whato Reeves,' I pipped, having ankled my way through the throng of near hysterical mourners and at length reached the South face of the promontory. 'probably best if we biff off now old tadpole, while the biffing's good eh?'

'I figure I'll stick around a while.' He rasped.

'What's that Reeves?' I boggled, 'For a giddy moment there I could have sworn you just announced that you were staying put.'

'Ah, I reckon I'll dig in here at the Academy if it's all the same to you.' He declared airily as he fastened my chest strap.

'Good gracious Reeves. You don't mean to tell me that you set some store in all of that piffle?'

He paused in mid-buckle.

'Dude.' he said, dealing me a look that contained a distinctly worrying dose of peace, serenity and inner spiritual conviction. 'What would it actually take, to get you to believe in something?'

'Whatever can you mean old thing?' I enquired, mystified by this turn of events.

'Well,' he said patiently, 'if not the evidence of your own eyes, what would constitute, for you, sufficient proof that Whisted was the one?'

I heaved a sigh.

'Well let me see. How about a spot of proper respectable scientific research for a start, and maybe a soupcon of actual empirical evidence.'

'But Whisted warned you man.' He smiled, slowly shaking his head whilst connecting my leg loops, 'he told you his discovery could be shown to work but that any test he passed, you would subsequently conclude was susceptible to error.'

'Well he would say that wouldn't he.' I retorted testily.

'A cynical mind,' Reeves lamented 'will always find a way to doubt.'

'I think what you mean Reeves is that a critical thinker imposes a burden of proof upon a theory, beyond the simple fact that it happens to appeal to him.' I parried.

He seemed both saddened and amused by my attitude. 'Logic will only get you so far man,' He said, as though addressing a simpleton, 'eventually you gotta take a chance and have faith.'

'If it was all about faith, then why did Whisted go to such lengths to affect scientific respectability for his claims?'

'You gotta talk to people in a language they understand.' He shrugged, switching on my g.p.s. and checking the release mechanism of my reserve parachute.

'But he pretended to be a psychologist for heavens sake.'

'Oh right, and you heard that from the same people who told you he was a murderer and a terrorist huh?'

'Tish and pish Reeves!' I ejaculated, 'All that business about psychology being the product of evolution? The mind being just a brain and a brain being no more than a computer? Well that's a definite scientific hypothesis, so it's entirely appropriate to evaluate it by scientific standards.'

'But he showed us man. He showed you, remember?'

'Au contraire mon brave.' I objected, 'He didn't show me anything, he placed the idea in my mind. He didn't reveal it, he suggested it powerfully to me and then he opened my mind to permit its ingress.' I decided to give a little ground, 'Look here Reeves, I'm not necessarily saying that Whisted's model of the human mind is wrong. Just that hypnotising people into believing something doesn't constitute proof. Maybe it is true, or partly true at least. It sounds reasonable enough certainly. But even if it's bang on the money and we are all - what was it he said? - 'shackled to an obsolete evolutionary psychology', the point nevertheless stands that anything and everything which according to Whisted, follows from this knowledge is merely his personal agenda. It simply does not automatically logically follow. No ought from is Reeves.'

Reeves minutely inclined an eyebrow in such a way as to suggest a lack of assent to this view.

'Seeing is believing.' Opined he.

He was being maddeningly obtuse and I decided to try a different tack.

'Look at this bunch Reeves,' I said, indicating Whisted's congregation, who were milling around the amphitheatre in huddled groups, half mad with shock and grief. 'Does it not strike you that they have rather more in common than a strong consensus on matters of tonsure?'

'What are you driving at?'

'Lets face it Reeves, they have all been carefully hand chosen for being, what you might call, not to put too fine a point on it, lame ducks.'

'Lame ducks?'

'Yes dash it!' I stormed, 'lame ducks Reeves. Wet lettuces. Sad acts. Hapless Harrys. For Whisted's 'trickster' archetype, read: lame ducks.'

The uncomfortable silence that followed this explosion, hung in the air for a few moments like the aroma of a passing sociology student.

'I mean they're spiffing fellows to a man Reeves,' I back-pedalled, 'but in most cases, its hard to believe that in making the decision to go in for a life of monastic isolation, they first had to weigh against the proposal, a whole range of wildly tempting alternatives.'

Reeves looked blank.

'One cannot see them, for instance, being plagued with offers of high octane sex, in a penthouse in the Amsterdam area, with the members of the Swedish ladies Olympic, beach-volleyball team.

He adjusted his implacable features by a nanometre or two, so as to convey the impression that further amplification of this point was required.

'Look, with the possible exception of Serge,' I continued, 'these fellows would probably follow you to the end of the world if you told them they had, what was it? 'virtually unlimited biological mental potential,''

'So, given that Whisted selected you too, wouldn't that make you a lame duck also?'

'Very probably Reeves.' I admitted, 'but at least this duck is sufficiently ambulatory to walk away.'

He turned and looked fondly at the Academics for a long moment.

'All I see are fine people, patiently pursuing wisdom, fulfilment, fraternity and excellence.' He said mildly. 'Perhaps the reason you see them as inadequate is because you emphasise the wrong things in your estimation of a person's worth. Their status for instance, their wealth, their physical beauty, their extraversion.' A bit rich coming from an American I thought but I let it go. 'These people have beliefs that work for them,' he continued, closing in for the kill, 'whilst you cling paranoically to a dull minded cynicism which effectively prevents you ever being happy.'

'The purpose of a belief is not to cheer you up.' I retorted, 'The purpose of a belief is to be true.' And I don't mind saying I was a trifle stung at being twitted by Reeves in this way. Who would have thought the fellow had been inwardly judging me all this time?

'Life's real truths lie beyond science,' he persisted, 'and at some level they are already known to you. If you would just open your mind.'

'Twaddle.'

He sighed. He was finding this as frustrating as I was. 'Have you any personal proof of the existence of genes or the expanding universe?' he asked mildly.

I could see where this was going.

'Well obviously not.'

'So you are taking it on faith that the scientific establishment wouldn't deceive you.'

I reflected that when one's grey matter is as race tuned as Reeves' it's bound to misfire occasionally.

'Can you actually be suggesting Reeves, that the method of scientific enquiry is simply another belief system?'

'It's a religion dude. Its prophets are Aristotle, Newton and   Darwin. Guys whose ideas, once established, acquired the status of knowledge by authority.' He said this slowly and clearly and in that infuriating manner which contrives to suggest that if you don't agree then you mustn't have properly understood.

'Hells teeth!' I blurted.

'Immunity to heretical criticism,' He added, and I could almost hear Whisted's voice as he said this, 'is a feature of any dominant ideology.'

'Science isn't about faith Reeves,' I said archly, hastening to rebut this awful drivel, 'it's about evidence. All the evidence in support of genetics and evolution is there to be inspected and reinterpreted by anyone at any time. It's only religion that depends upon the willingness to believe in something in which one has no reason to believe.'

'Surely there is every reason to believe in something if it works.' He countered.

'There is every reason to want to believe it Reeves. But there's no justifying reason. No reason having to do with it being true.'

'There are none so blind,' recited my former gentleman's gentleman sadly, his eyes filled with pity, 'as will not see.'

Whichever way you looked at it, all of this was clearly as water off the back of a differently able duck.

There was nothing more to be said. Reeves laid out my glider, checked my lines and then we said our final goodbye on the most strained of terms. Uncertainly I extended my right hand and although he shook it, the whole gesture fell a mile short of being convincingly matey.

As I prepared to launch he stayed to wave me off. His other arm was around Trinity's shoulders. Her eyes were red with crying. I would miss him awfully of course but he was a stranger to me now.

Gathering up my lines I reflected that although in butling circles he was without peer, and whilst I had come to think of him as nothing less than my right hand, perhaps it was after all, time that I started looking after myself. Whilst Whisted had forced me to confront my elemental self in order to gain mastery over him, with Reeves and me, as in all classic master servant relationships, there had always been more than a little reciprocity. He was to me as Yin to Yang. We had been locked together in a sort of weird symbiosis.

I took off and climbed out in a smooth, late afternoon thermal, barely conscious of the wing above me as I ascended. At cloud base I luxuriated for a while in the refreshing misty coolness, allowing it to cleanse me of the last residual shreds, of a strange and nagging anxiety, that perhaps in leaving Reeves behind, I was deserting my better half. That he was my heart and soul and I the disembodied ghost.

When this irrational feeling had passed, I gratefully set out on a glide, steering a South Easterly heading, striking out for The Lyceum, the gateway to the real world, which I reasoned I might realistically reach in the three hours remaining before sunset and where I could pass the night in relative comfort, and awaken to the dawn of the new millennium.

20 THE HEMLOCK MANOUVRE

'Man is nothing else but what he makes of himself'

Jean Paul Sartre

So had Whisted really been onto something? He was probably pretty firmly on the money in saying that flying, for some people, mostly but not entirely men, represented the expression of an ancient subconscious impulse to pursue a quest and prove themselves worthy. The essence of that knowledge though, was ages old. The fellow's real discovery had been in spotting the extraordinarily suggestible mental state that it produced in them. How, in a certain type of individual, only flying could quieten the incessant prattling monologue of the ego which otherwise drowned-out the whispered injunctions of the subconscious. Therein he saw his opportunity.

His big idea was to pass off hypnotic suggestion as insight. As revelation. He claimed that his technique would eclipse the dazzling glare of the consciousness which blinds the mind's eye to the firmament of the soul. The truth was that by using regression, he could manoeuvre his subjects into a state of trance where their minds would do his work for him. Would willingly generate material in support of whatever he suggested to them. We saw what he wanted us to see. We allowed ourselves to believe him.

The past life personalities generated by people in hypnotic regression are, of course, in reality, merely a projection of their own self image. In this state, a subject's mind will, if prompted so to do, improvise an entire composite identity. And it does so essentially out of a desire to please the therapist. In the pursuit of this end the mind will make use of any memories that it has to hand. It might for instance, to choose an example completely at random, use scraps and fragments of tweedy childhood fictional stories, or even the names of fallen soldiers from the county regiment, glimpsed amongst the hundreds of forgotten dead, emblazoned upon a war memorial, by the cricket field in a Sussex market town.

And once his subjects had demonstrated a willingness to cooperate in this fabrication, Whisted knew that we were of a mind to accept his post hypnotic suggestions as though they were their own personal experience.

Everyone who underwent his initiation, thought they knew for a certain fact, to which they had been witness, that the interior of their mind was no more and no less than a computer. That their attitudes, their behaviour, and their personalities were all determined by their inherited biology. They literally believed, as I did, that they had seen its anatomy. Could see it still. Inevitably they underwent an instant conversion to a new fundamentalism. Evolutionary psychology. A deterministic world-view so bleak, that they found they needed Whisted to give their lives meaning.

Having demonstrated himself to be a chap who knew about what he was talking, it was relatively easy for Whisted to tack on his philosophy of life too. He was able to disguise his values as revealed truths and smuggle them past their critical faculties whilst they reeled from the shock of the induction. An expert sophist, he was able to make it sound as though his views followed logically from the truth they thought they had seen. Ought from is.

And they believed him, because they wanted to. Because he relieved them of a life long sense of inadequacy, by rather sportingly placing the fault elsewhere. With a society that valued the strong, the brave, the beautiful and the smart, above the reflective, the thoughtful, the shy and the sensitive. They believed in Whisted because he offered them hope, and because he was who they wanted to be. He became their prophet. They his flock. Like the Cathar Monks in their mountaintop monastery at Montsegeur they had built a simple life of self imposed privation, sanctifying themselves against the seductive decadence and shallow consolations of the unexamined life.

The basis of Whisted's approach was that human nature is hard-wired, retrograde and unlikely to deliver the objectives of an enlightened society. Like the Cathars he believed that it was vital for humankind to elevate itself above its base animal nature. From this foundation, and being the sort of chap that he was, he reasoned that the interests of truth would best be served by converting others to the cause. By whatever means necessary. That people shared his world view was pretty much all that mattered. The minor detail that they had been tricked into doing so was no problem for him at all. Because in the end, he wasn't looking for the truth, he was looking for followers. For Whisted, it was entirely acceptable to mislead people for their own good.

The greatest balance of happiness over unhappiness. The end justifies the means.

The tragedy of the thing, was that whilst they believed that they were seeing into their souls, in fact they were being treated to a guided tour of his. Because ultimately what Whisted had showed us, amounted to the difference between apprehending something and comprehending it. Between actually seeing something and merely seeing what it is that somebody is saying.

Reeves, bless him, had been hopelessly wide of the mark in saying that science is just another religion. But then again, what Whisted was peddling was the baddest of bad science. I am reliably informed that the devil himself may quote scripture for his purpose. Not really my area of course but I do know that the screed of evolution too, can be used to clothe some pretty doubtful ideologies. And Whisted knew that when you replace god with science, creation with evolution and ritual with the scientific method, there remains a vacuum to be filled. A situation that he was ideally placed to exploit.

So, three years have now passed since the unpleasantness at the Academy. Each has been more prosperous and crowded with incident than the last, and you find me much altered. Mostyn the preternaturally gullible dupe; you know. With Mostyn the goannas friend; you are acquainted. And of Mostyn the spiritually annihilated husk; you are surely heartily sick. But what of Mostyn the kick-ass adventurer? What sayeth Mostyn the dissolute roister-doisterer? And wherein dwells Mostyn the artful seducer of beautiful women? For in every man these are inalienable component parts, shrivelled undernourished and vestigial in all but a few cases but there nevertheless, awaiting the call.[25] Well, happily, after the conclusion of the whole Whisted business, these qualities rather burst to the fore. Indeed as I type these words one-handedly on my new, state-of-the-art, titanium portable computer, you find me lounging upon a gigantic bed in my penthouse suite at

---

[25] *Look, I'm serious ok.*

the hotel de l'Europe in Amsterdam. Tastefully arranged about its satin sheets, in attitudes of profound sexual satiation, laze two naked, lissom limbed lovelies of incandescent beauty, their exquisite Scandinavian bodies, toned to perfection by a regime of sauna and beach-volleyball. As Inga decants a pre-prandial cocktail into the crystal tumbler in my left hand, she faux-clumsily overfills the vessel, artfully spilling few drops of ice cold pineapple daiquiri across Rosel's perfect breasts. Smiling coquettishly Inga dutifully sets about making amends for her carelessness with her skilful tongue, whilst Rosel begins to take each of my fingers in turn into her hot wicked mouth. I brace myself for yet another frenzy of high octane debauchery.

Much has changed then, since Whisted's death, and that which he showed me in Annecy and which thereafter remained so vividly clear to me; the anatomy of my unconscious mind, I can see no longer. Mercifully, the cataract has reformed across my minds eye. Now I simply feel the presence of the influences that he described, calling to me across the generations. Feel them in the curious way that one is aware of things which have no other existence beyond one's awareness of them. As I feel the presence of the dead parents that I never knew. And I have learned to make this new intuition work for me too. To help me accept what I am. A highly evolved animal, bent on survival and reproduction.

The post hypnotic suggestions that he placed in my mind may have been washed away but my memories of the Whisted affair generally, have remained absolutely pin sharp, despite the passage of time. And amongst this vivid tableau of recollections, there is one detail in particular that I prize above all else in this world. It is a captured moment in time lodged at some neural address or other deep within my brain. A frozen glimpse of the shiny object, glistening with moisture, that Inga is holding in her hand at this very moment. And I will take it with me to the grave for the following reason:

Two millennia ago, when the state of Athens put Socrates to death, it was putatively for corrupting the minds of the young men of the city. The plan backfired because as the old man raised the hemlock to his lips, he made lifelong acolytes of all those there present. This state of affairs was not lost on Whisted it seems, who realised too, that the very best thing that he, as a visionary, could do to perpetuate his ideas, was to become a martyr. It would send his followers the strongest imaginable vindication of their ideology. That it was perceived as a threat by a system which absolutely depended on people remaining chained to predictable, acquisitive and self destructive drives that could readily be put to work on its behalf.

Fortified with this knowledge, his disciples would surely elevate their beloved mystic to the status of avatar. The fact that the revelatory excursions on which he escorted them, would never be duplicated in subsequent generations of the movement, was of no more significance than that the disciples of Jesus Christ are unable to reproduce the miracle of the fishes.

And it is to Whisted's credit that he was able to put this plan into effect in such a way that I suspected nothing, until the very moment at which the old man lay dead at my feet. Until I knew everything but could do nothing. Knew that I had been his creature throughout our acquaintance but knew also that no one would ever believe me. My credibility with the Academics was at its lowest ebb, and at that moment, above any other, their faith in him was unshakeable. Whisted had already furnished them with an explanation for his imminent death that they were desperate to believe, and he had primed them to expect nothing from me but cynical doubt.

Perhaps though, I should at least have tried.

Two hours out from the Academy, as I approached the line of total commitment to the downwind dash, beyond which there is no turning back, I was still considering this angle. Climbing slowly in a mellow evening thermal, the light beginning to fade, I removed my sunglasses, intending to stow them in the latest in a long line of receptacles to be pressed into service in this capacity. Locating the item in the side pocket of my harness, I contemplated it for a long moment and was reminded of Whisted's prophecy, that the task, by means of which, I had contrived to test his claims, and which would no doubt go down in the lore of the

Academy as 'the miracle of the pineapple daiquiri', I would subsequently conclude, was in fact susceptible to error. Of course it must be conceded that one of the more precipitous pitfalls with which the career path of fabulously rich and ultra-promiscuous sensualists such as myself is beset, besides the constant state of near exhaustion and the barely concealed envy of every male that you meet, is that your mind's eye is permanently fogged with lust, as after-images of hard-core sexual athletics linger upon its retina. Nevertheless, I promise you that the image that I jealously hoard in my memory, of the cylindrical object, scintillating with beads of condensation, which Inga is, even now, using to elicit a gasp of delight from Rosel, I can still picture with perfect clarity, three years on, as I frolic atop the 'Rosie Cheeks' empire; global publishers of porn and highly predictable murder mysteries. This image has been revisited regularly since that day at the Academy and in fact on each and every occasion that I have experienced the slightest doubt about my decision to leave. It is certainly something that I shall be sure to have it about my person when I meet St. Peter at the gates to heaven. The image shows the cocktail shaker that I won in a game of cigar cutter roulette against Leonardo Ping, the Chinese gondolier that I met in Zanzibar. Like my silly, posh accent I have kept it as a souvenir of the Whisted affair. In fact, to be exact the image shows the interior of the item as I saw it when I glanced inside, just before taking off from the Lyceum on the way *to* the Academy on that December morning in 1999. And on inspecting it, one cannot help noticing, almost immediately, that the object is unaccountably un-infested by poison-filled vials of any description whatsoever. Because if such a thing had been present, then I could scarcely have overlooked it, as I retrieved the pair of slightly effete sunglasses, based around the principle of the two way mirror, which, at that time, it was my custom to store inside the trinket for safekeeping. The picture has been carefully tagged and entered as evidence in the trial of a man accused of committing a terrible act. The taking of a human life, no less. It proves Whisted guilty of suicide.

Bertrand Whisted had been an illusionist to the last. He knew, better than anyone, that people always remember what they think they saw, and not what really happened. He was known to be an accomplished close up magician, skilled in the art of misdirection and in dividing his mind to perform two tasks at once. A fact further testified to, by the slight of hand with which he had secreted the vial of poison in his palm and deftly transferred it into the pineapple daiquiri.

I could but begrudge him a measure of respect for pulling off this sly deception. Whichever test I had proposed he would no doubt have twisted it to fit his purpose, but I had been more than obliging. Triggered by the sight of the machete, the pineapple and the stylophone apparently accidentally littered around the speaking rock, I had reflexively disgorged the trick that Leonardo Ping had shown to me in the piano bar of the

Zanzibar Hilton. Without stopping to ask myself who in turn might have shown it to him.

I could not seriously expect anyone at the Academy to take my word against that of their messiah. Whisted was just too good. He had played me. As the most susceptible of the original twelve followers, he had singled me out and cast me as his Judas. He had put me to sleep for five years and activated me when the need arose.

I popped my mirror sunglasses into the, really rather nasty silver cocktail shaker and replaced the cap, inwardly giving thanks for the fact that glasses cases are so easy to lose. My odyssey into the heart of dorkness, was at an end. I had sought the grail and found a poisoned chalice. The decision was made. I resolved to continue South, to the Lyceum. And for the first time in six years I felt philosophical, exultant even, to be bowing out of an argument that I simply couldn't win.

A glorious sense of calm descended upon me as I passed the point of total commitment. I was doing what I do. For I am a cross country pilot. A nomad. I was in the zone. Where I landed I would sleep. My only witness, the empty sky. Wrapped in my heat reflective survival blanket and a sublime tranquillity.

One hour later and an incandescent, crimson sunset was smouldering on the Western horizon. The sepulchral, silver moon already rising in the East was exquisite beyond words. Everything was as beautiful as it could be. I lazily circled in the restitution lift. Topping out at cloud base one final time. Nearer to the gods no mortal may approach. At last I was afforded one of the most delicious sensations that cross country paragliding is capable of delivering; the realisation that my goal was within glide. That I had done enough. I started on the long descent into the Lyceum with a light heart. A new millennium beckoned. And besides, I was looking forward enormously to renewing my acquaintance with Les and Derek.

ABOUT THE AUTHOR

Simon Forbes spends half of the year freelancing in the UK television industry and the other half paragliding in the Southern hemisphere. He is not married but does have a rather adorable daughter.

22206631R00176

Printed in Great Britain
by Amazon